The
Righteous
Cut

Other titles in the series

The Righteous Cut

A Wesley Farrell Novel

Robert Skinner

Poisoned Pen Press

Poisoned Pen Press
6962 E. First Ave., Ste. 103
Scottsdale, AZ 85251
www.poisonedpenpress.com
info@poisonedpenpress.com

Printed in the United States of America

For Jean,
I wish it was more

*Who ever perished, being
innocent? Or where were
the righteous cut off?*
Job 4:7

*Even when someone battles hard,
there is an equal portion for one
who lingers behind, and in the
same honor are held both the coward
and the brave man; the idle man
and he who has done much meet death alike.*
Homer
The Iliad book I 1 318

*"If you want trouble,
I come from where they make it."*
Raymond Chandler
"The King in Yellow," March, 1938

New Orleans Times-Picayune
Monday, December 8th, 1941, Page 1
Dateline: Honolulu (AP Wire)

In the early hours of Sunday, December 7th, hundreds of fighters and torpedo bombers launched from Japanese Imperial aircraft carriers hit the army and navy installations around Honolulu, Hawaii. Although actual numbers are not yet available, military and civilian authorities estimate that perhaps hundreds of military personnel and civilians were killed or wounded in the early morning attack.

Bombers and torpedo planes smashed into the unprotected fleet in the harbor, sinking many capital ships while at anchor. Military aircraft at Pearl Harbor and Hickam Field were destroyed wholesale on the ground...

NEW ORLEANS CRIME BEAT
[column] by Art Frizzell

*"Shooting at Lake Pontchartrain
caps week of violence."*

…eyewitnesses report that gunshots were exchanged between a man holding a woman hostage and a second man. Police state that the pre-dawn show-down in Bucktown was connected to a week of gang violence that rocked the Crescent City…In a related incident, police finally identified the "love-tap killer" who was responsible for at least three murders…

Chapter 1

Wednesday, December 3rd, 1941

The moon cast a pale milky glow over the Jefferson Parish countryside as the engineer of the Illinois Central locomotive began to lean on his whistle. From his vantage point in an empty boxcar, a big man with shaggy dark blonde hair watched the meager traffic on U.S. 90, which paralleled the IC tracks. A lot had changed since he'd last seen that highway. There had been almost nothing out here ten years ago. Now the lights of houses, gasoline stations, and an occasional store or tavern could be seen winking along the right of way.

As the train neared the Orleans Parish line, he felt the train's speed begin to diminish. He shrugged his big shoulders inside his leather jacket and pulled his sweat-stained hat down over his eyes. He had better, more expensive clothing in his valise, but for the time being he was strictly a bum. He grinned as he remembered how he'd left here with his tail between his legs. All the years of waiting, the months of planning were over. He was back to get what rightly belonged to him.

The harsh racketing of the wheels gradually slowed to a dry, monotonous clacking, signaling that his journey was finally at an end. He retreated into a shadow as the slowing train eased into the curve at the Carrollton switching shack. A hundred yards further, he swung easily down from the boxcar and faded into the shelter of a large willow tree. When the train was safely past, he made his way down the tracks to a street crossing where he turned toward Downtown.

Signs in the darkened store windows advertising everything from decorations to candy reminded him that Christmas was coming. If things went as he planned, Christmas would come early for him this year.

It wasn't long before he turned a corner and saw a tavern open. He entered quietly, finding it deserted but for the bartender and a group of three drinkers. The man made his way toward the telephone booth at the rear of the room, unnoticed by the four men who bunched around the bartender's radio, listening spellbound to the lugubrious voice of H. V. Kaltenborn as he lamented over the war news from Europe and Asia.

Leaving his valise just outside the booth, the big man dropped a nickel into the slot and asked the operator for a Downtown number. It rang a half-dozen times before the owner picked it up.

"Hello?"

"I'm here," the man said.

"When did you get in, Pete?" The other man's voice was flat, polite without cordiality. It was the greeting of an associate rather than a friend.

"Stepped off an in-bound freight about twenty minutes ago. What's the story on those boys I asked you to get?"

"Johnny Parmalee gave me the okey-doke last week. He and his brother can start tomorrow if you give the word. My other men can handle anything else that comes up."

"Swell." He paused for a moment. "Have you got a message for me?"

"Everything's in place. Don't worry about a thing."

Pete's brows puckered and something like disappointment crossed his face. "Okay, then." Pete's voice was grim. "Give everybody the word. I'm ready to get this show on the road tomorrow."

"It's been a long wait, hasn't it?" the other man said.

"Not as long as being dead. I'm gonna ring off now. I'll find myself a room somewhere so I can get a bath and a haircut and a good night's sleep. Tomorrow I'll move out to that place you rented and make my headquarters there."

"Okay, Pete. I'll be talkin' to ya."

Pete hung up and left the booth. As he passed the bar on his way out, Kaltenborn was still cataloging the dead and missing in China.

⊗⊗⊗

The church bells at Saint David's Church on Saint Claude Avenue were chiming 11:00 p.m. as a well-dressed Negro named Merced Cresco eased out the back door of a two-story stucco house. The kisses of the married woman inside were still warm on his lips as he tiptoed through the alley. She was some hot mama and no lie—one man would never be enough for her, no sir, uh-uh. Cresco paused as a sedan with its high beams on slid past the house on the way back Downtown, then stepped quietly out onto the sidewalk.

It was chilly tonight, but Merced Cresco was still plenty warmed up. He'd been this woman's back-door man for about three months now and had never had it so good. She never got enough. He sometimes reflected that it was a good thing her husband was only out of town twice a week. More than that, and Merced would be walkin' bowlegged. He laughed out loud as a mental image of himself staggering down the street on convex legs came into his mind.

As he headed Downtown, he began to whistle. He had a mellifluous, high-pitched whistle that echoed up and down the deserted street. He paused at an intersection just as he finished "Let It Snow," and that was when he heard the soft sound of footsteps behind him. He stiffened, then quickly crossed the street, picking up his stride. He didn't like the sound of footsteps behind him on this street. Saint Claude could be rough after dark, and he wasn't carrying a gun or a razor. He hadn't thought he'd need them for the deacon's wife.

He walked as fast as he could without breaking into a run. He was certain that if he ran, whoever was behind him might just decide to shoot him for his money and his watch. He needed some cover and a weapon, and he needed them soon. He crossed another street and recognized a restaurant he frequented. It was closed this time of night, but there was an alley and in the alley there were always empty whiskey bottles and pieces of wood. The entrance to the restaurant stuck out from the other buildings, providing just enough of a blind for Merced to duck into the alley unseen.

Near the kitchen door he found a couple of cases of empty whiskey bottles. He snatched one by the neck and ducked into the shadowy recess of the kitchen door. A minute went by, then three. Five minutes passed, then ten. He was beginning to think he'd imagined the entire episode, and began poking fun at himself. Damn 'fraidy cat. Actin' like a kid 'fraid of spooks. Shit.

He listened carefully, then poked his head just past the recessed doorway. Nothing. Not a damn thing. He stepped out and ran head-first into the hardest thing he'd ever felt. He grunted painfully as the blow knocked him sideways. Before he could recover, big hands grabbed him by the lapels of his coat, shoved him up against the hard brick wall and held him there with his feet dangling.

Merced Cresco groaned, tried to unfasten the hands at his throat. "Lemme—lemme go. Chokin' me—lemme go."

His captor began to slap his face, forehand and back. He kept it up until Merced Cresco began to whimper. As Cresco's vision cleared, he saw a square, black face staring at him. The man's visage was like something hacked out of ebony, with eyes that burned like hellfire. As his wits began to return, a thrill of horror went through him as he recognized the face.

"Boy," the apparition said. "You know who I am?"

"Easter C-Coupé? You ain't Easter Coupé, are you?"

"You ain't as stupid as you look, Cresco," Coupé said. He slapped Cresco some more, harder and harder until the blows were like fire against the man's skin. Cresco began to weep like a lost child.

"Please, man. Please don't kill me. I got money. Take it. Take it all. Take my watch and my lodge ring, too. They worth fifty, sixty bucks easy, just lemme go, please."

Coupé laughed mirthlessly. "That all your life's worth, Cresco? Two hundred bucks, say? Hell, I could get that from a wheelbarrow load of nutria skins and they won't stink near as bad as you do. You done shit yourself, ain't you?"

"S-sorry, Mr. Coupé. Sorry as I can be. Please, lemme go and I'll clean up, I swear it."

"You know why I got you in this alley, boy?" the big man asked. "You got even the smallest idea?"

"N-no, man, I swear, I dunno, but gimme a chance, I'll make it right, whatever it is."

"You gonna take back fuckin' Deacon Charles's wife for the past three months? Tell me, boy, how do you un-fuck a broad? I'd like to know, case I ever find myself in the shit you're in right now."

"No, y'see, it was like—" Before he got the words out, Coupé slashed him across the face with an iron backhand.

"Shut your hole. Next thing, you'll tell me it was all the woman's fault. You do that, I'm liable to get sore."

Cresco knew he was doomed. For years he'd heard of Easter Coupé, and had seen him pointed out in bars. Coupé was somebody you hired when you wanted somebody hurt until they begged for death. Somehow Deacon Charles had found out about him and Mrs. Charles. Instead of praying to God to make it right, Deacon Charles had hired Easter Coupé. Sweet Jesus.

Coupé began to work him over, slowly and methodically. He was a man who knew his work and did it well. Cresco felt his nose break, then several of his ribs. Coupé held him easily against the wall with one hand while he belabored him with the other. Cresco knew he was going to die, and he sobbed his grief out into the empty alley.

Cresco peered through his swollen lids at the man who was killing him, saw Coupé's pitiless eyes staring back. He knew the killing blow was coming, and saw the big black man draw back his fist. Then something happened. Coupé opened his left hand and Cresco slid out of it to the ground. He's gonna stomp me to death, the beaten philanderer thought. He braced himself, but the kicks never came. He craned his neck painfully, saw Coupé staring at him with a peculiar look on his face.

"Listen to me, Cresco. When you can stand up, you get the bus to the railroad station. You get a ticket on the first train goin' outa here and you get on it. Don't you never come back here, you hear me?"

"Y-yeah, boss, I h-hear you. You—you ain't gonna k-kill me?"

Coupé drew a long, shuddering breath. His face was still a pitiless ebony mask, but the hot mad rage no longer animated his eyes. They were downcast. "Stop wastin' time, boy. Get on your feet and get to hell away from me."

As torn up as he was, Merced Cresco knew better than to look a gift horse in the mouth. He found a support and dragged himself erect. He hobbled past the huge black man like a three-legged dog and disappeared out the mouth of the alley. Easter Coupé remained there for a moment, staring at something only he could see, then he turned and departed in the opposite direction.

⊗⊗⊗

Frank Casey nodded to the patrolman who stood at the head of the stairs on the top floor of the Bella Creole Hotel on Conti Street. The patrolman pointed silently down the hall where several detectives stood waiting.

"Evening, Ray," Casey said to the rail-thin detective who stepped away from the others. "What we got here?"

"Jack Amsterdam," Ray Snedegar replied. "Somebody gave him a bigger thrill than he was counting on."

"Humph," Casey grunted. "For a guy neck deep in illegal gambling, he sure made a wrong bet."

Snedegar led Casey past the other men into a small, dingy room lit by dim light from a dirty ceiling fixture. A naked man in his middle-forties lay spread-eagled on an unmade bed, his sightless eyes fixed on the ceiling. His face had a stupidly placid expression, marred only a little by the two small red freckles over his right eye.

"What did they use?" Casey asked.

"Looks like a .22. He died quick."

Casey noticed a skinny old man standing nearby. He was dressed in a gray suit and vest that might have been pressed the year Roosevelt entered office. The only shape it had was that which his bony body gave it. He had a crumpled fedora on the back of his head and a dead cigar butt in the corner of his mouth. "You the house dick?"

The old man turned his gaze to Casey, took the limp butt from his mouth. "Yair. Otis McKelvey."

"You know this man, Mr. McKelvey?"

McKelvey nodded complacently. "Yair. Mr. Jack Amsterdam. A big man around here, Mr. Amsterdam. A-Number-One to Councilman Whit Richards. Reckon I know him, all right."

Casey could not quite keep the distaste he was feeling from his face. "What's he doing here?"

McKelvey turned a dead stare to Casey. "You mean what's he doin' in this room, or what's he doin' bein' dead in this room?"

Snedegar's mustache almost disappeared as his lips retreated from over his teeth. "Crack wise like that once more, McKelvey, and I'll kick you down the stairs."

The house dick's face grew pale and the cigar butt slipped from his tremulous hand.

"Let's start with why he's in the room," Casey suggested.

McKelvey avoided Casey's eyes as he shrugged. "Reckon he liked to get away from the house oncet in a while. Prob'ly thought this was a nice, restful place, which it is." He stuck his thumbs in the armholes of his vest and assumed a self-important air. "I like to keep it that way for the customers."

Snedegar moved across the room in a single long stride, grabbed McKelvey by the front of his vest and jerked him to his toes. "So quiet you didn't hear two gunshots through these cardboard walls?" He shook the house dick like a rat in a terrier's jaws. "Tell the Captain what that stiff is doin' here and do it right-Goddamned-now."

McKelvey's face went slack. "He—he was gettin' his ashes hauled. He did it regular—oncet a week, at least."

"For how long?" Casey demanded.

"Two, three years, mebbe. I dunno. I didn't keep a calendar on the guy. He drew a lotta water in this town." As Snedegar's grip loosened, he backed gently away and tugged his rumpled clothing back into place.

"Who brought the whores up here to him? You?"

"N-no, I swear it. It was prob'ly that li'l dago bell captain, Johnny Ferrara. I ain't no pimp."

"You ain't no pimp," Snedegar sneered.

"Did he have a regular girl?"

"No, I don't think so. Just whoever they could find." McKelvey smiled ingratiatingly. "Mr. Amsterdam, he liked 'em all, blondes, brunettes, red-heads. Hell, he liked a shine gal once in a while and a Chink if he could get one."

Casey backed McKelvey into the wall. "For somebody who didn't have anything to do with the late Mr. Amsterdam's sex life, you seem to have cataloged his habits pretty well." He turned and glanced over at where Amsterdam's clothes were draped over a chair. A boyish, blonde detective in a maroon corduroy hat was going through them. "Find anything, Mart?"

Mart shook his head. "What you'd expect, Skipper. Wallet's empty, watch and rings are gone."

Casey shook his head. "Rolled by the girl, probably. Amsterdam must've tried to stop her and the pimp was near enough to stop him, permanently." He turned and stared at the house dick again, his eyes flat. "Ray, get the bell captain in here. Let's see if he tells a better story."

Snedegar jerked his chin at Mart and the young detective left silently. McKelvey took the opportunity to slide down the wall away from Casey and Snedegar, his steps hampered by the knocking of his knees. Mart returned a moment later shoving a skinny olive-skinned man in a red jacket ahead of him.

"You Johnny Ferrara?" Casey demanded.

"I'm Ferrara," the man said sullenly. A sheen of sweat gleamed on his pock-marked face.

"McKelvey says you brought girls up here for Amsterdam. What about it?"

Ferrara shot a glance of exquisite hatred at the house dick before returning his gaze to Casey. "I ain't no pimp."

Snedegar laughed nastily. "He ain't no pimp either, skipper. Don't that just slay you?"

"Yeah, he's a regular choirboy. Are you saying you didn't bring girls up for Amsterdam?" Casey snapped. "Think hard, because the penalty for perjury is a lot worse than it is for pandering. You want a minute?"

Ferrara's mouth worked as he tried to generate enough spit to loosen his tongue. "Sometimes I'd get a girl for Mr. Amsterdam. Just as a favor, not for money or nothin'."

Casey smiled humorlessly. "What about tonight?"

Ferrara tossed a quick glance at Snedegar, saw violence staring back at him. "Y-yeah. I found him one. For a favor, like I told you."

"Who was she?" Casey demanded.

"I—I never seen her before. She looked like his type, you know, so—so I thought he'd like the variety."

"You never saw her before? Who's her pimp?"

"I didn't get her from no pimp. She was just hangin' around, offered me—" He broke off suddenly as he realized what he was about to say.

Casey put his hand flat against the bell captain's chest, shoving him up against the wall. "You were about to say that she offered you part of what she made. Is that right? I said is that right?"

"Y-yeah. Yeah, that's what she did, all right."

"What'd she look like?"

He shrugged, not looking at Casey. "Average size, good figure. Long red hair."

"What color were her eyes? How tall was she? What was she wearing? C'mon, Ferrara, give, or I'll treat you to Christmas dinner at the parish prison."

"Hell, she was just a chick, you know? Maybe five-five or so. She was wearin' high heels and it might be she was smaller'n that. I didn't look at her eyes or nothin'."

Casey sighed. "Yeah, I know what you were looking at. Take both of them down to headquarters, Ray. Book them both for pandering, then let 'em spend the rest of the evening with some mug books."

"Christ's sake, I ain't done nothin'," McKelvey whined.

Snedegar grabbed the house dick, whirled him around by a shoulder and snapped cuffs on his wrists. Mart, taking his cue from his sergeant, did the same to Ferrara. They pushed the protesting men into the hall and down the stairs.

Casey turned as a dark-haired man in spectacles got to his feet across the room. "Get anything, Nick?"

"Something but not much," Nick Delgado replied. "A couple of red hairs from the bed, and the shell casings. Western long rifle Super Match. A .22 is a pimp's gun, right enough, but that's high-grade target ammo."

"That's interesting, all right. What about prints?"

"I've dusted the room and found plenty of prints, but we'll have to get the prints of the hotel staff so we can eliminate them from suspicion."

Casey snorted. "If those two are a sample, we probably can't eliminate any of them."

Casey heard voices in the hall and turned to find a fleshy, dark-haired man in an expensive overcoat standing in the door. His dark mustache stood out on his pale face like it had been scrawled there with a grease pencil.

"Jack. My God, Jack." The man rubbed his face, his mouth hanging open. He stared at the body for a long moment, then looked up at Casey as though surprised to find him there. "Who did this?"

"We don't know yet, Councilman Richards. He came here to use a prostitute, and it looks like he may have gotten rolled by the girl or her pimp. We can't say for sure until we investigate further." Casey spoke softly, but without sympathy. Richards owed his position to graft and the dead man was part of that. Amsterdam had brought hundreds of thousands into Richards's political coffers running illegal gambling operations that Richards protected with the power of his office. One dirty hand washing another.

Richards went closer, staring down into Amsterdam's sightless eyes. "Jesus, Jack. Jesus Christ."

"Sorry to drag you away from home this time of the night, Councilman, but we figured you'd want to know."

Richards appeared not to hear him. "Twenty years we been together and now you let a fuckin' whore kill you. God damn you, Jack."

The men with the coroner's ambulance appeared at the door with their stretcher. A look from Casey halted them. He moved to Richards' side and took him gently by the elbow. "They've got to take him to the morgue, Councilman."

Richards let Casey move him to the side, and watched dumbly while the ambulance men wrapped the corpse in the bed sheets, then moved it to the stretcher. He remained with Casey until the corpse had been carried into the hall, then he followed it with a heavy tread.

Casey stared after him for a moment, then followed everyone down the stairs to the lobby.

Chapter 2

As dawn broke over D'Hemecourt Street, Skeeter Long-baugh drove his Model A touring car down the alley to the shed behind the shotgun double where he lived. The young Negro yawned hugely, feeling contented. Three nights out so far this week, each time with a different chick and every time a score. Sometimes his luck amazed him.

He left the car and stumbled through the back yard to his kitchen door. As he bent to insert the skeleton key in the lock, he was briefly surprised to find it already unlocked. Musta forgot when I left last night, he thought. He pushed the door open, shrugging. He didn't have anything worth stealing anyhow.

He passed through the kitchen into his bedroom and stopped so short his feet almost went out from under him. A broad-shouldered white man lounged on his unkempt bed. Hard brown eyes stared out from beneath thick brows ridged with scar tissue.

"About time you got home," the big man said in a flat baritone. "You know you ain't got nothin' to eat in this dump?"

Skeeter swallowed hard. "Uh, huh. Say, man—who the hell are you and what you doin' in my place?" Skeeter almost jumped at the sound of his own voice. It sounded composed, even unconcerned. It did not reflect the panic he felt at all.

He heard a metallic click just behind him and started, jerking his head around. A second white man, smaller, with a narrow face and fine features straddled a chair. His snappy two-toned shoes looked totally out of place in the dingy room, but it was the switchblade knife in his hand that drew Skeeter's eye.

"Curious, ain't you, boy?" the knife man asked. His slit of a mouth resembled something that might have been a smile. Might have been, but wasn't.

"'Fraid you can't go to work just yet, Skeeter," the larger man said. "See, we got a li'l project in mind. Somethin' that requires you to make it work."

Skeeter swallowed again, feeling nausea cramp his stomach. "Job? Naw, man, ya see, I gots to get to work right away. Sister Malcolm'll chew up my ass and spit it back at me if I ain't there on time. Y'all just gotta excuse me, okay?" He began backing up toward the kitchen, but the slim, handsome white man got off his chair and blocked his path, the knife blade pointed casually at his guts.

The heavy-set man rose from the bed with an unexpected grace. His size made him more menacing than the other man's knife. "Settle down, boy. I ain't got no mind to hurt you, but you gonna do what I tell you. You don't and I'll beat you stupid, get me?"

Skeeter's eyes protruded from the sockets. "Yeah, boss, yeah. I read you loud and clear. You say the word and I'll *be* the word." All he could do was play along and hope he'd find some way to get away from this pair.

The heavy-set man grinned in a way that was almost friendly. "Good. You and me are gonna get along just fine, Skeeter. Let's go on out the back door, and let's us be real quiet, awright?"

"Right, boss. Like the grave." The moment he heard the thoughtless word in his mouth, Skeeter grimaced.

∞∞∞

Later that morning, City Councilman Whitman Richards smiled genially at the two men sitting across from him. One was about Richards' own age, with a tired face. The other, dark-hired, young, and vital. Neither smiled back at Richards. Another young man stood behind Richards' desk with his arms folded. His lips wore a faintly amused smile that didn't reach the dark, bright eyes that stared from behind the lenses of a pair of steel-rimmed glasses.

"What makes you boys think I'm in any position to help you?" Richards asked.

The older man, Mel Chastain, almost sighed. "Quit kidding us, Richards. Every time the chairman of the Zoning Board opens his mouth, your voice comes out of it. We need a zoning change in order to build our torpedo parts factory and he won't give it to us, as you well know."

The younger man, Tom Maxwell, snorted derisively. "Let's get to the point. You want something to get the Zoning Board chairman to approve the change, so why don't you spit it out and stop wasting your time and ours?"

Whitman Richards' eyes crinkled as a lazy laugh escaped his mouth. "Kid, you're the man for me. No beating about the bush." He cocked an eyebrow at Chastain. "This kid's going to make you rich, Mel." Richards sat up abruptly and leaned forward, his hands clasped on the desk blotter.

"Okay, fellas. You want my help, here's what it'll cost you. Two thousand up front for me, and another five Cees for the Zoning chairman. Cash only. That's for starts."

Maxwell's jaw got tight and his hands quivered gently. "What's the punch line, Richards? Twenty-five hundred's letting us off cheap."

Richards grinned again at Mel. "I like this kid. He thinks like me. Okay, I'll want ten percent of your company. It'll be put in the name of a special corporation my associate, Mr. Langdon there, runs for me. He'll handle all the details for you." He leaned back in his chair again, assuming a comfortable pose. "Once the factory's going good, you won't even miss that ten percent." He paused for the briefest of seconds. "Take it or leave it, fellas. I'm a busy man."

Mel looked tired and sad. He turned to his partner. "I guess you've made up your mind already, Tom."

Maxwell glared at Richards. "Mel, you and I both know that government contract isn't worth the paper it's printed on unless we get the factory built. We're being robbed, but we'll be ruined if we don't give him what he wants."

Mel sucked a tooth as he looked back at Richards. "I guess you've got a deal."

"Good," Richards replied briskly. "See Mr. Langdon first thing in the morning and he'll have the paperwork drawn up for you. You'll have your zoning change by Friday afternoon."

The two visitors recognized the dismissal and stood up. "Fine. You'll pardon us if we don't shake hands." He put on his hat and buttoned his jacket. "How do you sleep at night, Richards?"

The city councilman's face hardened and the lazy smile disappeared. "Like a baby, Mel. I dream about money in the bank and sleep like a baby. Now, if you'll excuse me, I've got city business to attend to." He ostentatiously pulled some papers from a basket and began reading them while Robert Langdon herded the two businessmen out of the office.

Langdon paused in the doorway as a pretty young woman with a stylish cap of feathery blonde hair appeared there. "Mr. Richards?"

"Yes, Meredith," Richards said without looking up.

"Captain Casey from the police is here."

"Send him in."

Langdon stood to the side and gestured for the policeman to enter the office. "Have a seat, captain." Langdon waited until Casey was seated, then took up his former position behind Richards' desk.

Richards looked up as the chief of detectives sat down across from him. "Well, what do you know so far?"

"Not much. The room hadn't been cleaned in months and they've picked up fifty different sets of fingerprints so far, not including Amsterdam's. It'll take time to check them all."

"A pity they can't pick up fingerprints on skin," Richards said bitterly. "I'll bet you'd find the broad's all over Jack."

Casey folded his hands across his stomach. "Yeah, that would be helpful, all right."

Richards glared at the detective. "What about the house dick and the bell captain? Did you get anything out of them?"

Casey smiled, but it wasn't friendly. "We kept them up all night looking at mug books, but it was no soap. We're holding both of them on a pandering charge to see if their memories improve, but I'm not very optimistic. The girl may be new in town, or maybe just new in that vicinity. We've got Vice Squad detectives combing the area with the girl's description."

Richards rubbed his face, his frustration evident in his glance. "What about the hotel staff? Could they have done it?"

Casey shook his head. "Doesn't look like it. The janitor is sixty-three years old and has a bad leg. McKelvey's spine is made out of rubber, so he makes a lousy suspect, too. Besides, the desk man and one of the bellhops say he never left the lobby. The bell captain was shooting craps with the other bellhops in the back."

Richards sagged in his chair. "Great."

"Tell me something, councilman," the detective said. "Had Amsterdam said anything to you about having a run-in with somebody, or maybe meeting somebody who had an old beef with him?"

Richards' face got red. "Nuts. Nobody in this town who knew anything would try to jerk the rug out from under Jack Amsterdam. They'd know better."

Casey uncrossed his legs and bent forward, staring intently at the city councilman. "Then why is he dead? I've been a cop for a long time and I've seen a lot of killing. A whore, caught in the act of rolling a customer, might slash the john with a knife or a razor, anything to slow him up while she made a getaway. But this is different. Amsterdam was killed by a pair of .22 target rounds to the head. A nice, clean kill."

"Fuck." Richards' voice was flat and cold, his body rigid in his chair.

Casey stared at him without an ounce of friendliness in his demeanor. "The trouble with this case is that you and I both know your office is nothing more than a machine to help you make money through graft and extortion. There are probably two hundred people within the city limits with a motive to kill Amsterdam—or you, for that matter. We both also know that you've got to keep your mouth shut because any information that would lead to the arrest of the killer would probably put you right beside him in Parish Prison."

Richards regarded Casey with a contemptuous sneer. "Don't think I won't remember this, Casey. I don't have to take any puke from you or any other cop. With one call to the mayor I could get you reassigned to some district on the West Bank where you spend all your time in a rowboat."

Casey got to his feet and put his hat on. "I guess you could, at that. We'll eventually get the woman. We'd find her quicker with a little cooperation, but we'll find her. Thanks for your time." He turned and left the office.

"He seems to think that the killer is somebody we've put the squeeze on," Langdon said when they were alone.

Richards gave his associate an ironic look. "I wonder why he thought that?" He sighed, then laughed and shook his head. "Jack had no sense about women. The chances are it was just what it looked like. She fucked his brains out and while he was half-asleep, she tried to make off with his goods. It was just his rotten luck he woke up too soon. We'd be in here laughin' about it right now. Instead..." He left the thought unfinished.

Langdon looked at his watch. "You're due in council chambers in about twenty minutes."

"Yeah. I got a thing to work out with Councilman Burkhart before the session starts. Take care of things until I get back."

"Sure, Whit. I'm sorry about Jack. You and he go back a long way."

Richards put on his hat as he went into the outer office. Meredith Baker, the junior secretary, looked at him worriedly, brushing his hand with hers as he drew near. He paused to look at her, letting a soft expression briefly cross his face before he turned to go.

Langon paused between the two secretaries' desks until Richards had departed.

"Is there any news, Mr. Langdon?" Catherine Landau, the older senior secretary, asked.

"Nothing, I'm afraid." He ran thin nervous fingers through his fine brown hair, his dark eyes flickering rapidly behind his spectacles. "You'd better cancel all of Councilman Richards' appointments for the rest of the day. If you get any calls from newspapermen, tell them nothing, you understand? Nothing." He nodded reassuringly at Meredith as she sat down at her desk, then went to his own office and closed the door.

⊗⊗⊗

At eleven o'clock that same morning, a twin-engine amphibian with private markings touched down at the hydroplane base near the New Orleans Lakefront Airport. It taxied slowly to the docks where a closed Cadillac limousine waited. After the hands made the large plane fast to the dock, the hatch to the passenger compartment opened. A wide-shouldered man with pale gold skin disembarked alongside a tall, elegantly dressed woman. The woman, her face hidden by a veiled hat, placed a gloved hand in the man's and allowed him to help her over the gangway. A barrel-chested Negro helped them into the limousine and placed their luggage in the trunk. Within a minute they were driving in the direction of the city.

"It's still pretty warm here," Savanna Beaulieu observed as she removed the veiled hat and placed it on the seat beside her. "Maybe we'll have a mild winter this year." She took out a compact and inspected the makeup on her dark brown face. The rose-colored face powder accentuated her high cheekbones.

"That would be all right with me," Wesley Farrell replied. "I've spent so much time in Cuba my blood's thinned out." He took Savanna's hand, leaned over, and kissed her on the mouth. "Welcome home, baby."

Savanna's gloved hand touched his face lightly. "I didn't think I'd miss it so much, but I'm glad to be back."

They drove in companionable silence down Canal Boulevard, reacquainting themselves with the sights of the city. Twenty minutes later the limousine pulled into the small parking lot behind the Café Tristesse. The Negro helped them get their bags out of the trunk of the car and up the iron stairs to Farrell's apartment before leaving them.

As Savanna went to freshen up, Farrell took the opportunity to make some calls. Finding his father absent from police headquarters, he called his cousin, Marcel Aristide.

"How much money do we have in the bank, kid?"

"Hey, Wes! I thought you wouldn't be here until tomorrow. Captain Casey's wedding is taking place on Sunday, right?"

"Yeah. We decided to come back a little early. How's the pretty girl from Brownsville?"

"She's still here," Marcel replied brightly. "She's developed a real taste for big city life, so I guess she's here to stay. Savanna come back with you?"

"Yeah, she was getting homesick for the people at her club and her friends. So how are things here?"

"I think we need to hire an accountant."

"An accountant? Things must be good."

"You better believe it. Margaret Wilde's doing a fantastic job with the lounge across the river, and we've had a banner year with our other businesses, too. The down side is that, with you gone, I'm the only person on the payroll who can handle the books. I'm running from one operation to the other to cover things and I'm beat."

"Damn, I'm sorry, kid. We'll hire one this week, then. I haven't had time to call anyone else yet. How are they?"

"Well, Israel Daggett and his wife are expecting a baby in April. Jake Broussard said he wanted to see you when you got in. And I think your dad's getting younger by the day."

Farrell laughed. "Well, a guy doesn't get married every week. I can hardly wait to see him."

"He may be busy this week with other stuff besides his wedding," Marcel replied. "I just got word that Jack Amsterdam was murdered last night."

"Murdered how?"

"Shot in a fleabag hotel, supposedly by a call girl." Marcel paused for a moment. "He was Councilman Whit Richards' right-hand man, wasn't he?"

Farrell's mouth hardened and his eyes glittered strangely. "Look, I'll call you again later after we're settled in."

"Great. Glad you're back, Wes."

"Same here." Farrell put the receiver back into the cradle. As he looked up, he saw Savanna standing in the bedroom door, shaking her long dark brown hair loose to her shoulders. She wore nothing but a diamond-studded platinum wristwatch that Farrell had given her for her thirty-third birthday. The stones winked and flashed against the deep brown of her skin.

"I was thinkin' of taking a nap. Would you like to come help me?" she asked.

"What if I'm not sleepy?" he asked.

She chuckled. "I bet we can fix that."

As he walked toward her, loosening his tie, he had a fleeting thought about the city councilman named Richards, feeling a coal of anger that he'd thought long extinguished begin to glow again. He grabbed Savanna around her bare waist and kissed her fiercely, forcing the anger back into the box where he'd kept it hidden for almost twenty years.

In the classrooms at venerable Sacred Heart Academy on St. Charles Avenue, the voices of the nuns quickened as they tried to get one more point across to their pupils before the 2:00 bell rang. Some were still talking, raising their voices to make themselves heard above the bustle and clatter of girls moving to their final class of the day.

Out on the grounds, an older girl walked purposefully across the campus toward her job in the headmistress's office. Sister Rosary was a peppery old thing who had let her know early in their association that she disapproved of tardiness more than any other human fault.

The girl was tall and slender with legs and shoulders that hinted at an athletic prowess. Long, dark red hair framed her pale olive face. Her cool green eyes missed nothing as she walked. She used her last free moments thinking about the freshman Christmas dance being held at Tulane University in another ten days. An old playmate, Joel Martins, had invited her to be his date, and she reveled in the knowledge. It was evidence that she was no longer just a kid, but on the cusp of womanhood.

She'd never been invited to a formal dance before, and her mind was full of ideas about the kind of dress and shoes and gloves she might wear, if she had enough money left in her clothing budget. It was suddenly hard to think about school and her job in the office.

As she entered a deserted cloister, her thoughts were briefly distracted by a moving shadow in the dim outdoor corridor. She stopped short, her breath caught in her throat. A young Negro stepped from behind a column, and she let out a nervous laugh. "Skeeter, you scared me half to death. What are you doing there?"

The young custodian grinned nervously. "Just fixin' somethin', Miss Jessica. Always somethin' needin' fixin' around here."

Jessica frowned as she studied the young man. His complexion, normally a healthy brown, had turned sickly gray. "Is—is something the matter, Skeeter? You don't look well. If there's—" Before she could complete the sentence, a rough wool blanket was thrown over her head and she felt herself lifted bodily from the ground. She shrieked and kicked out, but the cry was muffled and her effort to escape was checked by the overwhelming strength of her captor. Her arms pinioned to her sides, she felt herself thrown bodily over a broad shoulder as she was carried away.

Unwilling to give up even now, she thrashed and kicked, yelling as loudly as she could. Her captor stopped abruptly and spoke. His voice was deep, businesslike, but strangely lacking in menace.

"Girl, listen and listen good. No amount of kickin' and fussin' is gonna help, and it might get you hurt. You ain't big enough to hurt me anyhow, so just save your strength. We ain't out to hurt you."

Before she could reply, they were moving again. As frightened as she was, the man's obvious care in carrying her was strangely reassuring and kept her from panicking. She heard the squeak of metal hinges and realized they were going out the rear of the campus where they could disappear into the neighborhood unseen. Then she heard a familiar voice call out.

"You there—Skeeter—what's goin' on? Who you got in that blanket, man?"

Skeeter replied, his voice low and urgent. "Go 'way, Butterbean. Shut up and get outa here."

"Get lost, nigger," a new voice said. Jessica thought she heard a trill of apprehension beneath the bluster of it.

Butterbean became more truculent. "Hey, man, put that gal down." There followed the sounds of struggle, then a hard blow followed by a strangled gasp and the thud of something hitting the ground. A terrible silence followed, then came the voice of her captor, bitter with regret.

"You Goddamn fool. You didn't have to do that."

"No," the new voice said. "I coulda let him run off knowin' all of our faces. Like hell." The new voice was angry, resentful now, but still that trill of fear ran beneath the anger.

"Shut up," the first man commanded. "Let's get outa here."

It dawned on Jessica that the senior custodian, Butterbean Glasgo, was dead. The understanding was so overpowering that she felt faint. She heard the creak and groan of a door or hatch being jerked open, then the man laid her gently down on a hard, lumpy surface. As the hatch closed with a hollow thump, she realized she was in the trunk of a car. Despair settled over her and her mind went blank. She didn't hear the engine start or feel the car move down the street.

※

A man in a shabby room somewhere in the middle of the city stared at old framed photo that he tenderly held in a rough, thick-fingered hand. He stared at it quietly, his mind somewhere back in the past. As he sat there, the telephone began to ring. It rang three times before he set the photo down on the table and picked up the receiver. "Yeah?" The voice was that of the man Pete Carson had spoken to the night before.

"Is Carson here yet?" The voice was soft, muffled, but recognizable to the man in the shabby room.

"He arrived last night. He told me to turn the Parmalee brothers loose. I expect they've made the snatch by now."

"Good," the voice said. "Any time now Richards will be getting the news."

"I wish I could be there to see his face." The man paused for a moment. "Carson asked if there was any message for him."

"Tell him I'll get in touch with him when the time's right. I've got to get moving," the muffled voice said.

"Fine. We'll talk later." His thick-fingered hand put the receiver quietly back into its cradle.

Chapter 3

Skeeter looked across the rear of the blue Chrysler at Joey Parmalee's knife. Sweat leaked from under the band of his hat down his face. "Please boss, I won't say nothin'. Lemme go home and I'll forget I ever seen you."

"Like Hell," Joey said. His confidence had returned with Butterbean's death. He was cocky, confident.

"Get in the back seat with Joey, man," Johnny Parmalee snapped. "The longer we stand here, the more likely somebody's gonna notice us."

Joey looked at his older brother with the hard, bright light of murder in his pale blue eyes. "You and me are gonna have words before long, know that?"

"Get in the Goddamn car," Johnny hissed. "Or I'll leave you here."

Skeeter piled into the back, grateful for the reprieve. Joey got in beside him, the knife still in his hand. He looked at Skeeter as though he were a bug he planned to stomp. As the sedan moved up Cadiz Street, Skeeter tried not to think of the look of sick terror in Butterbean Glasgo's eyes as the knife plunged into his chest.

Johnny drove in stolid silence, smoothly working the wheel and gears. At Claiborne, they headed Downtown, sticking to the speed limit like law-abiding citizens. Joey watched Skeeter, playing with the switchblade with a relentl-ess monotony that had Skeeter close to screaming.

Joey checked his watch, his face impatient. "Man, you think you could hurry the fuck up? I got a place to go to."

Johnny laughed in his throat. "Oh, yeah? What's her name, pretty boy?"

"The fuck's it to you what her name is?"

"I already know her name," Johnny replied. "I seen her, too. You can sure pick 'em, li'l brother." He laughed mirth-lessly.

Joey snapped open the knife again, waved it in the air. "Keep pushin' it, man, keep pushin' it. This girl ain't some twist you can talk about. Gabby's a lady, get me?"

"Yeah, man," Johnny said. "I get you. Keep your pants on. We'll be there in time enough for you to make your date."

"I was supposed to see her last night," Joey grumbled. "Always some fuckin' shit goin' on to mess me over."

At the corner of Thalia, two teenaged boys in a Model A Ford roadster spurted wildly into traffic, just missing the Chrysler and two other cars. With movements too rapid to calculate, Johnny's foot hit the brake as his thick hands wrenched the steering wheel into a skid that left the sedan rocking on its springs.

Skeeter, his nerves on a knife-edge, saw his chance and took it. As the Chrysler heaved against its suspension, Skeeter popped the door open and rolled out into the street. Like a rubber ball he bounced to his feet and sped through traffic into the adjoining neighborhood.

"Stop, you Goddamn sonofabitch!" Joey jerked a long-barreled gun with target sights from under his arm and aimed it through the open door. Once again Johnny's reflexes exploded, his hand grabbing his brother's revolver around the cylinder, immobilizing it.

"Put it away," Johnny said in a low rumble.

"Goddamn it—" Joey sounded petulant, like a kid told he couldn't go out to play.

"Put it away, or I'll break your fuckin' hand off. He ain't gonna get far." As he felt Joey relax his grip, Johnny pulled the gun from his hand.

Joey hissed, rubbing his wounded hand. "How do you know how fuckin' far he's gonna get?"

"I know he'll run to a friend, a relation, or a woman, and it won't be hard to find out who them people are."

"How the hell you know how easy it'll be? He's a nigger. Who knows where they crawl to?"

"I know a man who can find him—and shut him up, too," Johnny replied easily. "Now sit tight and keep quiet. We gotta get the gal to the hideout and then we've got more work to do." He quickly put the car into motion as automobiles behind them began to honk irritably at the tangle blocking the street.

❈

Israel Daggett stood over the corpse of Butterbean Glasgo with his hands shoved deeply into his pockets. He said nothing as he inspected the scene.

"Poor old Butterbean," Sam Andrews said somberly. "I used to go to Sunday School with him when we were kids." He pulled the blanket off the body and studied the wound. "Single knife wound, right under the breastbone. Butterbean prob'ly didn't even make a sound dyin'."

"Nothing anybody could hear." Daggett squatted down opposite his partner and began going through the dead man's pockets. "Wallet, pencil, keys, pocket knife. No big money." He noticed that both of Glasgo's hands were clenched tightly. "Looks like he was fighting, or about to fight." He rotated the man's wrists, saw something caught in the left fist. "What's this?"

Andrews held the wrist as Daggett pried the fingers open. A piece of shiny metal rested in the pale brown palm. "What the hell's that? Looks like a li'l bitty horn."

"A clarinet," Daggett replied. "It's a tie clasp shaped like a clarinet." He picked it up at the ends and studied it. "This is a nice piece of goods. Twenty-four carat gold with enamel trim and diamond chips. Got a maker's name stamped on it."

Andrews held an evidence envelope so Daggett could drop it in. "Maybe somebody at headquarters can find out where this came from."

Daggett stood up and rubbed his chin. "Probably surprised them as they were going out the gate."

"Could be they had to kill him for another reason," a voice behind them said. Daggett turned to see Inspector Matt Grebb approaching from the direction of the school.

"What's that, Inspector?"

"We got another custodial worker missing," Grebb replied. "Kid named Skeeter Longbaugh. The head nun says he called in sick this morning. He's one of only five people with keys to the gates."

"What makes you figure him for this?" Daggett asked.

"We tried to reach him on his home telephone. No answer. You'd better see if you can run him down."

Daggett didn't like Grebb insinuating that the missing Negro was involved in the crime when there was no direct evidence, but he kept that to himself. It was one of the daily compromises he made as he worked with and for white cops. "Got a description?"

"The kid's twenty years old, five-nine, weight about one thirty-five, slender build. Skin, dark brown, hair, black, worn thick, eyes, brown. He rents half of a double at twelve-seventeen D'Hemecourt Street."

"Okay, Inspector. We're on it." They left the scene and drove out Napoleon Avenue, heading west on Claiborne until they reached Carrollton. Ten minutes later they turned into D'Hemecourt.

"Don't look like nobody's home," Andrews said.

"Let's try the other side of the double." Daggett knocked on the door and a few seconds later the door opened. An attractive light-brown woman of about forty-five stood behind the screen. "Yes?"

"Police officers, ma'am. Are you the owner of the house?"

She looked mildly flustered. "Oh. Well, yes. I'm Mrs. Coretta Ivy. Is something wrong?"

"We hope not, but we're looking for Skeeter Longbaugh."

"Dear me, he might be ill. He normally leaves for work at 7:00, but his car's in the shed behind the house."

Daggett jerked his chin at Andrews. "Take the rear. I'll see if I can raise him." He gave Andrews a couple of minutes to get around back, then he knocked loudly on the door several times. "Mr. Longbaugh, it's the police. Open up please." He pounded some more. When no answer came, he looked into the anxious face of the owner. "Have you got a key, ma'am? I'd like to make sure he's all right."

She reached into the pocket of her dress and brought out a small ring with two keys on it. Singling out the proper key, she handed it to him. It was the work of only a moment to unlatch the door and push it open. "Mr. Longbaugh? It's the police. Answer if you're in there."

"Ain't nobody here, Iz," Andrews called from the kitchen. "Back door was unlocked. Car parked in the shed."

Daggett walked through the house, taking in the rumpled bed, the dirty dishes in the kitchen sink. "Looks like he just sleeps here—when he sleeps." He led Andrews back to the front porch where the lady waited.

"Nobody home, Mrs. Ivy."

"Do you think something's happened to him?"

Daggett shook his head. "I don't know. Do you know if he has any close friends or a girlfriend?"

She put a finger to her chin as she thought. "No, not that I noticed. I speak to him just about every day and he seems like a happy-go-lucky youngster. Rather good looking." She smiled fondly. "I see him out with quite a lot of young girls. He never brings them here, of course. I made that clear to him at the beginning. He's been a good tenant. Never any trouble, always on time with his rent."

Daggett reached into his vest pocket and removed a white card. "Thank you for your help, Mrs. Ivy. If you see or hear from Mr. Longbaugh, would you please call us? It's really important that we speak to him."

She took the card, trying not to look worried. "Of course, officer. I do hope he's not in any trouble."

Daggett nodded. "We hope so, too. Good morning."

"Think she's a li'l sweet on him, herself?" Andrews asked when they were back in the car.

"She's just the motherly type. She didn't seem jealous of all his girlfriends."

"He sounds kinda girl-crazy to me, Iz." Andrews face took on a worried expression. "Girl crazy and a kidnapped white gal make a bad combination. He could be one of these fools who's just burnin' up to lay down with a white woman."

Daggett shook his head vigorously. "Uh-uh. Let's give him the benefit of the doubt until we can find him."

Andrews shrugged. "Sorry. Imagination run off."

"That's the trouble with this job. Even before you know what a suspect looks like, you automatically think the worst. We got to find him and get to the truth. It might be all the chance he's got."

When it became clear who the kidnapped girl was, Casey sent a radio car to pull Whitman Richards out of council chambers and drive him to his Coliseum Street home. Casey himself greeted the city councilman at the door.

"What do you know so far?" Richards demanded.

"Almost nothing," Casey replied. "Her books were found scattered about the cloister near the headmistress's office. A custodian was found stabbed to death near a rear gate."

"If you don't know anything, then why the hell are you standing around my living room?" Richards demanded. "Get the hell out on the street and find her, Goddamnit."

"I've got teams of detectives canvassing the neighborhood around the school and a dozen radio cars are tracking down the leads as they come in. In the meantime, we need you here to wait for the ransom demand."

"Of all the fucking bullshit," Richards exclaimed. "I can get thirty private detectives out on the street in less than half an hour. Maybe that's something I should do."

"Stop acting like a fool, Whitman." A strikingly beautiful red-haired woman of about forty stepped into the foyer. Her eyes flashed with barely repressed anger. "Give me a moment with my husband, Captain."

Casey withdrew, stepping onto the front porch. When they were alone, the woman looked at her husband with frank dislike. "If I were you, I wouldn't take it out on the police. They're the ones trying to clean up your mess."

He favored her with a blunt expression that matched her own. "I don't know what you're talking about, Georgia. I don't know anything more than what we just heard."

Her beautiful mouth hardened and her eyes struck sparks. "Who did you double-cross this time, Whit? Or is this some stunt you're pulling for your own reasons?"

The accusation momentarily silenced Richards. "Why are you so sure this is about me? We're worth three and a half million. Isn't that reason enough for a kidnapper?"

She folded her arms under her bosom and shook her head. "I'd feel better if that's all it was. I just have an uncomfortable feeling that this is somebody you knifed in the back." She came closer to him, lowering her voice. "If anything happens to Jess and it's your fault, I'll kill you, Whit. I swear I'll kill you." She turned on her heel and left him with his hands bunched impotently at his sides.

An hour went by, during which Richards paced up and down the hall, staring out the upstairs windows. He was passing the study door for the fiftieth time when the phone bell cut the tense silence like a razor going through ripe fruit. Forcing himself to maintain his poise, he entered the room, picked up the receiver and spoke into it with studied non-chalance. "Whitman Richards here."

"Well, how nice to catch you at home, Councilman," a man said. "Not spending the afternoon at the office?"

Richards listened to the voice, thought he heard something familiar there. "What is it you want?"

The voice laughed as detectives frantically bent over their wiretap equipment, whispering and gesturing to one another. "That's what I like about you, Rico. All business, right?"

At the sound of the nickname, Richards stiffened. No one had called him "Rico" in a very long time. He swallowed, his face frozen with dread. "That's what this is about, isn't it? You want to conduct some business?"

"Right. I have your daughter, and you want her back."

Richards forced himself to listen carefully. He understood now. "What do you want in exchange for her?"

"It's not going to be so easy as that. We'll have to see what you think the kid's worth."

Richards' stomach went into free fall and he closed his eyes as he fought to keep his equilibrium. "I see. Well, if it's money you want, I'll need to know how much."

"We'll talk again later, when the cops aren't listening." He hung up, taking Richards by surprise.

Casey looked at the wire men and saw from bitter head shakes that they hadn't gotten what they needed. He swore under his breath as he turned to the city councilman. "Well, it looks like he wants to play cat and mouse with you. Try to keep him on the phone a bit longer next time."

Richards slowly put the dead receiver back into its cradle. "Get your men and your stuff out of my house."

"What?"

"You heard me. I don't need the police to handle this. He wants to bargain with me. Swell, I'm going to give him whatever he wants. The longer you birds are sucking around here, the longer this is going to take, so get lost."

Casey folded his arms as he studied Richards' face. "You're out of your mind. You can't order us off the case."

"Goddamn you, get your shit out of my house. Do it, or by Christ I'll call the mayor and have your badges. Now get out, Goddamn it. Get out!" Richards' voice rose to a shrill scream, veins standing out in his temples as he pointed a quivering finger at the door.

Casey knew he was licked. Richards' money and influence had helped put Mayor Trask in office. He swallowed the bile in his throat. "I hope you don't live to regret this. You're playing with your daughter's life." He turned on his heel and quietly ordered his men to break down their equipment and evacuate the premises.

In less than fifteen minutes, Richards felt quiet settle over the house as the last policemen departed. He stood at the study window, satisfying himself that he once more ruled his own domain. He felt, rather than heard Georgia standing behind him.

"I was right, wasn't I?"

He turned, his expression cold and distant. "I don't know what you mean."

She choked back angry tears. "You know who took Jess. Who is it, Whit? Tell me who it is."

He rushed her with a speed that took her breath, shaking her by the shoulders until her teeth rattled. "Listen, you dizzy bitch. Jess is my daughter, too, and I'm not going to let anything happen to her. I'll get her back, do you hear me? *I'll* get her back. Now get the hell out of my sight." He shoved her violently from him, and was gratified to see her run down the stairs.

He closed the study door and bolted it. He knew exactly what he had to do. He sat down at the desk and unlocked the bottom right drawer. From it he lifted a second telephone, one of the new ones with a rotary dial. It was an unlisted number the police knew nothing about.

He already knew the name of the man who had called him Rico, just as he knew that, somehow, the man would know his unlisted number, and would call him on it. He willed himself to patience. Today was the other man's day, but the days were short in December.

⚕

Jimmy Doughtery parked his Hudson Terraplane across the street from Bockman's Shoe Repair on Magazine Street. He removed a pair of black bluchers from the floorboard and took them with him as he went inside the shop. He didn't really want any work done on the bluchers. They were camouflage, just like the shoe repair shop wasn't quite a shoe repair shop.

The little bell over the door announced his entrance, but there was nobody at the counter. "Hey, Hugo," he called. "Hey, you got a customer out here." He looked at his watch. In ten minutes he wanted to be down the street at Ubertino's Oyster Bar with a dozen on the half-shell and an ice-cold glass of Jax in front of him. He pounded the flat of his hand on the counter. "Hey, Hugo. Fer Christ's sake, man. I got places to go." He went around the counter and into the back where the work benches were.

The odors of new leather and shoe dye back there were strong enough make your eyes tear up. Wrinkling his nose, he continued to the door at the back that led to the room where the telephones and the safe were. He jerked it open, expecting to hear the usual hubbub of bookies taking bets over the telephone. He wasn't expecting the muzzle of the small-bore revolver that met him at eye level.

"What the fuck—?"

"Gimme the take," Joey Parmalee said.

"The—the take?"

Parmalee smiled gently. "I know the route, asshole. I know you already been to ten other parlors by the time you get here. This is the last one on your route. So make with the kale and do it quick. My hand's gettin' tired."

Doughtery looked past the gun at the man's face, finally recognizing him. He saw, too, the unnaturally small pupils of the gunman's eyes. He was higher than a kite on coke or morphine. "Joey Parmalee. You sonofabitch. You think you're just gonna take the money and go have a party with it?" Doughtery was shocked at the young man's effrontery. "Christ almighty, man—Vic D'Angelo'll nail your hide to a barn door and set the barn on fire."

Joey cocked the target revolver. "The money. Now."

Doughtery swallowed. He'd said the gunman's name out loud. He was starting to get an idea he didn't like. "It—it's in my coat."

"Take it off," Parmalee ordered.

Doughtery gingerly removed his coat, held it out with shaking fingers. The gunman took it.

"Thanks, Jimmy." The small-bore revolver snapped twice, the sound like firecrackers in the small room. The muzzle was so close to Doughtery's face that it burned all the skin around the ragged hole where his left eye used to be. Parmalee took several packets of bills from the dead man's coat and transferred them to his own. He dropped the coat across Doughtery's face. Joey snickered as he reloaded his gun, casting a last look back at the three other dead men stacked in the corner. "Got the world by the tail, Joey. The world by the tail." He snickered some more as he walked away from the shop.

⚎

Jessica Richards awoke in a drab, high-ceilinged room without windows. She sat up on a creaking cast-iron bed rubbing her eyes. The last thing she remembered was being tied up and dumped into the trunk of a car.

"H-hello?" The tentative word was immediately swallowed up by the emptiness of the room. Her head ached.

She got up and began to explore her cell. An old bureau sat in a corner, all three of the drawers empty. The mirror had lost much of its reflective silvering, and the image it gave was something from a bad dream. The girl shivered, turned away.

A dry sink supported a bowl and pitcher with some water in it. Impulsively she picked up the pitcher and drank from the spout, spilling some down her blouse. It cooled her, helped wash out the fear clotting her throat.

With her thirst satisfied, she continued the investigation, finding a smelly slop bucket with a badly fitting wooden lid, and a two-year-old calendar decorated with a grainy photo of a nude woman. The woman had tiny little breasts that she flaunted as she leered at the camera. Jessica blew a defiant raspberry at the picture.

She moved on to the door, finding it securely locked. As she turned, she saw a closet. Upon opening it, a flurry of dust rose, making her sneeze. It was empty save for a fifteen-year-old *National Geographic* devoted to Richard Evelyn Byrd's flight over the South Pole and a *Screen Stories* with Clark Gable on the cover. She removed the magazines to the cot, figuring they might help her stave off boredom later on.

A rattling of the latch startled her and she jumped, placing her back to the wall. The door swung open and a man stood there. He was big, with a square Irish mug, scar tissue thickening his heavy brow. He looked dangerous, but not cruel.

"W-what do you want?"

The man stepped into the room. He had a paper bag in his hands. "Brought you some chow," he said. He put the bag on the bureau then leaned against the doorframe, his arms folded.

She hesitated. "Why am I here? What are you going to do with me?"

The big man's expression didn't change. "Your old man has something another man wants. Your old man gives it up, you go home. It's as simple as that."

"My—my father? He's on the city council. He's rich. Is it money you want?"

The big man stirred uncomfortably. "It ain't up to me to tell you, kid. Eat your food and keep quiet. Your old man wants you back so it won't be long." He backed out of the door, closing it firmly behind him.

As she listened to the tumblers fall in the lock, she hugged herself to still the trembling in her limbs. It continued until her eyes lit on the bag, and she suddenly realized she was ravenous. She crossed the room in two long strides and dug into the food.

⊗⊗⊗

Farrell woke up and for a moment forgot where he was. He blinked, pushing the hair out of his face as he looked at the other side of the bed. Savanna was gone, but a note pinned to her pillow explained that she'd risen earlier to visit friends, and would meet him at her club at midnight.

He and Savanna had lived together in Havana without raising a public eyebrow for almost fourteen months, becoming practically inseparable. He was largely immune to loneliness, but it felt a bit strange to have her gone from him for the rest of the night. He saw from the clock that it was almost 5:00 in the afternoon.

A quarter of an hour later he was knotting a tie beneath the collar of an oxford cloth shirt when the house phone rang. He picked it up.

"Hello, Harry. How's business?"

"Okay, boss. A lady down here's askin' to see you."

"She give a name?"

"Georgia Miles Richards."

The name silenced him for a moment. They hadn't spoken since 1924, and it had been a bitter parting. He felt surprise that the sound of her name could gall him so badly, yet curiosity sank a spur into his flank. "Send her up."

He was waiting at the stairwell door as she mounted the stairs. She looked at him with her wide green gaze, her face still the same but for a few small lines around her eyes. Her hair was shot with silver strands, but he noted with chagrin that she was still a dish.

"Hello, Georgia. Come in, won't you?"

"Thank you, Wes. It's good of you to see me." She smiled demurely and offered him a hand. In the light he could see the strain in her eyes and a certain stiffness in her bearing. He took the red fox stole from her shoulders and draped it across the back of a chair.

"Can I get you a drink?"

"Pernod and water, if you have it."

He nodded. Pernod and water was what they had drunk together in the old days, and she was telling him she hadn't forgotten. He went to the kitchen and a couple of minutes later he returned with two tall glasses wrapped in paper napkins. He handed one to her then stood there, looking down into her eyes. "You're looking good, Georgia."

She raised her glass to him and took a sip. "You don't look so bad yourself." She blotted her lips with the napkin, leaving a red imprint on the paper.

Farrell sat down across from her. "After all these years, it must be something big to bring you here."

She put the glass on the table, not looking at him. "I need help. A kind I can't get from just anyone."

"What makes you think I can help you? I'm just a businessman."

Her green eyes flashed up at him, and he saw heat smoldering in them. Her face stiffened for the briefest of seconds, then she forced a smile. "You get too much space in the newspapers for 'just a businessman,' Wes. Unless trouble is your business."

"I've been in the wrong place at the wrong time a bit too often. I live in Cuba most of the time now, and I've got business interests that keep me busy."

She nodded, her eyes heavy-lidded. "Will you at least listen before you tell me no?"

It hurt him to see her. He hadn't realized until now how raw this old wound was. He felt foolish, and that galled him all the more. "I'm not stopping you."

"It's about my daughter, Jessica."

"What about her?"

"She was kidnapped from school this afternoon."

He hid his surprise. "Is the FBI in on it yet?"

She snorted. "Nobody's on it. The kidnapper called and right after Whit threw the police out."

Farrell raised an eyebrow. "He must be very sure of himself."

She glared at him balefully. "He's sure, all right. He probably knows who's got her. Somebody he's double-crossed. Or—"

"Or what?"

"Or whoever has Jessica took her on Whit's orders and he's using this kidnapping to cover some scheme of his own." She wiped a hand tiredly across her face. "I'm just guessing. I have no idea what's going on."

"Neither do I. I just got back from Cuba today."

She settled back in the chair and a look of utter weariness suddenly added years to her face. She bit her lip, hesitated, then spoke. "I know what you're thinking: that I've got a hell of a nerve coming to you after what I did." She dropped her gaze, biting her lip again. A single tear escaped her left eye and traced a line down the curve of her cheek. "I'll say it for you. I'm a miserable grasping bitch. I left you high and dry for a man with a lot of money and I didn't look back."

He snorted. "You don't have to write a song about it. I know what you did."

She held up her head, hearing the wounded pride in his voice. "I did what I did. I won't make any excuses for it. Would it help if I told you I made a mistake? If I told you he's a lying, thieving rat? That he's cheated on me with every tramp who twitched her ass at him?"

He studied her with his brows lowered down over his eyes, hiding the emotion in them. "So you found out he was no good, yet you stayed with him."

"What did you expect me to do? I was on the street when you and I met, and everything I had to sell I gave you for nothing. Did you expect me to leave a big house and my own car and a fat bank account because I was married to a heel? I did what I had to do." Her green eyes had fire in them now, and her flushed face complimented the deeper red of her hair. For some reason he liked this woman better than the one who'd crawled in and asked for Pernod to call up a happy memory. He felt the hardness in his face relax.

"You've got guts, Georgia. I always said that. I'm glad to see you haven't lost them."

She shifted around in her seat, breathing harshly through her nose and she clamped her mouth. She wanted to cry, but she knew she couldn't, not with Farrell. She let the bitterness in her run free. "Whit's got to be behind this. He's played footsies with every grifter and shark in the state. This is somebody he double-crossed, I know it."

He noticed the glass in his hand, and drank half of the liquid in it, suddenly aware of how dry his throat was. He set the glass on the table and leaned forward, bracing his elbows on his knees as he stared into her eyes. "I can see you're in a bind, and I'm sorry as hell about it, Georgia. Kidnapping is a filthy trick, but I don't know what I can do. I've been out of town for over a year, and some of the players have probably changed. Besides, the cops may be off of it officially, but don't think they aren't paying attention. They're probably sore right now, looking for somebody to drop a ten-ton safe on."

Her veneer of toughness had been pressed to the limit. She put a trembling hand to her face as her shoulders began to shake with sobs. "Wes, I haven't got anybody else I can turn to. Even the Feds can't know all the things Whit's done. They won't know the names of all the men he's connived with or against. And Whit won't tell them. He can't. They'd put him in jail, too."

He got up and walked to the window. The December sun was low in the sky and already the garish neon signs of Basin

Street were flickering, pushing back the encroaching darkness as the music clubs began to come alive for yet another evening. "Why did you leave, Georgia? You never said, not even as you walked out."

"Because—" She hesitated as she groped for the words. "Because I wanted somebody who was going to be around. Because I knew you'd always be on the move. And—"

He turned and looked across the room. "And what?"

Her voice trembled, but there was the ring of truth in her words. "Because I was scared—of what you'd do. I knew sooner or later somebody'd get in your way and you'd kill him for it. And—and I was afraid I'd be there when it happened."

He nodded. He understood now. "I guess you were right, honey. That's just the way things turned out." He raised his pale eyes to hers. "And that's why you came to me now, isn't it?"

A single word, hard and resolute: "*Yes.*"

He almost smiled. "Have you got a picture of her?"

The question startled her for a moment but she recovered, slipping a hand into her purse. She extracted a wallet, opened it, and removed a picture. Wordlessly she got up and took it to him.

Farrell received the picture and looked at it. It was a wallet-sized copy of a formal portrait. It showed him a beautiful young girl with a remarkable air of self-possession in her direct gaze. She had a high forehead, thick dark hair, and a firm mouth. Her eyes continued to draw his attention as he examined it. "A good-looking young woman. She favors you."

"So I've been told. She has red hair, too, but it's darker than mine. Green eyes. She's about five-eight."

"Hmmm. Tall." He cut his eyes at her. "Must've gotten that from daddy. Whit's about six-three, right?"

She tucked a tendril of red hair behind her ear. "Yes, about that."

He slid the photo into his shirt pocket. "All right. I'll start asking around. Maybe I'll get lucky."

She moved a bit closer, looked up at him. Georgia was smaller than Savanna, probably no more than five-four, but she carried herself like a lot more woman, one who still had power, and knew it. She reached up a tentative hand, and like a fluttering moth, her fingers brushed his cheek, his stern lips. "I'd have done anything you wanted, Wes. Anything. You know that?"

"Yeah, but I'm not twenty-five anymore. Go home, Georgia. Don't come here again. When I know something I'll get in touch with you. Remember, the cops might be watching all of you, and if they aren't, Whit probably is."

Her face froze for an instant. "I hadn't thought of that. I'll go now." She turned and picked up her stole from the chair where Farrell had draped it. "Goodbye, Wes." She looked at him bleakly. There seemed to be nothing else to say. She turned and walked to the stairwell door.

He heard the door open and close, then the faint sound of her high heels rattling on the stairs fading to nothing. He reached up with his right hand and began to massage the muscles in his neck. He had returned to New Orleans a bit reluctantly, remembering the trouble and violence, the dead friend that had made him quit the city last year. Now he was back, and already there was trouble waiting. What was that Georgia had said? "Trouble is your business." That was a good joke, except nobody was laughing.

⊗⊗⊗

A skinny, pock-marked man with one of those mustaches that looked like something caught under your thumbnail reached Barracks Street just as the sun was beginning to go down. He'd only been up for two hours, his workday beginning when the rest of the world sat down to dinner. His name was Butch Callahan, and he managed almost two hundred whores for Whitman Richards.

He parked his Nash sedan in front of Vesey's Bar, a place that he used for a headquarters, and prepared to go inside. He paused under the neon sign to light an Italian cheroot, and as he struck the match, he saw the young man. He studied the man as he puffed the cheroot into life, watched him flipping a coin up and down. Callahan's mouth bent into a frown. He didn't like hustlers hanging out in front of his joint.

The young man seemed to notice him for the first time as he shook the match out. He stiffened slightly, almost guiltily, Callahan thought. He sauntered toward him, watching as the slightly built man faded into the shadow in front of a grocery store. He waited there as Callahan drew closer, the light from a street lamp glinting off the glasses he wore.

"What're you doin' there?" Callahan demanded.

"Mindin' my own business," the bespectacled young man replied. He spoke in a low, husky voice.

Callahan laughed nastily. "You're new in town, huh?"

He shrugged. "There a law against it?"

Callahan's voice hardened. "Not on the books, but, ya see, this is my territory. You want to hang around here, you gotta have business with me, but you ain't because I don't do business with punks like you."

The young man laughed. "Do tell."

Callahan didn't like that. "Don't get smart with me, you pissant. I don't have to take shit like that from nobody. You know what's good for you, you'll get your ass up the road."

"And if I don't?"

Callahan threw his cheroot to the ground, ignoring the sparks that flew around his feet. "I'll show you what." Callahan grabbed his lapel, jerked the other man toward him, his right hand flying back to strike. Before the blow fell, Callahan heard two muffled reports as something struck his chest. Weakness flooded through him. He stepped back, looked down at himself. "You—you b-bastard." Too late, Callahan saw the silenced muzzle of an automatic in the other's hand now. He looked down at the blood on the front of his shirt, felt the hot fire of the wounds. A wave of dizziness hit him as the pavement rushed up to meet his face.

Chapter 4

Easter Coupé sat alone at his kitchen table. He read the NAACP magazine, *The Crisis*, while he drank rye whiskey from a tall glass. He'd spent much of his life alone, and had until recently been content with his lot. Lately, however, he'd found himself with questions he couldn't answer, and the uncertainty was vaguely troubling to him. He'd taken to reading Negro magazines. They helped him pass the time, and sometimes he found the stories about the achievements of other Negroes strangely compelling.

The telephone on the kitchen counter began to ring. The sound was unwelcome to him. The look on his face would have silenced a man, but it had no effect on the instrument. When it rang a fourth time, he reached out a reluctant hand and snatched it from the cradle. "'Lo?"

"Easter? That you? It's Johnny Parmalee."

"Hey, Johnny. How's it goin', man?"

"You okay, Easter? You sound like you been laid up."

"Naw, man. What is it?"

"I'm in a bind. Me and Joey are hooked up. Somethin' big. We pulled a job today, but we had a hitch."

"A hitch?"

"A guy. He seen some things he ought not seen."

"Uh, huh. Why you need me?"

"It's a colored kid, name of Skeeter Longbaugh. We put the arm on him 'cause we needed him to get us into a place. He got away. He shoots his mouth off, it's bad all around."

Coupé rubbed his hand stiffly across his face. "You want him shut up, is that it?"

"He seen us kill a guy."

"Uh, huh. Where's he live?"

"Twelve-seventeen D'Hemecourt Street. Don't reckon he's gone back there."

"No, but it's a place to start. If you got the price."

Johnny hesitated. "How much?"

"A grand," Coupé said with the air of a man who knows he's charging too much but doesn't care.

"Done. This guy talks to the wrong people and Joey and me step off for it. You fix it, okay?"

Easter Coupé's jaw tightened. "I get you. It's taken care of. I'll call you." Coupé hung up without giving Johnny time to reply. He and Johnny had fought on some of the same cards in the old days. They had an easy informality for men of two different races. That was why Johnny had come to him, that and the fact that Coupé always did what he was paid to do. Except he hadn't with Merced Cresco. Something he couldn't seem to understand had stopped him.

He pushed that thought aside as he rose from the chair. He went to the bedroom, knotted a tie around his neck and slid into a black alpaca jacket. He clamped a black hat on his round head, pulling the brim low over his dark, expressionless eyes. He paused for a moment, then reached up to the shelf again. He took down a .38 Smith & Wesson revolver with a two-inch barrel. He slipped the gun into his hip pocket as he turned and left the house.

⊗⊗⊗

Casey was on his way home when a radio call diverted him to Magazine Street. He pulled up across the street from Bockman's Shoe Repair, where three radio cars and the crime lab van were already parked. Ray Snedegar came out to meet him and conducted him toward the rear of the repair shop.

"What've we got here, Ray?"

"Looks like a slaughterhouse in there, chief." As he shoved the door open, the coppery smell of dried blood cut through the odor of leather in the workshop.

Casey picked his way across the floor, stopping to stare down at the ravaged face of a man who lay with his head in a puddle of blood. "Jimmy Doughtery."

"Yeah, and over there is Hugo Bockman, Spence Markham and Morrie Crowder. All gunshot wounds."

"A .22?"

Snedegar shook his head. "Maybe. They're all small-caliber, but there's no shells lying around."

Casey stood up, shoving his hands into his pockets. He looked about the room, taking in the phones, racing forms, and rifled safe. "A bookie joint full of dead bookmakers. I'll bet you didn't find any money."

Snedegar pointed at the coat thrown carelessly across Doughtery's corpse. "The pockets are all turned inside out. Doughtery was a bagman for Vic D'Angelo. What you want to bet this was the last stop on Doughtery's route?"

Casey snorted. "Sucker bet. But that's not what interests me."

Snedegar tipped his hat back from his forehead. "What're you getting at, chief?"

"Doughtery's a bagman for Vic D'Angelo. D'Angelo works for Whit Richards."

Snedegar blinked. "So this happens the same day Richards' daughter is kidnapped."

"And the day after Jack Amsterdam just happens to get murdered by a whore in a fleabag hotel." Casey shook his head. "There's just a shade too much coincidence there for me, Ray. Something's going on, and I don't like it."

Snedegar drew closer to Casey. "You think somebody's making a run against Richards?"

"I don't know what else it could be. And that could spell gang war."

Snedegar looked down at Doughtery's body. "Hell of a time for something like this to come up. Here you are gettin' married in a few days."

Casey grinned good-naturedly. "Well, Brigid's been around cops all her life, so she's no stranger to crime intruding on her personal life. We're just having a private civil ceremony in her living room."

"Wes Farrell's standin' up for you, huh?"

Casey smiled. "I know you've got reservations about him, but there have been times when he was the best friend I had. A man needs to stick by his friends."

Snedegar gave him a sidelong look. "Then you might need him for more than just a best man. This weekend's liable to be a pip."

At that moment, Detective Mart stuck his head in the door. "Captain, dispatch says we got another gunshot victim over by Vesey's Bar."

Casey looked at Snedegar." They got an identification on the dead man?"

"Butch Callahan." Mart paused. "He's another of Council-man Richards's cronies, ain't he?"

⊗⊗⊗

Whit Richards stared out the window, the waiting eating at his guts like a cancer. He had never been afraid of a fight in his life, but the theft in broad daylight of his only child had rendered him inert. Until his enemy called again, he wouldn't know the score.

When the phone on his desk rang, he leaped to his feet like a runner at the starting gun. It took a second ring before he recognized that it was his regular phone. He picked it up warily. "Hello?"

"Whit, it's Vic. Can you talk?"

"Yes, I got rid of the cops. You got some news?"

"Yeah, and it's all bad. Jimmy Doughtery and all the guys at Bockman's are dead."

"Dead? What the hell are you talking about?"

"Somebody got into the back room and slaughtered everybody. Jimmy was layin' there with his head blown off."

"The money?"

"Gone," D'Angelo said. "Whoever hit the place must've known Bockman's was the last stop on the route."

Richards swore at the top of his lungs, using every combination of foul words he knew. He went on like that for at least a minute before D'Angelo stopped him.

"That ain't all, Whit. I just got a call from Vesey. Somebody shot Butch Callahan to death outside the bar a little while ago."

"And they killed Jack last night." Richards' voice was hushed with awe.

"Somebody's pokin' holes in us, Whit, but who?"

Richards put a shaking hand to the back of his neck and squeezed like a man shutting off the flow of blood from a wound. "It's Pete."

That stopped D'Angelo for a moment. "Pete Carson? You're outa your mind. He's been dead for eight years."

"Like hell he has," Richards thundered. "I was talkin' to the rat this afternoon. He's the one took my kid. He's the one tearin' down everything I spent twenty-five years buildin' up. He called me 'Rico' so I'd know it was him."

"God—Goddamn." Vic sounded dazed.

"Snap it up, Vic. I want you to get on the horn to everybody who's still alive. Tell 'em to stick together in groups. Get at least a dozen of 'em out lookin' for Pete. He probably hasn't been in town very long."

"Wait a minute, Whit. Stop and think about this a minute. Pete Carson didn't just breeze into town with a whole fuckin' organization. Somebody already here is backin' his play, or he'd never be able to pull this off."

Richards was suddenly quiet as he recognized the truth in his henchman's argument. "But who?" He sat up in his chair, his eyes suddenly brilliant with anger. "We've got to find out. Tell the boys to tear this town apart brick by brick, but find out who's behind this, you hear me?"

"I hear you. They're pokin' holes in my ass, too."

"Then get moving." Richards broke the connection. He sat there seething for two or three minutes, then forced himself to calm down. He had to think.

It was obvious that Pete Carson was making a concerted effort to weaken him. Jack Amsterdam had controlled his illegal gambling interests in Orleans and Jefferson Parishes. Butch Callahan had managed a vast prostitution network. By killing them, Pete had taken out two of the three men Richards had depended on to keep money flowing into his operation. They had also been his two most capable fighters. Rob Langdon was a first-rate scrapper in a courtroom or a boardroom meeting, but otherwise he was a college boy with no experience on the street. Vic D'Angelo was okay in a street fight, but he was no thinker. Keeping track of the bookie joints was his main responsibility, and Pete had managed to hurt him there, too.

He squeezed the bridge of his nose, trying to figure Pete's next move. Pete knew him better than anyone, and he also knew enough about the operation to think ahead. He looked at his watch and realized Meredith would soon be going home. She was a clever girl. Talking to her might help him make sense of what was going on. He opened the drawer of his desk and took from it a Remington .380 automatic. He grabbed his hat and coat from the tree as he left the study.

⊗⊗⊗

Easter Coupé stared out the car window at the Negro tavern across the street, examining it thoroughly. It had a neon sign that spelled out THE PITTY-PAT CLUB. As he got out of his yellow De Soto and headed over, he reflected on the words of three different men he'd spoken to. Each of them had mentioned joints where Skeeter Longbaugh was a regular, but the Pitty-Pat Club was the only one that all three had mentioned. Acting on instinct, Coupé decided to try this place first.

As he entered, he cast a sharp glance at the few customers inside, noting each was deep in his own thoughts.

A handsome dark-skinned woman tending bar looked up from the glass she was polishing as he sauntered in. He placed a half dollar on the mahogany surface and pushed it toward her. "Seven Crown please, ma'am."

She gave him a roguish smile. "Nobody's called me 'ma'am' since I left daddy's farm."

"Mama taught me to treat every woman I met as a lady. Until she showed me different, that is."

She uttered a lazy laugh. "Most of the men in here don't remember nothin' their mamas taught 'em. Hell, most of them probably don't remember they had mamas." She laughed some more as she poured whiskey into a glass and placed it in front of him.

Coupé picked up the glass and toasted her with it. "Your good health, ma'am."

She leaned on the bar and studied his face, clearly intrigued by him. "I answer to Kate."

He grinned. "I thought it might be Pitty-Pat."

She grimaced. "That was the name when I bought the place. I was afraid to change it for fear of confusing the customers." She shot a sardonic glance around the room. "Some of these characters confuse pretty easy." She looked at him again. "Don't recall you ever been in here before."

"Ain't. Young fella I know mentioned the place."

"What was his name? Maybe I know him to talk to."

Coupé squinted at the ceiling as though deep in thought. "Has kind of a peculiar name. Scatter, Skipper—no, Skeeter. That's it. Skeeter Longbaugh."

She rolled her eyes. "Oh, him. I can tell you how he got that name. He purely loves to buzz 'round the females."

Coupé grinned. "Likes you a li'l bit, huh?"

Kate snorted. "If he ever met a gal he didn't like, I'd like to see her. I've fielded so many passes from that boy that I could be a receiver for the LSU Tigers."

Coupé put down his glass and she silently refilled. He placed his forearms on the bar and leaned on them. "Ain't seen ole Skeeter lately. Wonder where he's got to?"

"He's got so many women he ain't got time for no men friends," Kate replied. "Heard he's sweet on the kid sister of that woman who runs the bawdy house out by the lake."

"Hmmm. That'd be Miss Toni Mereaux's place, right?"

"Aw," she said, grinning. "You know it, huh?"

He shook his head primly. "Of it, Miss Kate. A smart man stays outa them kinda places. 'Sides, with women like you around, why would I bother?"

She lowered her lashes, letting him know he'd scored a point. "Hear tell Skeeter's also spendin' time with the woman who cooks at Ma Rankin's house on Mystery Street. She used to hook, but retired before it killed her. Skeeter'd never pay for his lovin' nohow. He ain't got no money."

Coupé finished his drink and put the glass on the table. "Well, reckon I better be movin' along, Miss Kate. Sure enjoyed your company." He stood up, looking down into her face, seeing the light of interest in her eyes.

She put her hand over one of his. "I aim to please. Think you might be comin' back this way soon?"

He reached up to tug his hat down over his forehead, smiling at her. "Reckon I might, Miss Pitty-Pat. So long now." He gave her hand a squeeze before turning to leave. By the time he reached the door and stepped into the street, his charming demeanor had disappeared beneath an air of calculation. He decided to check Skeeter's house next. He glanced at his watch, saw that the kid had been loose on the streets for over three hours.

As he got to his car and opened the door, he cast a wistful look back at the bar. He hadn't talked to a woman in a long time that wasn't a whore, and there wasn't much talk with one of them. His life had little in it but eating, sleeping, and hurting people. He felt a spike of some emotion he didn't recognize as he got into his car.

❈

Detective Sam Andrews eased the old Dodge sedan to a stop outside a gin mill on North Robertson called Chili's Place. He cut his eyes over at Daggett and grinned. "This might just be the scummiest hole you and me ever been in."

"It just looks that way because we been in so many of 'em. Let's go inside. Maybe we'll be surprised."

Andrews snorted. "The last time I was surprised, Herbert Hoover was president." He pushed open the driver's door and climbed out onto the pavement.

As the pair entered the juke joint, the blare of Charlie Parker's sax from the jukebox almost blew them back out into the street. They paused, squinting into the blue haze of tobacco smoke until they saw Smoker Cauvin sitting in the far corner with his back to the wall. As usual, the stubby dark brown man surveyed the scene through a pair of dark glasses, a cigarette smoldering in the corner of his mouth. The Negro detectives split apart and approached him from two directions, their empty hands swinging loose at their sides.

"What say, Smoker?" Daggett asked when they were close enough to be heard.

"Nothin', man. I ain't like a lotta cats, rattlin' their lips when they ain't got nothin' to say. I'm a man who chooses his words with great care, you dig?"

Each detective hooked a chair and straddled it. "We're lookin' for Skeeter Longbaugh. Hear you're thick with him."

Smoker sneered around his cigarette. "I'm that dumb-ass's first cousin, if you call that thick. He's family, so I gotta put up with him once in a while. What's that empty-headed motha-fuckah done now?"

"We just wanna talk to him. Seen him lately?"

Smoker removed the cigarette long enough to drink from a tumbler full of Four Roses, then he replaced the cigarette in the corner of his mouth. "Yeah, about a week ago. Hit me up for a sawbuck, like I'm made of money or somethin'. I give him a finif and told him to be grateful for it. Six days ago that motha-fuckah borrowed money from me and you think I seen him since? Shit, naw."

Andrews sighed. He was tired and his patience, never great to begin with, was wearing dangerously thin. "Smoker, you know we ain't prowlin' this shit neighborhood to listen to your trials and tribulations. Where is he likely to go with your five bucks weighin' down his pants pocket?"

Smoker's mouth curved into a smile. "When he's got money, he chases after Toni Mereaux's kid sister. She ain't trickin', cause Toni'd kill her, but she been givin' it to Skeeter all the same. Boy's as dumb as a ball peen hammer, but the chicks think he's just bein' cute. By the time they realize just how dumb he is, they done give him enough tail to keep six guys happy."

"Just in case he's run through that fortune you give him, where else could he be?" Daggett asked dryly.

"That ex-whore who cooks at Ma Rankin's house. Whole house fulla gals sellin' it as hard as they can, and fuckin' Skeeter finds the one gal there who'll give it to him for nothin'." He laughed, slapping his knee.

"Tell me, Smoker," Daggett said, leaning a bit closer to the smaller man. "Would you know if Skeeter was mixed up in some kinda trouble?"

"Shit, yeah, man. He's too dumb to keep a secret." Smoker laughed raucously. "You ain't got him pegged as no criminal mastermind, do you?" He laughed some more.

Daggett got up, Andrews a half-beat behind. "Thanks for all the help, Smoker. We'll see you again some time."

"Yeah, man, look forward to it." He laughed some more.

As they left the noise and the stench of Chili's behind them, Andrews paused to rub the back of his thick neck with a hand the size of a ham. "One of these days, I'm 'onna slap that li'l pissant through a wall."

"He's just another lowlife living from one buck to the next. With any luck the Army'll draft his ass soon, and *they'll* slap those dark glasses right off his nose."

Andrews laughed. "I'd enlist myself to see that."

"Forget that idea. You're too fat and I'm too old. They wouldn't take either of us, and anyway, we'd end up diggin' ditches. Even being a Negro cop in New Orleans is a better life than that."

"Say that again, boss. You wanna take a flyer out to Toni Mereaux's?"

Daggett shrugged and headed to the battered old Dodge. "We got to find Skeeter so let's give it a try."

Andrews opened the driver's door and slid his bulk under the steering wheel. "I ain't been to a high-class cat-house since I was in knickers."

As they drove west across town, Daggett fingered his chin as he frowned at the darkening street. "You know, Smoker talks big, but he's no dummy."

"I reckon," Sam said grudgingly.

"He said that Longbaugh was too simple to be mixed up in something and then be able to hide it."

Sam nodded slowly. "What d'you think that means?"

"I don't know. Let's see what else we can find out."

It took them about forty-five minutes to make it across town and out to the shore of Lake Pontchartrain. Toni Mereaux's three-story house was silhouetted against the moon as bright light from a dozen large windows spilled out into the yard. Through one of the open windows, they heard Artie Shaw's clarinet backing Lady Day as she crooned "Begin the Beguine." The house piano played behind them, skillfully embroidering the melody while not detracting from the pros on the recording. As they approached the house, Andrews began to snap his fingers, pleased little grunts emanating from the depths of his throat.

Daggett leaned on the bell, his badge in his hand. The door opened and a delicately featured mulatto girl stood in the door, the light radiating behind her small head like an aura. "Police. We want to talk to Miss Mereaux."

The mulatto girl sighed, gestured for them to enter with an elegant movement of her head. She led them past half a dozen girls in slips and peignoirs, some entertaining high rollers in zoot suits. One looked past his girl's shoulder and gasped when he recognized Daggett's face.

"Keep your seat, brutha," Daggett said softly. "Whoever you are, we ain't after you tonight."

They continued past a skinny Negro boy of about nineteen and realized he was the piano virtuoso they'd heard outside. Andrews grinned and grunted some more. "Sweet music, man. Keep at it—the Jelly Roll man and Fats both started out in one'a these places. You sound like you're ready to move on to Kansas City, playin' like that."

The kid gave the detective a shy grin. "Thanks, boss. Anything you wanna hear?"

"Anything, man, just keep playin'."

The girl led them down a hall to a room with a half-opened door. The girl knocked lightly, stuck her head through the opening. Daggett didn't hear what she said, but within seconds an older woman stood in the opening. Her bronze skin was so taut and smooth you could have bounced dimes off of it. Thick dark hair swung loose to her shoulders as she stared at them with a sullen mouth.

"I've already paid this month."

"We're not here for a payoff, Miss Mereaux. I'm Sergeant Daggett and this is Detective Andrews. We're out of the Negro Squad from Downtown."

Her large liquid brown eyes did a slow inspection of Daggett. "Sorry if I talked out of turn. What can I do for you?" She gestured for them to enter, and for the mulatto girl to return to the front.

Daggett took off his hat and held it down alongside his leg by the brim. "We're looking for a man named Skeeter Longbaugh. We were told your sister is friendly with him."

A frown creased the smooth tautness of her forehead. "I told her to stay away from that idiot. He hasn't got the brains God gave an animal cracker."

"Maybe, but it would be helpful to know if she's seen or spoken to him in the last forty-eight hours."

Toni Mereaux led them through what turned out to be a private apartment. The office door led through a small dining room into a room furnished like a parlor with very jazzy deco furniture in stark whites and blacks. A pretty girl in her late teens sat in a plump white armchair reading a novel with the words *Native Son* on the front of the jacket. She looked up as they entered and closed the book, holding her place with an index finger.

"Terry, these men are policemen. They want to know the last time you saw Skeeter Longbaugh." Daggett heard anger simmering in Toni's voice, but he kept his attention on the young girl's face.

She cut her eyes at Daggett and Andrews then back up at her sister. "What for?"

Toni's eyes got a hot, mad look in them. "Have you been sneaking out with that empty-headed little cock-hound?"

Terry lowered her eyes. "It's none of anybody's business if I do."

Daggett moved a bit closer to the girl, speaking in a patient, cool voice. "Listen, miss. A white girl was kidnapped from Sacred Heart Academy this morning. A Negro custodian was killed by the kidnappers."

"Skeeter's missing, too," Andrews added. "We need to find him so we can ask what he knows about it. If it's nothing, he walks, but the longer it takes us to find him, the rougher it's going to be when we do. Help us out, and help him out at the same time."

She looked up at both detectives, searching their faces for subterfuge. She cut her eyes briefly at her sister. "I—I saw him Monday, late in the afternoon."

"You little—" Before Toni could finish the thought, Daggett held up his hand to cut her off.

"What did he say?"

Terry shrugged her shoulders. "He'd just got off work and he seemed about the same. I got him to come with me to the Fat Man Lounge and we had a couple of drinks."

"He seem different to you?"

She shook her head. "No. He was his usual self, happy and smilin', whistling dance tunes. He's a lot of laughs."

Toni's face had become a thundercloud. She elbowed her way past Daggett, her hands bunched into fists. "He's happy because you keep letting him get his hand inside your pants, you little tramp. I told you to stay away from him and everybody like him. I told you—"

Terry jumped to her feet, the book held in her hand like a weapon. "You tell me to stay away from him while you peddle your ass and the asses of these other girls here. You got a hell of a nerve, you two-faced—"

Daggett saw it coming just in time to step in. Toni Mereaux's right hand flashed back and streaked toward her sister's face like a rocket. Daggett caught the wrist and checked the blow, interposing himself between the two women. "That's enough of that. If you two want to kill each other, do it on somebody else's time. You—" He turned back to Terry Mereaux, who remained in a crouch, her teeth showing in a snarl. "Did Longbaugh say anything else while you were with him? Cough it up or I'll take you Downtown."

Andrews had moved up behind the defiant girl, his face like a stone mask. "Tell him, girly. We're gettin' old listenin' to this kiddy-garden shit."

Andrews' bass voice hit Terry like a blow to the body and she dropped the book, glancing with scared eyes over her shoulder. "Only that he was short of money and was afraid he'd have to go back to being a mechanic because it paid better." She paused, thinking about it. "That was unusual.

Normally he lives from one day to the next. That's the closest thing to an ambition I ever heard out of him."

Daggett listened, watching the girl's face. She was shooting straight with them now. There was one other thing he wanted to know. "Does Skeeter carry a knife?"

Her face froze as she made the connection. "N-no. At least I never saw him with one."

Daggett nodded. "Okay, you're off the hook, but if you hear from Longbaugh, I want to know about it, understand?"

"Y-yes, sir."

Daggett turned to Toni Mereaux, who was sullenly massaging her wrist. "You're gonna think this is none of my business, but if you want to bring her up right, send her away to school. You believe that by keepin' her on a short leash you're protecting her from what you do for a living. It doesn't work like that, and it won't help her grow up clean."

She sneered at him. "I like that—a cop tellin' *me* what's right and what's not. I like that a whole lot."

Daggett's eyes grew cold and hard and his voice dropped to a cottony whisper. "I'm investigating a cold-blooded murder and a kidnapping, Miss Mereaux. If I had the time, I'd haul you in for contributing to the delinquency of a minor. Think about what I said, before I have time to come back here. Let's go, Sam."

They paused out at the car, Daggett using a handkerchief to wipe his neck and the sweatband of his hat.

"You got pretty wound up in there, Iz."

Daggett snorted. "Maybe. In a few more months, I'm gonna be a father. I have this strange feelin' it might be a girl. Maybe that's what I was thinking about."

Andrews nodded soberly. "I hear you. You wanna look up the gal at Ma Rankin's that Smoker mentioned?"

"It's the only other lead we got. Let's roll."

Chapter 5

Two hours after Georgia Richards left his apartment, Farrell took to the streets with his mind full of questions. Kidnapping was something he'd had little experience with, but it occurred to him that there could be only two reasons for such a move against Whit Richards: money or advantage.

The Quarter was the same as ever, street noise lightly mixed with jazz escaping the doors of juke joints and nightclubs warming up for the night's business. Eventually he reached the nameless club identified only by its trademark neon sign, the top-hatted crawfish with his two-olive martini. The colored kid at the door grinned his recognition and slipped him some skin as he passed through.

He saw immediately that his friend Little Head Lucas had spruced the place up since his last visit. Where the Wurlitzer juke box used to hold sway was a real bandstand, and on it were the Bones Melancon Sextette and Anna Lou Hamer just breaking into "Kick It," a number recently recorded by Krupa's band.

He located Little Head Lucas near the bar, his table now on a small raised platform. Oblivious to the music, the big man's dark face was bent over his chessboard as his thick fingers tickled the tops of the black chess pieces.

"I was afraid for a second I'd come to the wrong place," Farrell said when he was close enough to be heard.

The Negro lifted his head and turned, his face breaking into a huge grin as he recognized his old friend. He rose and pulled Farrell to the platform, enfolding him in a bear hug. "Man, I was afraid I wasn't ever gonna see you again. When'd you get back?"

"Earlier today. This is my first time out."

"And you come here first. I'm honored, my man. Sit down there." He snapped his fingers loudly and made a signal to the bartender as he returned to his seat. "What's it like in Cuba?"

Farrell removed his hat and ran his fingers through his thick reddish-brown hair. "Havana's a lot like New Orleans, pal. Anything goes if you got the price of the ticket."

Little Head's broad grin faded and an appraising look replaced it. "How you doin'? That was pretty tough, what happened last year. I never got a chance to tell you how bad I felt about Luis Martinez."

Farrell looked down at the chessboard, shaking his head. Even now he found it hard to talk about the death of his old friend. "Yeah. I know. That's all ancient history now." He was saved from further discussion by the arrival of two tall glasses full of lime juice and Barbados rum.

Lucas picked up a glass and touched it to Farrell's. "Good times, man. Let 'em roll."

Farrell smiled. "I hear you."

They drank in silence, listening for a while to Anna Lou croon words of love as only she could. Little Head watched Farrell covertly, concern in his eyes. He had known Farrell a long time, and recognized tension in the set of Farrell's body, the way his pale eyes moved restlessly across the crowd.

"What's cookin', Pops? I know you're into somethin', so don't be tryin' to jive me. Who you lookin' for?"

"An old friend visited me today. Said her daughter's been kidnapped. She asked me to help find her."

Lucas nodded. "That'd be Mrs. Georgia Richards. That story's all over town by now. Whoever snatched the girl also stuck a chiv into a brutha named Butterbean Glasgo. He left a wife and six kids."

"Damn. I didn't know. Georgia didn't mention it."

"No," Lucas said in a somber voice. "Don't reckon she did." He sipped some rum, ruminated for a moment. "Funny that should happen today."

Farrell cut his eyes at his friend. "Funny? In what way?"

"Seems like Councilman Richards is havin' a run of bad luck this week. Las' night, his right-hand man, Jack Amsterdam, got his lights put out in the Bella Creole Hotel. They sayin' that a whore rolled him."

Farrell studied his friend's face. "If that's a coincidence, I'll take up needlepoint."

"That's pretty much the way I feel, too."

Farrell rubbed a thumb over his chin. "If Richards weren't so big in this town, I'd be tempted to think somebody was trying to jerk the rug out from under him."

Little Head shrugged. "When you're that big, there's always somebody lookin' to take your place."

"But who's big enough to tackle Richards? He's got more than just guns going for him. He helped elect the mayor and Sheriff Tim Marrero has won three elections thanks to Richards' money and influence."

Little Head nodded. "That's all true, but the man's made some big enemies. I can think of several right off the bat that he hurt, but they all come back from it. And they all got money, men, and patience."

Farrell studied his friend's face, waiting for him to tell his story at his own speed.

"Number one on the list is Kurt Van Zandt," the big man continued. "He had a hell of a big gamblin' operation he operated outa some warehouses down river from here. Richards wanted a piece of it. When Van Zandt said no, Richards sent in enough guns to wreck it."

"Uh, huh."

"Next on the list is King Arboneau. When he wouldn't let Richards in, he used the Zoning Commission and various laws to condemn or confiscate most of the King's prime real estate. On top of that, he had King's son killed."

"I thought Tel Arboneau died drunk when a train smashed into his car at the Bywater crossing."

Little Head smiled. "Uh-uh, brutha. Lenny Schwarz, the coroner's stenographer, told me Tel was dead from a broken neck long before the train got there."

"Interesting. So who's number three?"

"Remember Old Man Tarkington?"

"Sure. He owned a big sugar refinery. I heard he was gunned down on a country road."

Little Head chuckled. "Uh, huh. Anyhow, Richards got his hands on the refinery and it gave him a respectable front—that's how he got what he needed to get started in politics, my man."

"How did he get the refinery?"

"Tarkington didn't have no family but a nephew, man named Neil Gaudain. Gaudain didn't know what the refinery was worth. Richards kinda made sure of that by scarin' all the other bidders off. By the time Gaudain understood how bad Richards had cheated him, a coupla years had gone by. The way I hear it, Gaudain's stayin' alive just so he can dance on Richards' grave."

Farrell drummed his fingers on the tabletop as he gazed at the Negro from under an arched eyebrow. "How the hell do you know all this stuff? Have you got a librarian working in the back room who compiles it for you?"

Little Head sighed. "No, its just when you sit in one spot all day, people is always comin' past and droppin' stuff where you can see or hear it. And then I got kind of a long memory."

Farrell nodded. "You've given me a lot to think about. Any one of those guys might have the resources and manpower to undermine Richards. There's only one thing missing from the picture."

"What's that, man?"

"There's not a really brave man in the bunch. Whoever's behind this has brains, but he's got more than his share of guts, too."

"Can't argue with you there, brutha. But I got one more name. Remember Fletch Monaghan?"

"Sure. He was hooked up with old August Milton during Prohibition. He's a gambler now. What's his beef with Richards?"

Little Head reached behind his head with a huge brown paw and massaged his neck. "From what I can tell, he just hates his ass on general principles. What they call a personality conflict."

Farrell gave the Negro a wry look. "Have you been reading the encyclopedia again?"

Little Head shrugged. "There might be a better reason for the hate, but that's a piece of information that ain't walked through the door yet."

Farrell grinned. "The night's young. And you're not the only man in town who soaks up loose talk."

"Let's have another drink then," Lucas said. "You can tell me about Cuba and maybe that information will come sit down beside us."

"Little Head, I like the way you think."

⊗⊗⊗

Whitman Richards lay on his back in Meredith Baker's bedroom. She sat astride his thighs and ran her fingers through the thick dark hair on his chest. Pale amber light from a lamp with a mica shade gave her skin a golden glow. Her head was bowed and blonde hair fell over her face, shading it from his view.

"Who is this horrible man, Whit? Why is he doing this?"

"His name is Pete Carson. We were partners—once."

She moved her hips slightly, causing the breath to catch in his throat. "There must be more to it than that."

"Be sure you want to know before you ask, Merry. I've told you enough about me by now for you to know I'm no angel."

"I love you, baby. I can take it."

He looked up, trying to see her bright blue eyes within the shadow of her hair. "There was a man named Tarkington, eight or nine years ago. He had a business that I needed in order to give myself a respectable front. I tried to buy him out, tried to go partners with him, but he was stubborn. He wouldn't give in."

"He sounds like a stupid man," she said.

He smiled. "He was that. Pete was for killing him outright. But then, Pete was getting too big for his britches. I found out he'd been shorting me on the take. I'd trusted him and he'd been stealing from me."

She began to move above him, her breathing quickening. "So what—did you—do?"

"I had somebody else kill Tarkington. Then I found a way to let the cops believe Pete had done it. He had to leave town, of course. Since I didn't have as many cops or judges in my pocket then as I do now, I couldn't help him."

She laughed. "Not that you wanted to." Her fingers kneaded the muscles of his chest.

His own breathing was starting to quicken. "No. I needed him gone, and once he was, things began to fall into place. I even got word he'd been killed. Cut in half by a train, but that was crap. Somehow, he figured out how I tricked him, and now he's back. It's too bad."

Her face was right over his now, and he could see her eyes were closed as she worked up and down on him. His body didn't seem to belong to him now, it felt like it was floating past him. He grappled and clutched at her, giving in to the convulsions tearing through him, trying with all his heart to blot out the fear that sucked at his mind like a vortex.

❧

Darkness had fallen by the time Joey Parmalee eased his Studebaker convertible behind the old farm house off

Fillmore Drive. He carried a valise full of the money he'd taken from the shoe repair shop through the back door where he found his brother and Pete Carson sitting at a table.

"Joe," Johnny said. "This is Pete Carson. My brother, Pete."

Carson stood, towering over Joey. He had a hard, fit look that reminded Joey uncomfortably of his brother. Carson held out a hand. "Good to know you, Joe. How'd it go at Bockman's?"

Joey grinned as he held up the valise. "Like shootin' fish in a barrel. Here's five grand, Mr. Carson. That operation's closed out. Permanent."

Carson took the bag, his eyes suddenly gone narrow. "You sayin' you killed Bockman?"

Joey shrugged. "Bockman, his boys. Jimmy Daughtery, too. They knew who I was, so I took care of 'em."

Carson blinked slowly. "Nobody told you to kill anybody, kid. I wanted the operation knocked over, not wiped out. Those guys all knew things that would've been helpful later on."

"Hell," Joey said, defensively. "They was just a bunch of bookies. They're a dime a dozen in this town, Mr. Carson." Joey saw Johnny looking at him, and felt his guts twist into a knot. All his life he'd been trying to please Johnny, and it was never enough. Carson was giving him hell, and Johnny would give it to him again. He felt sick to his stomach.

Carson stared down into Joey's eyes, holding them for a long minute before nodding imperceptibly. "Okay, you made a mistake. Don't make another one. Richards threw the cops off the kidnap case, but every time somebody gets killed, cops start snooping around. The more dead men, the more cops snooping. Am I gettin' through to you, kid?"

It took all of Joey's strength not to wilt under Carson's piercing green gaze. "I understand you, Mr. Carson. No more killin' unless you say so. I got it, all right."

Carson nodded. "Okay. I got to make some calls in the other room. Take a load off for now." He walked away, leaving the other two men alone.

Joey walked to the stove, poured himself a cup of coffee as he studiously avoided his brother's eyes.

"What is it with you, Joey? We got a shot at a sweet deal, with a guy who's goin' places, and you piss all over his shoes, for Chris' sake."

"Don't start wearin' my ass out, Johnny. I'm warnin' you—"

Johnny stood up quickly, looming over his brother. "You dumb fuck. Are you tryin' to get killed? Pete Carson ain't some drugstore cowboy you can lip off to." He paused, shaking his head. "I've watched you, Joe. You like killin' way too much. Don't tell me you couldn't of just stuck those guys up. No bookie's gonna risk his life over a few bucks. They ain't made that way."

Joey turned slowly, anger and fear warring within him. His right hand twitched with the desire for a gun, but Joey knew better than to pull iron on his big brother. "Get the fuck off my back, Johnny. You can't scramble eggs without breakin' the shells. You think them four guys was gonna give me the money for my looks? They pulled iron and I shot first. I ain't big like you. I don't scare nobody. A gun's the only size I got."

Johnny blinked uncertainly. He smoothed the anger out of his face as he considered Joey's story. Maybe he was in the wrong this time. He shrugged, took Joey by the arm and drew him close, looking down into his eyes. "Don't screw up anymore, little brother. I'm sick of bein' a leg-breaker to a loan shark. I could have class. I could be somebody. *We* could be somebody." He let Joey's arm go and his eyes wandered down the front of Joey's clothes. "Say, where's that nifty li'l tie bar I gave you for your birthday? The one shaped like a clarinet?"

Joey slid away from his brother, not looking at him. "Aw, it's around here someplace. I just mislaid it is all." He made his words casual, and Johnny bought them.

"Okay. Sorry for the tiff. Wanna play some pinochle?"

"No. No thanks, Johnny. Think I'll siddown and listen to the radio for a while."

"Okay, kid." Johnny walked away, leaving Joey stroking the place where his tie bar should have been, a nervous sweat beading on his upper lip.

⌘

It was immediately apparent to Easter Coupé that Skeeter hadn't returned after his escape. His car was still in the shed, and Skeeter's clothing and shaving things were all where they belonged.

Not having eaten since early that morning, Coupé decided to check out the boy's larder in the hopes of locating a snack. The icebox had a pint of milk gone sour, a half-stick of oleomargarine, and two shriveled oranges. In the bread box he found a wrapper with a few slices of white bread remaining. They were stale, but he was too hungry to care.

He continued through the apartment, noticing in the glow of his flashlight just how little the youngster owned. There wasn't enough furniture to entertain any company. Moreover the boy owned neither radio nor phonograph. There were no books, magazines, nor any newspapers. In a bureau, Coupé found an address book with the names and numbers of at least thirty women. Kate had been right about him.

In the drawer of a rickety writing table, Coupé found an invoice from a garage in Gerttown owned by somebody named Blessey. The bill total was $15.00, yet below the sum was scrawled the words "NO CHARGE." Coupé frowned at that. Automotive repair was a thing that people without money either handled themselves or did without in these times. For the equivalent of a week's salary to be so cavalierly dismissed suggested a relationship of some kind.

He looked about the dark rooms, thinking how much they were like his own, empty of past and holding no promise for the future. Once again he felt that strange stab of emotion that had hit him outside of Kate's lounge, but he rolled his shoulders, frowning as though it were a sore muscle as he exited through the back on the way to his car.

⊗⊗⊗

Pete Carson dialed the Downtown number again and listened to it buzz several times before the owner picked up. "It's Pete. Can you talk?"

"Yeah, I'm alone. I got the word about Bockman and Daughtery and them. Joey Parmalee do that?"

"Yeah," Carson replied. "The trigger-happy punk. He brought five grand back with him."

"My boys knocked over a couple of other joints. They brought in about twelve grand between them. We're already better off than when you got off the train." The man paused for a moment. "I got word of somethin' a li'l while ago, Pete. It's not bad news, but it ain't particularly good neither."

Carson frowned as he heard the note in the other man's voice. "What is it?"

"Jack Amsterdam got killed in a fleabag last night. They're sayin' a whore done it."

"Hell. Amsterdam was the lynch pin to Whit's gambling rackets. That's damned bad luck for us."

"Maybe," the man said dubiously. "He and Richards had been together from the start. I ain't sure you could've bought him. Scared him, maybe, but no other way."

"We'll never know," Carson growled. "Of all the frigging bad luck. Christ."

"Richards is pullin' the rest of his men back," the other man said. "Amsterdam gettin' killed woulda thrown him off balance, but he ain't stupid. My guess is that as soon as he got word about Bockman and Daughtery, he started pullin' everything and everybody back inside his hole. His men are gonna be real cautious now."

Pete grinned into the receiver. "Well, I expected that after we talked on the phone. I know from experience he's no slouch in the brains department."

"We all know that," the other man said. "But he never seen the kidnapping comin'. This was the prize sucker punch of all time. How long you think it'll be before he starts to buckle?"

Carson's eyes flickered. "Can't say for sure, but Rico's tough. I know him better than anyone else. We may have to hit him again."

"Give me the word and I'll send my men out again," the man said. "I've been waiting for this for a long time."

"Then you won't mind waiting a little more," Carson said. "We've got to do this right or not at all."

"I hear you, Pete. Don't forget how long I've already waited."

"Sure," Carson said. He paused for a moment and licked his lips. "You got a message for me yet?"

"No, but I wouldn't worry. You'll get a chance to talk before much longer."

"Yeah, I guess you're right. Good night."

"'Night." The man hung up.

Carson put his receiver back into the cradle. He felt a momentary sense of disquiet that he quickly shrugged off as he went to get some food and coffee.

Chapter 6

Frank Casey sat at the end of a blue-textured sofa in Brigid Longley's Jefferson Avenue apartment. She was lounging contentedly in the crook of his arm while her console radio quietly leaked the music of Xavier's Cugat's Waldorf Astoria Orchestra into her living room.

"You look tired, Frank."

Casey smiled and hugged her. "You'll get used to it."

"Oh, no. I've got things in mind for you, mister, and there won't be any room for you being tired." Before he could reply the phone rang. "Who could that be at this hour?" She rose and picked up the receiver. "Hello?"

"Hi, Brigid. How's the happy bride?"

"Wes, I was hoping you'd call. Did you have an easy trip back from Havana?"

"Like a breeze. Is the groom there?"

She looked over at Casey and smiled. "He hasn't moved in yet, but he sure takes up a lot of space. Here he is." She handed it to Casey, who'd gotten up to join her.

"I was wondering if you'd call tonight," Casey said. "When did you get in?"

"Before noon today. I tried calling you at the office and they told me you were off on a case."

"Yeah, it started off with a kidnapping and got worse from there. I think somebody's playing king of the hill with Whit Richards as the target."

"I think you're right. I heard about Jack Amsterdam."

Casey was momentarily surprised by his son's knowledge, then shook it off. Farrell was obliquely informing him that he had some interest in the case and might be able to help. "What have you heard so far?"

"Only about the kidnapping from the girl's mother, and about Amsterdam from Little Head Lucas. I suspect there's more, from the way you're talking."

Casey laughed gently. "Since this afternoon, we've had a bookie joint in the back of a shoe repair shop wiped out, Jimmy Daughtery among the dead, and Butch Callahan assassinated outside Vesey's on Barracks Street. Unless Richards got the word out fast, there are probably a few more dead or missing by now." Casey paused for a moment. "What's the girl's mother to you?"

"It's kind of a long story, Dad. She and I were together for a while almost twenty years ago. She left me for Richards, and I imagined she was living happily ever after. That's not quite how it turned out. When Richards pushed you guys out of the case, she figured it was some old enemy of his that he couldn't afford to have the cops knowing about."

"That's my take on it, too. He may have pushed us off the kidnapping, but the killings are keeping us in the game. Besides the dead among Richards' crew, there's also a dead Negro that Daggett's working on."

"Butterbean Glasgo," Farrell said.

Casey grinned to himself. His son had only been in town a day and already he was clued in to the entire caper. "There's another Negro custodial worker named Skeeter Longbaugh who's missing. He may just be off on a drunk, but we'll know for sure when we find him. But enough of that. I'm sure glad you're home. It's been lonesome without you."

Farrell's voice sounded tired and far away. "I've missed you, too, Dad. I meant to come back sooner, but business kept me tied up for months. How are you?"

Casey returned Brigid's impish grin. "I've never been better. Why don't you come to the office tomorrow and we'll have lunch. I want to hear all about Cuba."

"It's a date. Give Brigid my love."

"I will. See you tomorrow."

"'Night, Dad."

"Good night." He put the receiver into the cradle. "He sent you his love."

"That's swell. But why didn't you tell him?" Brigid asked.

He looked blankly at her. "What?"

"Why didn't you tell him that I know he's your son?"

He put his arms around her waist and looked at her with an earnest expression. "There's a reason. I wanted to be looking him in the eye when I told him. I want him to know that what I feel for you has nothing to do with his mother. I don't want him to think that you're some kind of replacement for her. Do you understand?"

She took his face into her hands and looked into his eyes. "Yes. Yes, I do." She smiled again. "It's time for you to go home."

He gave her a hangdog look. "Must I?"

She affected an impatient expression. "Well, I guess we could talk about it, but don't get any ideas."

⊗⊗⊗

As the day drew to a close, Skeeter began to recognize just how desperate his situation was. The police undoubtedly suspected his complicity in the kidnapping and murder. He was certain, too, that the big white man and his knife-crazy friend were also looking for him.

His best hope for salvation lay with his Uncle Howard Blessey. A semi-retired car thief, Howard was wise in the ways of the underworld. He'd served three years in Parchman Prison and, according to family stories, had also survived several gun battles with rival thieves.

He'd tried phoning Howard several times, but each time a mechanic had said the old man was out on the road. It was now past eight o'clock, and Skeeter was tired, hungry, and emotionally spent. If he didn't find a place to hide soon, he would surely be picked up by the police.

With desperation chipping away at his nerves, he left the corner bar where he'd been killing time and walked out into the gathering twilight. Entering City Park near the Delgado Trades School, he eventually reached the Carrollton Avenue park entrance. He crossed the broad avenue at the equestrian statue of General Beauregard and made his way over the Bayou St. John bridge to Esplanade Avenue.

It was fully dark when he turned into Mystery Street. At the end of the street, he walked around to the kitchen door of a big frame house. He knocked gently as he smelled the aroma of ham frying through the screen.

A pretty brown-skinned woman turned. Peering at his silhouette, she held a ten-inch butcher knife in her hand. "Who's there?"

"Mabel, it's Skeeter," he hissed.

She pushed open the screen and looked down at him. "What in the world you doin', boy? Come on in here quick, now." She stood aside and held the door for him. When she saw his face she knew there was trouble.

"What in God's name you done now, Skeeter? You look like death warmed over."

Skeeter's limbs suddenly felt all loose and rubbery. He slumped into a kitchen chair and began to tremble uncontrollably. Recognizing emotional exhaustion when she saw it, Mabel reached quickly into the cupboard for a bottle of Early Times and filled a tumbler to the rim. She gave it to him, her eyes widening as he drank it down in a single draught.

"Skeeter? Skeeter, you listenin' to me? Answer me, boy." She grabbed his shoulder and shook it roughly.

"I'm listenin', I'm listenin'. Please, quit, Mabel."

"Then tell me what's wrong. The truth."

"The truth ain't gonna make neither of us feel no better, Mabel. Two white men forced me to help them kidnap this rich white girl who goes to school where I work, and they killed Butterbean doin' it. I managed to run off."

Mabel's mouth hardened into a stern line. "So now you got cops and kidnappers both lookin' for you. Jesus wept." She put the bottle on the table and sat down across from him.

"Listen," Skeeter said in a hoarse voice. "If I can get to my Unca Howard, he'll know what to do, but I can't find him. I need someplace to stay so I can try again in the mornin'. Can I stay here?"

"I reckon, but I'll have to tell Ma Rankin that the cops are looking for you. Now how about somethin' to eat? You look like a half-starved dog."

Relief flooded through Skeeter but he felt weaker than ever. "That—that'd be swell, Mabel. I ain't had nothin' but a cup of coffee since early this mornin'."

"You smell like you had plenty beer, though." She shook her head as she turned to the stove. In a moment she'd dished up a platter of fried ham, succotash, stewed tomatoes and cornbread. She put it in front of him along with a pitcher of sweet tea. Skeeter grabbed a fork and knife and went through the platter in about seven minutes. Mabel refilled the platter and he quickly worked his way though that one. After he'd mopped his plate with a piece of cornbread, she gave him a bowl full of blackberry cobbler with cream and a cup of chicory coffee before sitting down again.

She regarded him for a moment as she sipped her own coffee. "Boy, you need to do somethin' about your life, know that?"

He wiped his mouth on the back of his hand. "Huh?"

"For over a year you've showed up here about twice a week. You eat everything in sight and then we go up to my room and fuck. The next mornin' you leave and I don't see you until the next time you got an itch to scratch. I ain't sayin' it's all your fault. If it wasn't convenient for me, I'd of kicked your ass out into the street long before now."

He looked at her, dumbfounded.

"Now you're in some kinda shit," she continued, staring into her cup, "and I'm guessin' the white gal these men done kidnapped is somebody else you go sponge off'n and fuck while you ain't here with me."

"No, that—"

"Shut up, Skeeter. You got to act like a man is what I'm sayin'. I'd of married you three times by now if you'd of had sense enough to ask, but you don't never think about doin' nothin' responsible. Why do you suppose that is?"

Skeeter shrugged, finding it hard to meet Mabel's eyes.

"I—I dunno, Mabel. I'm sure sorry if—"

"Shut up, Skeeter. Don't be tellin' me how sorry you are, 'cause you don't know what it is to be sorry. If these men catch you, you'll be six kinds of sorry, but then it'll be too late. Now get on. You know where my room is, so be quiet. I don't want any of Ma Rankin's customers bein' disturbed by your clumsy-ass foolishness. Go on, now."

Skeeter felt wounded and confused by Mabel's tirade. She'd never talked like this before, and it shocked him to hear her criticism. He walked up the back stairs to Mabel's room, wishing he could think of something intelligent to say. The sudden recognition of a missed opportunity stabbed him like an old maid's hatpin. He undressed and lay down, falling into an exhausted sleep.

※※※

Farrell visited several places that evening that housed illegal gambling operations before a card shark, Uther Kalbfischer, told him where to find Fletch Monaghan. It was approaching ten-thirty when he pulled up in front of Ledet's Bar across from Holy Name of Jesus Church on LaSalle.

Ledet's had a Mexican bouncer named Maldonado who Farrell knew from Prohibition times. Twice they had fought, and twice Farrell had licked him. It was Maldonado's glory and his curse that no matter how many fights he lost, he was always ready to fight again. He stood near the entrance as Farrell entered, immediately recognizing his old nemesis.

"What you want, Farrell?"

Farrell shoved his hands into his pockets in the hope of disarming the Mexican. He looked at him with an air of boredom. "No trouble. I just want to talk to Monaghan."

Maldonado's eyes made a slow examination of Farrell's person, his dark mustache twitching occasionally from an upper lip that wanted to sneer. When he saw no tell-tale bulges in Farrell's clothes, he moved his head to the right. "He's at that table in the corner. He ain't makin' no trouble, and neither are you, see? I got two other men here, and you can't take all three of us, *comprende?*"

Farrell somehow managed to keep the annoyance he felt from his face. "I said I only wanted to talk to him. If I wanted trouble, you'd know it already."

Maldonado carefully inspected those words for a challenge. "Go on over there, then. But if he don't want to talk to you, you drift, *sabe?*"

"*Si, senor. Gracias.*" Farrell made a slight detour around the bouncer and threaded his way through the crowd of drinkers to the table in the corner. As he drew near it, Monaghan lifted his narrow, handsome face from the game of solitaire laid out before him. His hat was tipped to the back of his skull, allowing a lock of curly black hair to dribble over his left eye.

"Hello, Fletch. Long time, no see."

"The name of this game is solitaire, Farrell. Be a good fella and dust."

Farrell ignored the rebuff, pulled up a chair and sat down across from the gambler. "Been here long?"

Monaghan's dark eyes flashed on either side of his long, thin nose. "You and me got nothin' to talk about."

"How about Whit Richards?"

The gambler's eyes flattened for a brief second, then shifted back down to his cards. "How about him? Did he fall down an open manhole? Or maybe did a bus flatten him like a Derry pancake?"

Farrell smiled. "You're trying to convince me that you don't know two of his top men have been murdered in the last two days? Or maybe nobody told you about his kidnapped daughter? That's funny, Fletch. I'm gonna bust a gut laughing in a minute." He put his elbows on the table and leaned toward the gambler. The frigid gleam of his gray eyes stabbed out at Monaghan.

"I don't give a damn about you bustin' a gut, bhoyo. If ya don't get your face outa mine, I'll bust somethin' else for ya, by Christ."

Farrell didn't move, nor did his expression change. "I don't know why you'd want to. I know what Richards did. It happens he's pulled a thing or two on me. If you're behind all his bad luck, I'd like to shake your hand. I might even ask your permission to kick his ribs in."

Monaghan held Farrell's gaze, then his thin lips twisted into something suggesting a grin. "I forget you're an Irishman, too, Farrell. The Irish have that well-known sense of humor. Okay, you've amused me. Get lost and let me play with me cards in peace."

Farrell had played Monaghan more than once, and knew how impenetrable the man's poker face could be. He was giving nothing away tonight, either. "You could use a friend, Fletch, if you're bucking Richards. Jack Amsterdam and Butch Callahan might be out of the running, but he's still got Vic D'Angelo playing on his team, and for such a funny little fat man, D'Angelo's good."

Monaghan yawned. "It's a fine package of somethin' you're sellin', Farrell. I wish I could use it, damned if I don't. But ya see, I'm sittin' here in front of God and all playin' cards and mindin' me own business. Now be a good lad and let me do it, okay?" Monaghan turned his attention back to his cards.

Farrell saw he was getting nowhere. He got up and left without another word. He paused at the bar and waited for the barkeep. It was someone he recognized. "Hello, Mike."

"Wes Farrell," he said. "What the hell you doin' in this dump? Slummin'?"

Farrell grinned. "A shot of Monagahela for the road, Mike." He paused while the red-haired bartender dumped a jigger of Old Overholt into a glass. "Tell me, how long you been on duty?"

Mike shrugged. "Since four this afternoon. Why?"

Farrell shrugged. "How long's Monaghan been here?"

"He was here when I came on."

"Alone?"

"Couple people been over there talkin' to him. Nobody I recognized. None of 'em stayed long. I don't know why he's in here. He ain't played a game all night."

Farrell downed the shot. "Thanks, Mike. I'll be seeing you." He turned and left the bar. He paused at the door long enough to take a cigarette from his case and light it. He watched Monaghan, but saw nothing but a man intent on a game of solitaire. After a while, he left the building and drove back Downtown.

※※※

It was past ten by the time Daggett and Andrews reached Ma Rankin's house. At the sound of the bell, the door opened and a woman of about sixty stood there.

"Hello, Daggett. Married life gettin' you down, son?"

"Mrs. Rankin, we'd like to speak to Mabel Evans."

"Mabel give up pleasurin' men," Ma Rankin said. "She ain't doin' nothin' but cookin' and housekeepin' now."

"Ma, we ain't got the energy to stand here listenin' to a lot of who-struck-john. Are we gonna have to call for a wagon to take every Goddamn person in here Downtown?" Andrews, red-eyed and greasy-skinned, was out of patience and didn't care who knew it.

Seeing they were in no mood to be fenced with, Ma Rankin flung open the door. "Why didn't you say it was business? Hell, I'm a law-abiding citizen."

She conducted them with great ceremony to the kitchen, talking loudly enough to let everyone know a pair of cops was coming. They found Mabel washing dishes.

"Mabel, these two p'licemen want to ask you some questions," the old woman said by way of introduction.

Mabel turned from the sink, wiping her hands on a towel. "You're Israel Daggett," she said.

Daggett studied her face. "Do we know each other?"

Mabel shrugged. "You raided a place where I used to work. You took me Downtown, but you were nice about it. What you want with me?"

Daggett took off his hat and rubbed his scalp. "We understand you're friends with Skeeter Longbaugh."

She took a package of cigarettes out of her apron pocket and put one in her mouth. As she fumbled for a light, Daggett stepped in and snapped a kitchen match on his thumbnail. She gently took his hand and held it while she pushed the end of her cigarette into the flame.

"Thanks," she said, exhaling a puff of smoke. "I know him. We have a few laughs every once in a while. Why?"

"He's wanted for questioning in a kidnap/murder."

She smiled. "Skeeter? Kidnap and kill somebody? No, he's way too timid to do anything like that." She inhaled again, let it out gently. "There's gotta be some mistake."

"Tell that to Butterbean Glasgo. He's in the morgue."

She grinned indulgently. "Listen, Sergeant. All Skeeter cares about is lovin'. If he ain't home, he's prob'ly layin' up with one of his other ladyfriends."

"When's the last time you saw him, Miss Evans?"

Mabel had been waiting for the question, but even so, when it came, she had to pause to take another drag from the cigarette. She held the smoke in for a moment before letting it feather out of her nose. "He was here last Friday. Spent the night in my room, left in the mornin'."

"It ain't helpin' him to not tell us where he is," Andrews said. "If he's in trouble, we're his best bet."

Mabel stared, stony-faced. "That why so many of us is in jail? 'Cause y'all are just dyin' to help us out? Don't make me laugh, copper."

Daggett felt his jaw muscles tighten, but he kept his temper. Shooting a warning glance at Andrews, he said, "Just because you've had a couple of run-ins with the law is no reason to think we're out to get Skeeter. If he's in a jam, we want to help him. He might be the only person who knows where the kidnap victim is."

"If I see him, I'll tell him what you said." She held the cigarette stub under the faucet and ran water over it. The sizzle of the fire put a period to their conversation.

"C'mon, Sam. Let's go home." Daggett turned on his heel and stalked back toward the front door. Andrews gave Mabel a hard look, then he followed his partner out.

Ma Rankin, who had listened stoically, followed them into the hall. In a minute she returned. "Is he upstairs?"

"Yes'm, but I'll get him out in the mornin'. I didn't mean to bring no grief here."

Ma shrugged. "It didn't cause no trouble. They couldn't search the place without a warrant nohow. But you oughta pay heed to Daggett. He's straight—for a cop."

"I'll think about it. G'night, Ma."

"'Night, Mabel."

Mabel sagged against the sink feeling suddenly weak in the knees. She knew enough about Israel Daggett to appreciate what a terrible chance she'd just taken. She was disgusted with Skeeter and his immaturity, but her feelings for him were too strong to simply give him up. She walked to the back stairs, hoping a night's sleep would help her see things more clearly in the morning.

"What do you think, Iz? Was she lyin'?" Andrews asked as he put the Dodge into gear.

"She didn't seem surprised by anything we told her, but we had no cause to take her in or search the place. If we don't get anywhere tomorrow, we'll come see her again. Maybe by then she'll be scared enough to talk." He paused, rubbed a hand over his face.

"Iz, you ever get tired of people thinkin' you're the problem, that *you're* the bad man tryin' to hurt 'em?"

"Yeah, pardner. I surely do."

It took Georgia some time to calm down after Whit manhandled her. As rotten a husband as he'd been, he'd never before raised a hand to her. For the first time in many years, she confronted the fact that he was a violent criminal, regardless of the respectable persona he presented to the public at large.

She paced the floor of her bedroom, smoking cigarettes until her throat was raw. She knew it was too early to call Farrell, knew it was unwise after he had specifically told her not to call him. Whit would tell her nothing; besides, he was probably off with his tart. Knowing he was off sleeping with another woman while their child was God knows where enraged her almost to the point of violence. She was staring out at the dark street when an idea came to her.

She went to the telephone and asked the operator for an Uptown exchange. It rang only twice before a man answered.

"Yes?"

"Rob, it's Georgia."

Rob Langdon hesitated for the briefest of seconds before he replied. "Hello, Georgia. How are you?"

"Terrible. Whit's thrown the police off the case and he's off with that Baker woman. I'm cut off here, Rob. I don't know anything and there's no one to ask."

Another hesitation. "I—I'm not sure what I can do, Georgia. I don't know much more than you do. Whit's handling this, and so far he hasn't confided much to me."

Georgia tangled her fingers in her hair, fighting to keep the hysteria from overwhelming her. "Rob—I meant something to you once. Please, I'm begging you. Do you know who has Jessica? Please, tell me."

Rob Langdon hesitated. He and Georgia had enjoyed an affair of ten months' duration not long after he went to work for her husband, but as his involvement in Richards' dealings had deepened, Rob had no longer been comfortable with deceiving him. With some reluctance he had terminated their affair, but his feelings for Georgia had persisted. "I'll try to find out what I can, Georgia. Vic D'Angelo is running Whit's action on the street, and he owes me a few favors. I'll see what I can find out from him."

Georgia managed to stifle the sigh that had risen from her chest, but her voice was shaky. "Thank you, Rob. I—I won't forget you for this. Do—do you know who's behind this yet?"

"Please don't ask me that, Georgia. Whit's got good reasons for keeping the lid on this. My fortunes are tied up in Whit's continued control of things, just as yours are. I can't do or say anything that might put him on the spot later. Do you understand?"

"So you know who has Jess."

"Georgia, I've said too much already. Let me make some calls and as soon as I know something, I'll call you."

"All right," she replied. "I suppose I'll have to settle for that now. Thank you." She paused for a moment. "I've missed you, Rob. More than I can say."

The confession seemed to startle him. He cleared his throat before he replied. "I—I'm flattered. Good night, Georgia."

"Good night." She replaced the receiver, stared at it thoughtfully for a moment before going into the bathroom to draw a bath.

❈❈❈

The man listened as Pete Carson broke the connection, then put his own telephone into the cradle. His thick, rough fingers drummed a tattoo on the tabletop as he stared at the old framed photograph. The youthful couple in the photo reminded him of better times, times when he had hope for the future. Those hopes were gone now. All that remained was the thirst for revenge, but he wondered if it were getting out of hand. People were dying and would probably keep on dying for a while. He had set that in motion, and had to live with it.

He thought about Jack Amsterdam, whom he had known once, years ago. He almost felt sorry for him, dying the way he had. It had been senseless, just bad luck, really. Whoever had killed him may have done them an inadvertent favor, though. Amsterdam had been tough. There was no guarantee that he could have been handled, if he still lived.

He got up from his chair, picked up the photograph and went to bed.

Chapter 7

Louis Bras and his Sizzlin' Six were the featured act at the Club Moulin Rouge that night. As Farrell entered, Louis dropped his cornet to his side and began to croak the lyrics to "I Got It Bad and That Ain't Good." Farrell gave him a two-finger salute off the brim of his hat as he strode to the stairs and took them to the second floor.

He found Savanna in the living room with her shoes off. The radio was turned down so low that only the essence of a song reached him from across the room. "Hello, sweetheart," he said. "You look all tuckered out."

She smiled up at him. "You don't know the half of it. 'Tee Ruth and Margurite took me all over creation today. I saw folks I haven't talked to in ages. They all begged me to stay home for a while."

"No reason why we can't," Farrell said as he hung up his hat on the way to the kitchen counter. He built himself a rye highball, then took it to the sofa and sat down close to her, rattling the ice in his glass. He leaned his head back and let her smooth the hair from his forehead.

"What's on your mind, honeychile?" she asked.

He cut his eyes over at her and saw that look, the one that reminded him they had no secrets. "A kidnapping."

"Uh, huh. Whose kid got napped?"

"City Councilman Whit Richards's."

She studied him thoughtfully for a moment. "What's the rest of it?"

He stalled for a moment, wondering how he could put it. "The girl's mother came and asked if I could help."

She smoothed his forehead again and looked deeply into his eyes. "You don't look very happy about it."

He shrugged. "I'm not happy or unhappy."

She snickered. "Bull. You like to pretend that you have no reasons for stickin' your nose into other people's trouble, but that's crap and we both know it. Every time you play this game, you have a reason."

"Maybe." He took a sip of his drink to give his hands something to do. "Maybe I don't know what it is yet."

"Let me try out a little woman's intuition on you, baby. You pretty obviously haven't been in touch with this woman for years before she came to you with her sob story, but if I've added things up right, I'd have to guess she left you instead of the other way around. Right?"

He swallowed, not looking at her. "I guess."

"Tsk, tsk. You're not too bright about women, sonny. I never met a man yet who didn't have a thing about some woman who done him wrong. I'm guessin' from that hound-dog look that this is that woman in your story."

"It must be great having all these insights into the male psyche," he said, nettled by her intuition. "You're not gonna charge me for this, are you?"

"No, but from where I stand, this is one of those times you ought to've minded your own business and given your pride a rest. We got it awful good these days for you to risk blowing it up." She kissed him lightly on the lips, then spoke in a gentler voice. "I'm used to havin' you around after this past year. If anything happened to you, I'd get over it, but I wouldn't like having to."

He drew her close. "I could just butt out of this now, before I get in any deeper."

"Baby, I'm not gonna nag you to stay home and do the dishes and walk the dog. That's not the kind of life we'll ever have. I know that you probably gave your word. When you give your word, you keep it. If you didn't, you'd be a kind of man I wouldn't *like* having around."

"I guess I'm stuck, then. I did give my word."

She slipped a soft hand over the hard line of his jaw. "That's right. So whatever your problem with this old girlfriend is, get it fixed. I'm not jealous, but I won't share you with anybody else, you hear?"

"I hear you."

"Good, so come to bed. I need a back rub."

⚬⚬⚬

Jessica Richards felt tired, but sleep seemed out of the question as she made the hundredth circuit of her prison. She'd had to use the chamber pot several times, and the smell had taken some getting used to. The nude calendar photo began to annoy her, so she shoved it into a drawer.

The single light bulb didn't give much light, but she was in no mood to read about Richard Byrd or Clark Gable anyway. Under most circumstances she'd be asleep in her own bed, the image of which almost brought tears to her eyes. But there was steel in Jessica Richards. She clenched her jaw and ruthlessly choked the tears back. She walked more briskly about the room, her green eyes flashing with the heat of sudden anger. She couldn't allow herself the luxury of sentimentality, not if she was going to survive this.

She had eaten the last of her food hours ago. The fact that they'd brought her so much suggested that her kidnappers had some vested interest in maintaining her good health. If they'd planned to kill her, she reasoned, they'd have done so already.

Once upon a time she might have considered praying, but she had reached an age where she subscribed to something her parents' cook was fond of saying: "God helps them what helps themselves." Bessie Mae was a Baptist, and had learned the hard way that prayers alone don't always help.

The walking and thinking gradually relaxed her enough to sleep. After removing her shoes and her skirt, she pulled the light chain and crawled into bed. A thin line of yellow light leaked from beneath the door, teasing her with evidence of the world existing just the other side. She turned on her side and closed her eyes.

As she lay there, she let her hand brush against the cool metal of the bed frame. It was soothing in some strange indefinable way. She allowed her fingers to explore the shape, pressing and tugging. Eventually the fingers met a piece of steel that was loose. It felt as though it might be eight inches or so in length, and perhaps a half-inch across. It was held in place by metal screws, but they were loose. She began twisting the screws and felt them loosen further. Jessica's eyes came open slightly as she began to imagine the possible uses of a loose piece of steel.

⊗⊗⊗

Easter Coupé had never been to Toni Mereaux's bordello, but he knew of it by reputation. She paid plenty of sugar to the cops to remain open, and also had the tacit support of certain members of the Negro bourgeoisie. She, herself, was said to be the mistress of a white man named Larson who'd made a fortune in oil. Coupé found that amusing. A certain type of rich white man always seemed to like having a black woman for his fun, while some Negroes were consumed with the desire to sleep with a white woman. You always want what you can't have, he reckoned.

As he drew near the house, he began to wonder how he should play this. People to whom he'd spoken had made it plain that Toni Mereaux kept her kid sister away from the johns. He had a feeling, though, that Skeeter had probably sampled some of the house girls, even if the younger Mereaux sister was giving it to him for nothing.

At his knock, a delicate little mulatto girl with brown hair cut boyishly short opened it and invited him in.

"Good evenin', suh. Can I get you a drink?" she asked.

"Seven Crown, if you got it, with a li'l water, missy."

She offered him a shy smile. "We got it. Why don't you have a seat over there and I'll bring it to you."

He sauntered over to a cushioned bench under a window that seemed to offer some privacy. As he made himself comfortable, he checked the other faces in the room, noting a couple of local business owners, three well-known musicians, and the head of surgery at Flint-Goodrich Hospital. He smiled as he watched them laughing and talking to the women they'd chosen.

The little mulatto girl came back with his drink, and he invited her to sit down with him.

"You sure, suh? We got some other gals who ain't workin' just now. Maybe you'd like to look 'em over." She fluttered like a bird under his gaze, and he wondered how long she'd been a whore.

"You'll do fine. Sit down and tell me your name."

"It's Patience, suh."

"That's a pretty name. You can call me Frank Brown."

"Okay." She looked down at her hands. "You, uh, wanna go upstairs now?"

"In a minute. How'd you come to be here, Patience?"

"Oh, I come over from Lafayette after my mama died, hopin' to find some secretary work, but nobody was hirin'." She shrugged. "I run outa money and needed a place to stay and, well, somebody told me 'bout this place." She shrugged again, looking down at her hands.

"You still wanna be a secretary?"

She looked at her hands again. "Well, I learned all that typin' an' shorthand an' all. It's nice, clean work." She looked up suddenly, as though fearing she might have given offense. "But this is okay, too, most of the time."

"Most of the time?"

"Well, every now and then we get a fella in here who don't know how to behave. Miss Toni don't hold with any carryin' on. If you're too drunk or loud, she has Elwood throw you out on your ear after he knocks you around some. I can tell you're a gentleman, though. You ain't hardly touched your drink. I hope it ain't too strong."

"No, missy, it's just fine. Why don't we go up to that room of yours and see what it looks like."

"Okay. Uhm, Miss Toni, she likes us to tell you up front that it's five dollars for a couple hours, and ten for the whole night. It's kinda expensive, I reckon."

"For a fine lookin' young woman like you? I should say not. She oughta charge more."

Her complexion deepened and she ducked her head as she stood and took his hand and led him up the stairs.

The room was clean and neat, as he'd expected, and there was a fresh seersucker spread on the bed. Patience turned on a small lamp, then closed the door. She turned her back to him as she undressed, neatly folding her things over the back of a chair. She wore a look of fierce concentration as she took his coat and unbuttoned his shirt and vest. He almost smiled at the methodical way she went about undressing him, but recognizing she was nervous, he made no comment.

She finally led him to the bed. He noted as she turned back the covers that there was a studied way about how she went about her work, as though she'd been well tutored but was yet unskilled enough to feel the need to give each immediate project her full concentration. She was even more delicate looking in the nude. Her skin was a dusky yellow, with a tiny patch of light brown hair at the place where her legs came together. He felt strangely excited.

The sex had a leisurely quality that was quite out of Coupé's experience. Most whores were in a hurry to move on to the next customer, but Patience was everything her name suggested. When it was over, she collapsed on top of him, her heart thudding against his chest.

He gently turned on his side and caught her in his arm as she slid off. "You didn't wear yourself out, did you, Patience?" he asked in an amused voice.

She pushed light brown bangs out of her eyes and smiled at him, her expression a bit self-conscious. "I'm sorry. It's supposed to be for you, but I forget sometimes."

He looked at her, stroking her bare shoulder with his blunt fingers. "Don't be sorry. It's supposed to be fun."

"Well—thank you, suh—I mean, Frank."

"How long you been at this place?"

"Oh, not long. About six months, I reckon."

He grinned. "You're pretty experienced for only six months. You're just a natural woman, I reckon."

"Oh, hush," she said, grinning self-consciously.

"This is my first time out here. Know a young fella who talks about it, so I thought I'd come see for myself."

"A young fella? What's his name?"

"Calls himself Skeeter. Funny name, ain't it?"

She flushed. "Oh, him. I reckon he's tried every gal here when Miss Terry weren't payin' no attention."

"Miss Terry?"

"She's Miss Toni's sister. Miss Toni don't 'low her to do what the rest of us does, but Miss Terry's kinda sweet on Skeeter. I seen them sneak into empty rooms when Miss Toni's not around. But he still does it with others whenever he gets the chance."

"You, too?"

"Oh, no. I feel sorry for Miss Terry, and I wouldn't do her that way."

He nodded gravely. "You don't meet many people with ethics nowadays. That's right fine of you."

"Thank you."

"I ain't seen Skeeter lately. Wonder where he got to?"

"Well, he useta work for his uncle. I forget his name, but he runs a garage somewhere in the city. Lately he's been workin' at that Catholic girls' school out on Saint Charles. I went by there once on the streetcar. It's a grand lookin' place, Frank. Wish I could work there one day."

"Well, maybe you will. That garage you was talkin' about, that wouldn't be Mr. Blessey's garage, would it?"

She nodded. "That's the name. You know him?"

He shook his head. "Know of the garage, but not Mr. Blessey personal. It's over in Gerttown, I think."

"That sounds right, but I never been over there."

"You don't wanna go. It's rough."

She ran her finger along the ridge of scar tissue on his jaw, but she didn't ask how it got there. "Thank you for that piece of advice, Frank. You're a real gentleman."

She was a screwy little dame, but her innocence had somehow penetrated the callus over Easter Coupé's soul. He rolled over on his back, pulling her along until she lay atop his thick chest. They teased each other gently with their fingers and lips and teeth until she finally melded her body to his once again. Easter Coupé genuinely regretted that he'd have to leave soon. As they rolled and pumped and squeezed each other, he felt a strange, indefinable sadness.

❈❈❈

Joey Parmalee remained at the kitchen table late into the night, opening and closing his switchblade knife. He finally got up and paced around the room, bored out of his skull. The crap on the radio made him sick. He looked at his jacket hanging from a chair, thinking of the bindle of cocaine in it. Johnny had told him to lay off of it.

Momentarily forgetting the loss, he reached for the missing tie clasp which he had used as a spoon for his coke. As his fingers rubbed the vacant spot on his tie, he felt a sickening dread that he had lost it when he'd killed the Negro earlier that day.

One more failure. One more thing to get Johnny on his ass. He'd go nuts for fear the cops would find it, and through it find them. Joey was less worried about the cops than he was about his brother.

He found himself pacing the floor again, playing with the knife as worry gnawed at his guts. He halted abruptly, turned to the coat and dug the bindle out of his pocket, taking two quick snorts off the point of the knife blade. Within seconds, he was leaning against the wall gasping as the drug bit into the membranes of his nostrils. As his heartbeat gradually slowed, his mood lifted dramatically.

As his confidence began to return, he got to thinking about Jessica Richards. He hadn't had a woman in almost a week. His mouth got wet as he imagined fondling, licking the red-haired girl's long legs. She would be sweet like honey. Sweeter.

He turned and walked up the stairs. The taps on his shoes clicked rhythmically on the risers as he imagined peeling off her brassiere, seeing the smooth, cool flesh tumble out into his waiting hands. The pictures in his mind had the fevered quality of a dream threatening to go bad, but he was too caught up in the sexualized images to pay heed. His senses heightened by the drug, he fancied he could hear her breathing, the whisper of her movements. He unlocked the door, letting it swing open. A trapezoid of light fell into the dark room, casting his shadow on the floor. He started, distracted by the distorted image, disquieted by its size and shape. It was his shadow, but it seemed outsized and grotesque, a large, dominating figure. All day he had faced men bigger and stronger than himself. He thought of the terror he'd seen in the eyes of Jimmy Daughtery, of Butterbean Glasgo. He'd cut them down to size, but there was no end to them. Whatever victory he'd earned by killing them, Carson and Johnny had stolen with their disapproval earlier that night.

Jessica's long bare arm hung off the cot, but the jagged outline of the shadow drew his gaze. He tried to turn away, but the image metamorphosed into the round head and thick shoulders of the Negro he had murdered. His movements seemed to mimic the Negro's defiance, even in death. Joey shot a glance at the sleeping girl, but the desire that had driven him here had ebbed, leaving him with a hollow, useless feeling.

Like a man awaking from a nightmare, he pulled the door shut, locking it with fumbling fingers. The strength in his legs gave way to trembling, and he slid to the floor, biting his knuckles to keep from crying.

⊗⊗⊗

Whitman Richards lay staring up at the mirrored ceiling of Meredith's bedroom, listening to her breathing as she lay in the crook of his arm. Normally he had no trouble sleeping after making love to her, but he was too keyed up tonight. He kept telling himself that Carson had no chance to keep himself, or Jessica, hidden forever, but there was a nagging doubt that would not let him rest. He recognized that he had been too willing to believe that Pete was dead. A smart man believed only what he had, himself, done.

Pinning Tarkington's murder on Pete was a clever thing to do, but he realized now that killing him would've been smarter. He should have arranged for it to look as though Pete and Tarkington had killed each other.

But be honest, you wanted Pete to know you'd outsmarted him, he told himself. That competitiveness had always been there between you. Pete was always faster, stronger. But you wanted him to spend the rest of his life knowing that you were better.

He gently disengaged himself from Meredith and got out of bed. There was the barest suggestion of winter's chill in the dark apartment, so he pulled on a flannel robe and walked into a living room bathed in silvery light from a pregnant moon.

It took something like this to remind a man that he can push his luck just so far, he thought as he poured a drink. Sure, they'd get Pete, but this incident made him recognize that in spite of his power, his relationships made him terribly vulnerable.

He looked toward the bedroom, and realized that although Jessica would soon be away at college, once he and Merry were married, he'd still have the same vulnerability. He shook his head. The very thought wearied him, made him feel his own sense of mortality. He sipped the scotch, grateful for its fiery trail down his gullet. Moments later, feeling somewhat better, he returned to the bedroom.

Meredith was still breathing deeply and regularly, her face in her pillow. He dropped his robe across the foot of the bed, then crawled in beside her. The feel of Merry's warm, taut, youthful flesh against his relaxed him instantly. He stared up at the mirrored ceiling, comforted by the certainty of a reflected image that he could not see.

∞∞∞

Coupé lay in Patience's bed until midnight, then he eased out and dressed himself. Patience lay on her stomach, her bottom shining up at him from the tangle of sheets. He pulled the spread up over her, then knelt beside the bed.

"Patience. Patience, I got to go now."

"Uhmmm," she said, opening one eye. "'kay."

"Here's ten for your boss and ten for you. I'll try to get back out here before long."

She smiled dreamily at him, then closed her eye and went back to sleep.

In the busy downstairs parlor, the piano player was doing some interesting things with some of the old standards, but Coupé had no time to stay and listen. He got into his De Soto and headed back in the direction of town. He turned on the radio, something he rarely did, and listened to a succession of white chicks croon love songs that were unfamiliar to him. The lyrics were all about a world of which he knew nothing, but which intrigued him. It made no sense, but it added to the sense of disquiet he'd felt since the beginning of this job.

He got home around one and went inside. The house seemed unnaturally quiet after the company of the car radio, but he owned no radio for his house. He sat down on a tattered love seat that represented a third of his living room furniture. He looked at the telephone on the small end table for two or three minutes before he lifted the receiver and asked the operator for a number. It rang several times before a man answered.

"Yeah?"

"Johnny, it's Easter."

"Hey, man." Johnny spoke in a low voice, as though he were not alone. "What the hell you doin' callin' this time of the night? You found Longbaugh?"

"Been at it all day. I got a pretty good lead tonight, but I can't do nothin' with it until mornin'." He paused, not quite sure of what he wanted to say. "This kid you want taken care of. What you know about him?"

"Not much," Johnny replied. "He's a janitor at the Sacred Heart. He lives alone, a real tail hound. Why?"

"Just wonderin'. Tryin' to understand him."

"Understand him?" Johnny was mildly incredulous. "Man, he's just a job, a target." Johnny paused, lowered his voice. "Listen, I'm working for a guy named Pete Carson. He's here to jerk the rug out from under a heavy hitter. He does that, I get my own action, and you come in for a piece. That's what this is about. The kid's just somethin' in the road. You run over it and forget it, see?"

Coupé listened, his unwinking eyes focused on the blank wall in front of him. "Yeah," he said slowly. "I see. Sorry I called so late."

"Forget it," Johnny said. "Lemme know if I can help you out, okay?"

"Okay. 'Night, Johnny."

"See you, Easter." Parmalee broke the connection.

Coupé slowly put the receiver back into the cradle. He got up and walked through the dark to the room where his bed was. When he got there, he lay down in his street clothes and went immediately to sleep.

Chapter 8

Friday dawn was just breaking when a telephone began to ring in a dark bedroom. It took seven rings before the rough, thick-fingered hand snaked out from beneath a blanket to pull the receiver from the cradle. The man coughed several times and hawked up some phlegm before he spoke into the receiver. "Yeah?"

A soft, muffled voice spoke. "You sound like you're dying. You want me to call back after you're finished?"

"Do you know what time it is?" the man asked in a weary voice.

"I call when I can. What's the next move?"

"The next move's up to Richards," the man in the bedroom said. "Our men have hit him pretty hard since yesterday. He's out several men and about twenty grand. Carson's idea is to weaken him enough so he knuckles under."

"Knuckles under?" the voice on the phone said. "Is that all you want? You think knuckling under is going to pay us back after what we lost?"

"We ain't never gonna get back what he took, but we can bleed Richards white if we play this right."

"Listen." The caller's voice grew harsh. "I waited for you. I waited for you to get your scheme together because you promised we'd make this right, once and for all. Okay, Carson's here now. Let's use the girl to finish it."

"Stop talkin' crazy," the man protested. "You can't wreck this now. There's too much at stake."

"Don't tell me what's at stake. I've waited as long as you have. I put myself on the line to get Carson down here to help us."

The man rubbed his face tiredly as he stared out into the darkness of his room. "Carson's been askin' to talk to you. He seems pretty anxious. Maybe you better call him or somethin'."

"Later. We've got business to take care of first."

The man was quiet for a moment. "What happened up in Seattle? What did you promise him to come down here?"

Low, sibilant laughter came through the receiver. "Use your imagination. But be careful. Imagination can be a dangerous thing. Ask Jack Amsterdam."

The man stiffened in his bed. "Jack Amsterdam? You're not sayin' that you—"

"He and Richards were together in it all, don't forget that. Now he's out of the picture, along with his pal, Callahan. Richards'll have to fight us on his own, now."

"Jesus Christ! Pete didn't want those guys hit. He wanted them alive, to bargain with. If he finds out—"

"Then you'd better not tell him." The caller abruptly broke the connection, leaving the thick-fingered man feeling a chill that his blankets couldn't stave off.

❧❦❧

Savanna had Farrell up by 6:00 Friday morning and made him poached eggs and coffee. The night's sleep had done him good. He felt none of his earlier misgivings.

Farrell drove back to his place, where he showered, shaved, and changed into fresh clothes. On his way out, he walked into the office and unlocked the desk. It took only a moment for him to slip his razor, a Luger automatic, and a couple of spare clips into his clothing before he left.

Cutting across Downtown, he took the bridge across Bayou St. John to Wisner, and drove north to Robert E. Lee Boulevard. Cool air from the north had shrouded the swampy ground along the road in fog, from which long-billed egrets occasionally made ghostly exits.

Farrell turned onto Beauregard, following it until he reached Oriole. A friend had once told him Kurt Van Zandt played nine holes of golf out here every morning.

Leaving the car, he walked through a stand of pines to a grassy knoll where he halted. Farrell heard the murmur of men's voices gradually increase in volume until a party of four became visible. Two carried heavy bags full of golf clubs while another pair walked ahead of them. One was blonde and fair-skinned, his upper body thick and soft. He did most of the talking while his golf partner, a man Farrell knew as Lenny Raskowitz, nodded occasionally. Farrell let them get close before stepping out of the trees.

A muffled word from one of the caddies cut off the flow of the blonde man's words and he stopped short. As Farrell drew closer, he noticed that Van Zandt's eyes were like those of a reptile, watchful and still.

"Van Zandt, I'm Wes Farrell. Can I talk to you?"

Van Zandt hesitated, then spoke in a blustering voice. "You take chances, mister. Where'd you come from?"

"I parked my car on the street and walked through the woods. I heard you played golf every morning."

Van Zandt studied Farrell's face, measuring him. "I saw you once, a long time ago."

Farrell nodded. "I remember. I saw you first."

The recollection seemed to make Van Zandt uneasy. He shifted his feet. "What do you want?"

"I came to talk to you about Whit Richards."

Van Zandt shrugged elaborately. "What about him?"

"Somebody's making some king-sized trouble for him."

Van Zandt's mouth cracked, revealing two rows of large white teeth. "So what?"

"Maybe I'm glad," Farrell said. "Maybe I want to congratulate the guy who's making the trouble. Maybe even help him make some more so I can get back what the louse took from me." Farrell spoke in a flat, bitter voice.

"Well, well, this is a revelation," Van Zandt said. "So Richards even took a bite out of the great Wes Farrell."

"I'm nothing special. If we were to form a club of the people Richards has cheated and stolen from, they'd overflow the Blue Room at the Roosevelt. Thing is, I've got my own bone to pick. It'd be simple for you to let me put my foot on Richards' neck while you've got him down."

Van Zandt handed his club to one of his henchmen. Farrell noticed as the man took it that he had his right hand out of sight behind his hip. He watched Farrell without subtlety, his stare baleful. Van Zandt began to walk again and he beckoned Farrell to fall in beside him. Lenny Raskowitz faded wordlessly behind with the two caddies, but he, too, was watchful and tense.

"You're taking a lot for granted," Van Zandt said. "What makes you think I kidnapped Richards' daughter?"

"Who said anything about kidnapping?" Farrell replied, smiling. "There's been nothing in the news about that."

Van Zandt grinned. "This is a small town, Farrell. I knew about the kidnapping almost as soon as the cops. I also know they haven't a clue as to who pulled the snatch."

"That mean you do?"

"If I did, I'd be a real sap to tell you. Kidnapping's a Federal beef, or haven't you heard?"

"Nuts. Richards threw the cops off the case. So far as I know, the Feds aren't involved. That tells me Richards knows the kidnapper and is giving him a clear path."

Van Zandt shot him a sudden surprised glance. "Well, good luck to whoever it is. I hope they grind him flat."

Farrell made a careless gesture with his hand. "Well, it's too bad. I'd have given you an even split of whatever I could squeeze out of him. Sure you don't know anything?"

Van Zandt snorted. "I don't need to prove anything to you. Sure, Richards jerked the rug out from under me once, but I got back what I lost and more. I'm out of the rackets now. With the war coming on, I can make a lot of money, strictly legit, you get me? Now get off my land or I'll have you thrown off."

Farrell didn't move, but he paid attention to the trio of men standing just past Van Zandt's right shoulder. "Don't get too tough with me, Van Zandt. I remember that time we saw each other just as well as you do. You came to kill me, but you saw me and ran like a rabbit."

Van Zandt swallowed, his eyes suddenly damp, blinking.

"Yeah, you remember it, too," Farrell continued. "Common sense would dictate that a man like you should stay a hundred miles from a plot like this, but he hurt you once, and I think you're just small enough to want to knife him in the back. See you later, Van. Be careful, hear?"

When Van Zandt failed to reply, Farrell walked to the copse of trees and faded into it. Five minutes later he was headed back to the city.

✖✖✖

Early that morning Skeeter was awakened by Mabel's touch as she gently made love to him. It seemed to him that her kisses were more ardent this time, her touch a bit more urgent. Her dark nipples seem to burn his bare chest as she clutched him to her. They made love three times before Mabel collapsed against him. He tried to speak, but, with her face hidden in the side of his neck, she pressed her fingers gently against his mouth.

After a while, she got out of the bed and went to the washbasin. She silently bathed herself from head to foot, then drew on fresh undergarments and a clean house dress. She paused at the door, speaking softly over her shoulder. "Get yourself together and I'll make you breakfast." Before he could reply, she opened the door and slipped through it.

Melancholy settled over him as he lay there. He remembered what Mabel had said last night, feeling unhappy in a way he didn't recognize.

After a wash, he dressed and walked quietly downstairs. As he sat down, he noticed that Mabel did not turn from her work at the stove. A few minutes passed before she brought over a plate heaped with flapjacks and bacon, poured him a cup of coffee then went back to her work. After he poured sulfurated cane syrup all over his cakes and bacon he ate steadily, occasionally pausing to look at Mabel's back. When he was finished, he pushed his plate away.

"That was mighty fine, Mabel. I sure do thank you."

"You need to get goin' now."

As she turned to look at him, he saw the tracks of tears on her cheeks. "What's wrong, Mabel?"

"Skeeter, you're a sweet boy, but a boy's all you are. It might be all you'll ever be. One thing I know, if you're gonna grow up, grow up now. You need to start actin' like a man, today, you hear?"

"Yeah, Mabel. Mabel, I—I love you."

"I know. Now go on, and don't be comin' back."

Skeeter's face fell. "You—you don't mean that, honey. You couldn't."

She took a dishtowel and pressed it up to her face, shaking her head. "Please, just go. Try not to let them kill you. Go someplace else, while you got the time, but just go." She began to weep quietly into the dishtowel, turning her back on him again.

Skeeter wanted to comfort her, but he turned away and walked out. Today he seemed to have no future.

He didn't know Jessica Richards except to speak to, yet he felt as much a victim as the girl. There should be something he could do to get his life back, but the dull weight of misfortune hindered his thinking.

He pulled his cap out of his pocket and put it on as he walked to Esplanade Avenue. A bus honked as he crossed the avenue without paying attention to its approach.

When he reached the vicinity of the old U. S. Mint, he made a beeline to a telephone booth. A few seconds later, he listened to the buzz of the line at Howard's garage.

"Blessey's," a voice said.

"Mornin'. Is Howard there today?"

"He is, but he's talkin' to a fella. You wanna wait?"

"Yeah, reckon I better."

⊗⊗⊗

Easter Coupé woke at daylight. His plan was to reach Howard Blessey at opening time. If Skeeter was there, he knew he'd smell him.

He dressed in a dull black business suit and a black narrow brimmed Dobbs hat. From his bureau he removed a shoebox, from which he took a .22 automatic pistol with a silencer. He checked the magazine, replaced it in the box, and left the house. Instead of taking the De Soto, he went to the rear of the house and entered a small garage where he kept an old brown Plymouth.

Leaving his neighborhood at six, he stopped at a diner for ham and eggs and coffee before continuing on. Alone with his thoughts, he found them invaded with images of Patience and the bare little apartment where Skeeter Longbaugh lived. He irritably shook the images from him as he left the counter.

Like many who haunted the Negro underworld, Coupé was intimate with Gerttown, a place where every kind of vice found haven and sustenance. Coupé didn't know Blessey, but if things ran true to form, the man was probably a thief, quick to smell a phony line.

He entered Gerttown from Fig Street at the edge of Notre Dame Seminary. As he made the turn into Olive he saw that Blessey's outfit occupied most of the block. A high metal fence surrounded a salvage yard, a two-bay sheet metal garage, and a faded blue shotgun cottage. Coupé could hear the sounds of hammer on metal, the hiss of a welding torch, and the noise of a radio.

Parking the Plymouth across the street, he walked to the nearest bay and squatted until he could see hands wrestling with the cover of a universal joint. "Hey, 'scuze me, man. Mr. Blessey around?"

A pair of eyes rose above the edge of the grease pit. "Over there." He jerked a thumb.

"Thanks." Coupé got up and walked until he saw an open door. He found an old man at a desk making notations on an inventory sheet while another Negro sat propped against the wall playing with a fuel pump. On a wall shelf, a dusty Philco radio blared. Coupé had to shout several times before the old man looked up. Blessey started to speak, then got up and beckoned Coupé outside.

"Goddamned racket," he growled as he tugged at his bristly gray mustache. "One a these days I'm 'onna throw that damn radio out the door. What you want, mister?"

"Lookin' to get a tune-up 'fore I leave town. Young fella I talked to said y'all did fine work."

The old man looked at him sharply. "Young fella?"

"Yeah, had a funny name. Skipper, Scooter—no, Skeeter. That's it, Skeeter."

The old man snorted. "My nephew. Used to work with me here but he didn't like gettin' grease on his hands. Said the gals didn't like it."

"Well, he seemed to know somethin' about cars. I been havin' this knockin' noise when I get her above thirty-five. He said a good tune-up would set her right as rain."

The old man cast a glance across the street. "That your Plymouth? I reckon I can look at 'er t'morra." He tossed a look back at the work bays, then scratched the back of his neck. "Should have it ready for you before noon."

"Fine. My mechanic moved to Los Angeles a while ago. Didn't know of anybody else until I spoke to your nephew."

"Yeah, he's a good enough kid. Just triflin' and girl crazy is all. Could'a made a decent mechanic outa him if he'd hung around longer. Well, lemme get back, Mr.—"

"Brown, Frank Brown. I'll see you tomorrow then."

Coupé walked back to his car, then drove out of the neighborhood. Blessey was sharp, but his responses to Coupé's remarks about Skeeter had been too spontaneous. If the kid were there, he'd have been more guarded.

Coupé drove around the edge of the neighborhood, reentering two blocks down from Blessey's compound. From there, he had an unobstructed view of anyone approaching. He took a pair of army surplus binoculars out of the glove compartment and put the gun on the seat behind him. He wanted this over, so why did he dread it so much?

⧉⧉⧉

Frank Casey hadn't been in the office very long before Nick Delgado appeared. Casey considered the lab man an indispensable member of his team, but the man, himself, was self-effacing to a fault. "Hello, Nick. Got something?"

"A beginning," the lab man replied. "Jimmy Doughtery and the other men at the shoe repair shop were killed with a Smith & Wesson .32, but the Amsterdam and Callahan killings were both done with the same .22 automatic, same kind of ammunition."

"A .32's not much gun for a stick-up artist or a hired killer," Casey mused.

"Smith & Wesson manufactures a target grade .32 with match sights and oversized grips," Delgado replied. "A different gun, but still a sharpshooter's weapon. Could still be the same shooter. Two of the four guys at Bockman's were shot twice, just like Amsterdam and Callahan."

Casey fingered his chin. "Amsterdam and Callahan were two of Whit Richards' closest associates. I think they were targeted and stalked by a pro. The massacre at Bockman's is too heavy-handed to be the same man."

"Maybe," Nick replied. "I'm checking all the ballistic evidence with other cases to see if we can find a match."

Casey grunted. "What else?"

"Been working on that tie bar Daggett found. I didn't think it'd be worth much, but I kept playing with it."

"Uh, huh."

He put an eight by ten color photo on Casey's desk that brought the small details of the tie bar into sharp relief. "For one thing, this is a very nice piece of goods. It's twenty-four carat gold with diamond chips in the valves. The manufacturer is a firm in Kansas City."

"Really? Were you able to get in touch with them?"

"Caught them this morning. Apparently these were a special order for a local distributor. The office manager there said that they'd placed them in four different men's stores here, just a handful in each one because they're pricey, about thirty-five bucks apiece."

"Big money. You get the names of the shops?"

"Sure did. They're all located Downtown."

"I don't guess you found any prints or anything?"

"Didn't really expect to, chief. The way the thing's been engraved and detailed."

"Well, that would've been asking for a miracle."

"There is one thing I did find. It's no immediate help, but it's worth telling your investigators."

"What's that?"

"Embedded in some of the engraving I found traces of powdered cocaine. The owner probably used the tie bar to spoon cocaine to his nose."

Casey nodded. "That might be worth something."

"Let me get back to work on that ballistic evidence. I'll call you when I've got something more." He excused himself and departed for the lab.

Casey pulled the telephone toward him and dialed an internal number. "Ray, this is Casey. I've got a line on that tie bar Daggett found. We need to send some men Downtown to check a few men's stores." He gave Snedegar a few details then hung up.

He leaned back in his chair and rubbed his face. More than a day after the kidnapping and not a single real lead yet. He hoped Farrell was having better luck.

Chapter 9

Daggett and Andrews gave up their search for Skeeter Longbaugh not long after visiting Mabel Evans and drove home. Daggett found his wife, Margurite, awake when he arrived. She was long past the nausea and vomiting stage of her pregnancy, but she sometimes had trouble sleeping because of backache. Daggett shared a cup of mint tea with her, then rubbed her back and legs until she slept.

Daggett had come to cherish these moments. The pregnancy was unexpected, but he was happy about it. Knowing he had a child on the way had somehow mellowed him, made his job seem easier to bear.

When he and Andrews arrived at the office Friday, they found Detective Merlin Gautier waiting for them with news.

"Even though this Longbaugh kid has no priors, I kept asking people about him," Gautier explained. "I eventually found somebody who knew him pretty well."

"How well?"

"The fella's a mechanic, and he knew Longbaugh from working in a garage with him," Gautier replied. "Nobody else we talked to mentioned that."

"No. The kid doesn't seem to have many friends."

Gautier grinned. "Too busy chasin' the skirts, my man. But that's not the good part."

"So what is?"

"Man said the garage he and Longbaugh worked at belongs to Longbaugh's uncle, a man named Howard Blessey."

"And?"

"Blessey's a car thief. He went down for a three spot at Parchman in 1919. I pulled his sheet and discovered he's a pretty hard old boy. He's had twenty-seven arrests since then, but never gone to trial. He's believed to have killed several rivals, too."

"Nice work, Merle. Where's Blessey's garage?"

"On Olive in Gerttown. You get anything last night?"

"We talked to a couple of his girlfriends, but they couldn't or wouldn't help us."

"The way I figure it," Gautier said, "the kid's got no place else to turn but his old uncle the car thief."

Daggett nodded. "Let's take a ride."

∞∞∞

Howard Blessey returned to his office and saw his employee still fiddling with the fuel pump, the radio blasting wide open. Blessey noted the telephone receiver standing on end and spoke to the man. "For me?" he shouted.

"Huh?"

Uttering a growl, Blessey reached up and shut the radio off. "The phone. Is it for me, you Goddamn knucklehead?"

"Oh, yessir. Sorry. I plumb forgot."

"Get outa here before I put a boot in your ass."

As the man ran out, Blessey grabbed the phone. "Yeah?"

"It's Skeeter, Unca Howard. I got some bad trouble."

"What kinda trouble?"

"Two white men forced me to help 'em kidnap a white girl yesterday. They killed my friend Butterbean doin' it. I reckon they lookin' for me now. Prob'ly the cops, too."

"Hell," the old man growled. "I reckon now you wished you'd stayed here in the grease pit, don't you?"

"Yessir, but that ain't helpin' me just this minute."

"How far away are you?"

"Down Esplanade. If I catch a bus I might could get there in forty-five minutes."

"Okay, but be careful. By now the cops know you're related to me, and if they know that, they know I ain't the friendly neighborhood grease monkey. Come in from the east. You can see if anybody's hangin' around before you get here." The old man paused as something occurred to him. "Tell me, you been talkin' up the garage to anybody lately?"

"No, I don't think so."

"How about a man named Frank Brown? Deep black skin, hard around the eyes and a bad scar along his jaw."

Skeeter was silent for a moment. "Don't recollect nobody like that."

"Get your ass over here. Now."

The boy hung up without further conversation.

As the old man walked to the office door he saw a black Dodge slow to a stop across the street. Howard made them for Negro cops as soon as the three men got out of the car. He went back into the office as though he hadn't seen them.

He was at his inventory when the door opened. Blessey looked up at a tall, lanky brown man. "Help you, mister?"

The tall man opened his hand, revealing a gold star and crescent shield. "Sergeant Daggett. Are you Mr. Blessey?"

"I am. What can I do for you?"

Daggett led two more men into the office. "This is Detective Andrews and Detective Gautier. We'd like to ask you some questions about your nephew, Skeeter Longbaugh."

Howard poked out his lip thoughtfully. "Hell, I ain't seen the boy in weeks. He in some kinda trouble?"

"Some kind. A white girl was kidnapped yesterday and a man was murdered. Skeeter hasn't been to work, and he hasn't been home, either. In fact, nobody's seen him."

Blessey waved a dismissive hand. "Man, you're barkin' up the wrong tree. He ain't got many brains, but he's got enough not to do that." He laughed in a dry clatter.

Daggett nodded. "Maybe, but the fact that he disappeared looks bad for him. I've got a hunch, though."

"What kind?"

"Your nephew hasn't got a black mark against him and everybody speaks well of him. It could be he was forced to help the kidnappers." Daggett pushed his hat back off his forehead and gave the old man a sympathetic look. "The only way we can clear him is to find the criminals."

Blessey shook his head tiredly. "Man, this gettin' to be a tough ole world when a boy can't mind his business without a bunch of ofays draggin' him into their shit."

"Who said anything about white men?"

Blessey lifted his head and saw Daggett staring at him. "Sorry, I thought you did. Makes sense, though—these folks kidnapped a white gal. Our kind would know better'n to do somethin' as crazy as that."

"Do him a favor and get him to turn himself in."

Blessey nodded solemnly. "If I hear from the boy, I'll talk to him, Sergeant. You can take that to the bank."

Daggett rested a foot on the seat of an empty chair, stared down at the old car thief. "Mr. Blessey, I believe in being fair. We know you got a record, and there are people at headquarters who think you're still in the hot car racket. If I find out you've been hiding Skeeter, I'll send you back to prison. That's something *you* can take to the bank. Let's go, fellas. We're through here."

Blessey maintained a straight face through Daggett's threat, and he watched silently as the detectives filed out of the office. When their car pulled away, the old man spat in the waste basket. "You're just as slick as glass, ain't you, Mr. Nee-Grow Detective? Shit." He went to the door and shouted into the garage bays. "Lonnie. C'mere a minute."

A skinny brown man in grease-stained overalls and cap came at a lope. "What'd the cops want, Howard?"

Blessey grinned at him affectionately. "You can sure smell one, can't you, Lonnie? Skeeter's knee-deep in shit. We got to get him outa town tonight. Get that Oldsmobile ready and fill up the tank. You're takin him to Houston."

Lonnie nodded wisely. "He can get lost but good there in the Fifth Ward. I'll get right to it."

"Good. Keep your eyes open, too. People liable to be snoopin' around here, if they ain't already."

"Cops?"

"Cops and worse, boy. Lots worse."

⊗⊗⊗

"Take us to that sweet shop over on Telemachus," Daggett said.

Andrews turned the wheel at Pine Street and took them past Xavier University to Dixon Street. "What now?"

Daggett already had the microphone off the dashboard clip. "Inspector 51 to Dispatch."

"Dispatch. Go ahead Fifty-one."

"Have Officer Park meet us at Shallowhorne's Sweet Shop on South Telemachus Street immediately, over."

"Park to Shallowhorne's on South Telemachus, wilco."

Daggett replaced the microphone and turned to look at Gautier. "Merle, I want you and Eddie to take a plant on Blessey's place. My gut tells me the kid's not there yet, but the old man's too cool about it. That tells me he already knows the whole story. If the boy comes close enough for you to grab him, bring him downtown. If you see him enter the garage from the other direction, call for backup. I'll get more cars in here and we'll box him in."

"Sounds simple enough," Gautier said.

Daggett grunted. "If it is, I'll buy you a steak."

⊗⊗⊗

Whit Richards left Meredith's apartment before sunup, driving back to his Coliseum Street home, where he showered, shaved and changed into fresh clothing. He was back in his study when he heard the dulled whirring of the private telephone in his desk drawer. Unlocking it quickly, he brought it out and spoke into it. "Hello?"

"Morning, Rico," Pete Carson said.

"Don't call me that, you damn louse. Where's my kid?"

"Now, now, Whit. Let's not get our bowels in an uproar before breakfast. Very bad for the digestion."

"Goddamn you, what the hell do you want so badly that you've got to kidnap a helpless kid? If you want a piece of me, tell me where to meet you and we'll settle it like men."

Carson laughed. "That's good, coming from you. You decide to kill Old Man Tarkington, then you set me up to take the fall for it. Now you've had a good long run without me here to get a share of it. There's no such thing as a free ride, Rico. You got to pay the fare."

Richards felt his neck swell and tore open his collar. "What do you want?"

"Well, Whit, I guess you can say that I want it all, including you. See, I don't want you dead. You're no good to me that way. I need your contacts in the government to make sure our little family enterprise keeps us nice and fat. Then there are all those legitimate businesses you're in, the businesses you bought into with the money we stole together. I'm going to be your silent partner from here on out."

"Sure, come on down and take the office next to mine," Richards sneered. "We'll have a rare time, you bastard."

"It won't be quite like that, Whit. But I'll be around, and I'll have men watching Georgia, and Jessica, and that cute little doll you've got on the side. Yes, I know about her, too. I could reach out and take her just like I took Jessica, so you'd better start thinking about how we're going to work together, brother of mine."

"Brother," he said in a raw voice. "We had the same mother, but don't dare call me your brother."

Carson's voice thickened to a growl, his words hot. "Suit yourself, Whit, but if you won't play ball, then we'll just see how many of your womenfolk have to bleed."

As the enormity of Carson's plan hit him, Richards felt his legs go rubbery. He sank into his desk chair, all but numb.

"Y-you leave Merry alone. Leave her alone or I'll—"

"You'll do nothing. I'll give you until tomorrow night to think it over. If you don't come across, I'll have my men hit a few more of your money factories. Once you understand that you can't lick me, we'll talk again."

"You sonofa—" Before Richards could complete the curse the connection was broken. He tapped the cradle to get the dial tone and quickly dialed Meredith's number. It buzzed three times before she answered. "Merry, it's Whit. Don't talk, just listen. The man who kidnapped Jess has just threatened—well, it doesn't matter what he said. You need to be careful, understand? I'll send Rob to get you for work and take you home, at least until this is cleared up. I don't want you going anywhere by yourself, do you hear?"

"Why, yes, Whit. Of course. This man, this Pete Carson. He's trying to use me against you, isn't he?"

"Yes, sweetheart, I'm afraid he is. But he isn't going to get the chance. Make sure your door is double-bolted and don't answer it until you know it's Rob. I'm calling him now to give him instructions."

"Darling, I'm frightened. Don't let him hurt you." She spoke earnestly, seemingly without concern for herself.

"He won't. I—I love you, sweetheart."

"I love you, too, Whit. Don't let him beat us."

"No. He won't." He broke the connection, then he got up and left the study. He found Georgia standing in the hall, her eyes like flint.

"Taking care of business, Whit?" Her voice was harsh, guttural, her words layered with contempt.

He stared at her coldly. "Stay in the house, Georgia. I'm going to ask the sheriff to station some deputies outside to make sure nobody tries to come in."

"Why how thoughtful. You actually care whether or not somebody kidnaps or kills me?" She began to laugh. She kept laughing as Richards pushed past her toward the stairs.

The ground fog had burned away as Farrell headed back to the city. He lit a cigarette, remembering the old days when he and King Arboneau had been the bitterest of rivals. Farrell knew that "The King" would remember, too.

Farrell turned off Canal to Derbigny Street and slowed to a crawl. He took the left at Conti Street and pulled to the curb across the street from a corner market. The store, Farrell knew, was a front for a bookmaking operation upstairs. He knew, as well, that Arboneau's men sold gange and heroin from the candy counter inside. Kids Arboneau hooked on dope, he then put out to whore or steal. That was just penny ante crime, though. Arboneau controlled all the gambling and narcotics in this part of town, and a vast network of prostitutes. Many were older women who were nearly played out, but the King found plenty of suckers to lie down with them and pay for the privilege.

He crossed the quiet street to the market, pausing to drop his cigarette on the pavement. Casting a quick look around, he entered the store. Inside, he found three dusty aisles of canned food, bread, and packaged goods. A beefy white man in a blood-stained butcher's coat looked up from slicing a rack of pork ribs, shooting a quick glance at the boy who lounged near a cash register cleaning his fingernails with a watermelon knife. As he moved deeper into the store, Farrell noticed a pretty, fair-skinned girl with her hair tucked up into a net. She looked up with a wary expression from the pan of potato salad she was making. As Farrell's eyes met hers, she looked quickly away.

The butcher leaned a hairy forearm on the counter top. "What'll it be, mister? Got some fresh pork chops, some Gulf shrimp if you're interested." He showed Farrell a smile full of yellow teeth and insincerity.

"I want to talk to the King."

The butcher's face flattened. "You said which? What king you talkin' about, mister?"

Farrell saw a flicker in the butcher's eyes and knew the cashier with the knife must be closing in. "I didn't come to make trouble. I just want to talk to Arboneau. Tell him Wesley Farrell's down here. He'll recognize the name." As he spoke, Farrell pivoted on his right foot, surprising the cashier. The narrow blade in the boy's hand was waist high, his thumb poised on the ricasso for a quick thrust.

"Stay where you are," the butcher said. He turned to the startled looking girl. "Gabrielle, call upstairs to the boss and ask him what he wants to do."

As Gabrielle moved to do the butcher's bidding, the boy found himself facing Farrell's icy gaze. He blinked nervously, his knife hand wavered. He was used to handling kids, rubes, and drunks. Slowly, he lowered the knife.

Farrell nodded slowly. "That may be the first smart move you've made this week. Now fold that thing up before your hand does something your brain didn't intend."

The boy folded the long thin blade into its handle and slid it into his hip pocket, then backed away until his rump bumped into the checkout counter. Behind him, Farrell heard the girl speak softly to the butcher.

Farrell turned at the butcher's approach, saw him stop abruptly a few feet away. "The King said you can come up, but you've got to stand for a frisk. He don't 'low no guns up there." The butcher stepped closer, holding his hands out.

Farrell's gun appeared like cards from a magician's sleeve, stopping the butcher dead in his tracks. "You won't put your hands on me." He ejected the magazine from it, then proffered the empty Luger to the butcher, who took it gingerly, eyeing Farrell warily.

"Take the stairs," the butcher said hoarsely.

"Thanks." On the other side of a swinging door, he mounted a dusty staircase to the second floor. At the head of the stairs, he heard telephones ringing and the murmur of men taking bets. He saw an open door on the left and stepped through it.

A fat, white-haired old man and a reedy, bespectacled youth sat at a large desk counting money into bundles that they bound with rubber bands. They looked up as Farrell's shadow fell across the desk. The old man stared through beady black eyes set deeply on either side of a prominent nose. "What do you want, Farrell?"

Farrell straddled a chair. "How long have you operated out of this dump?"

Arboneau glowered, but his eyes were cloudy with regret. "A long while now. What's it to you?"

"Nothing. Just remembering the old days."

"The old days are gone. What do you want, Farrell? You didn't come in here just to goad me."

"How's to talk without the audience?" Farrell said, jerking his chin at the teenage boy who still busied himself counting money. He appeared unaware of Farrell.

"Don't worry, he's deaf as a post. Hell of a bookkeeper, though. Great concentration. Speak your piece."

"Whit Richards."

Arboneau's eyes became hooded as he leaned back in his chair. "What about him?"

Farrell smiled. "You need to work on your poker face, King. You don't seem surprised."

"I hear about him all the time. What of it?"

"So somebody snatched his kid, as if you didn't know. There's an interesting symmetry in that."

"Cemetery? What're you talkin' about?"

"No, symmetry. It's when things are in balance with each other. Richards had your son killed, now his kid's missing. Interesting, huh?"

Arboneau stood up, his face suddenly pale. "What the hell you tryin' to pull?"

"Sit down, King. We're not through talking yet. And tell four-eyes there to put both of his hands on the table. For a deaf man, he seems awfully nervous. If he twitches one more time, I'm liable to cut his arm off."

The youngster's head jerked up, his eyes wide behind the thick lenses. When he saw Farrell's eyes on him, he slowly placed his hands flat on the surface.

Arboneau grimaced at the boy. "Wait outside, Cal."

"Yes, sir," he said. He got up and left the room.

"You were always too quick to shoot from the hip, King. Richards is no friend of mine. Maybe I'd like to take a whack at him while he's on his knees."

"That's nothin' to do with me, Farrell. I own this part of town and it's been good to me. Richards don't want no part of it, and that suits me fine."

"Wait until somebody else wants to buy it," Farrell said dryly. "The zoning board chairman'll be over here and the next thing you know, you'll be sitting on the levee in your skivvies. You're talking like a man who's gone soft."

"Maybe I have. I ain't young no more, and I ain't got nobody to help me do better." His lined face was sullen.

"Don't kid me, old man. You use this dump for a front while you make book, peddle dope, and run whores who aren't old enough to vote. Thanks to that, you own most of this neighborhood and everything in it."

Arboneau shrugged. "Make up your mind. Either I'm washed up or I'm a tycoon. You can't have it both ways."

Farrell laughed cynically. "You know, I've conducted an unofficial poll. Nobody in the city has more reasons to hate Richards than you do, and you're one of the few who's got the brains to test him." He leaned forward, crowding the white-haired man. "But you haven't got the guts to do this by yourself. Who's working the string, Arboneau?"

Arboneau's face grew red and his hands bunched into fists. "I don't know what you're talkin' about. Sure, Richards hurt me plenty. It's taken years to build myself up again. Y'think I'm gonna risk losin' it again? Do you?"

"Not even to pay him back for your son?"

Arboneau raised a fist, then turned jerkily away, letting his arm fall slowly to his side. "God damn you," he said, his voice cracking with emotion. "Tel was all I had. Ain't it enough that he's dead without you comin' over here to rub it in? Tel had a big mouth. I told him. I told him more than once not to shoot it off about Richards." He turned back to Farrell, his dark eyes blazing, brimming with unshed tears. "All these years later, and still I feel like my heart's been torn out by the roots. No." He shook his head wearily. "I'm tired and I'm sick. Richards is too big for me, Farrell. He proved it twice." He turned away, his face pinched by something that might have been shame.

Farrell stared at the fat man's back, feeling the defeat and grief come off Arboneau in waves. Was it real or was the old fox slipping him a load of hay? "Okay, King. You're as innocent as a newborn babe and you're yellow clear through. If that's what you're selling, I guess I'll have to buy it. Sorry I bothered you." When Arboneau didn't reply, Farrell turned very deliberately before walking through the door. In the hall, he found Gabrielle in a huddle with Cal. She had a protective arm about him, a hand stroking his face as she spoke to him in a low voice. Neither looked at or spoke to Farrell as he passed.

Returning to the ground floor, he retrieved his gun from the nervous butcher before walking to the car. As he turned the ignition and fed the Packard gas, he fought a sense of frustration. He was no closer to finding Jessica Richards than when he'd begun.

As he drove back toward Canal Street, he noticed on the dashboard clock that it was nearly noon. He turned in the direction of police headquarters to meet his father for lunch, wondering if he had any better news.

Chapter 10

Farrell arrived at his father's office to find him talking on the telephone. With a quick grin, he gestured for his son to enter as he concluded his conversation.

"Cuba agrees with you, son," he said as he placed the receiver back in the cradle. "You're losing that gambler's pallor." He came around the desk to throw his arms around Farrell. They slapped backs affectionately.

Farrell took Casey by the shoulders and looked at him critically. "I think you're getting younger, Dad."

"Well, I feel younger anyway. It's been so busy around here that I can't quite believe the wedding's in two days. It was great of you to come back to stand up with me."

Farrell laughed. "You needed a best man, didn't you?"

"Sit down," Casey said. "We can go grab a bite as soon as White shows up to look after the office. Want to hit that little dump on Poydras and have some étouffé?"

"Great. What's the latest on the Richards case?"

Casey gave a rueful grin. "Confusion. The Amsterdam and Callahan murders were professional hits with a pro's weapon. A .22 High Standard automatic. The bookie joint was something else entirely."

"How so?"

"It looks as though it was a heist. Snedegar believes it was the last stop on Jimmy Daughtery's route, and the killer knew that. He took the money, then shot all of the witnesses. This one seems to fancy himself a sharpshooter, too. According to Delgado he used a .32 Smith & Wesson target revolver."

Farrell plucked idly at a hair growing on the back of his hand. "I've never known a hit man to vary his weapon. The target gun angle must be a coincidence. Besides, the crimes are completely different. Amsterdam and Callahan were two of Richards' closest confidants. The kidnapping of Jessica Richards has to be connected to those murders."

Casey frowned, nodded slowly. "That would mean the killer's boss wants to isolate Richards from his best brains. Once he weakens Richards enough—bingo."

Farrell rubbed his chin. "Before I left town, it was Callahan, Amsterdam, and Vic D'Angelo calling the shots in Richards' organization." Farrell paused to tug thoughtfully at his earlobe. "I'd hate to be Vic D'Angelo today."

"You know it," Casey replied. "You pick up anything in your travels?"

Farrell sat down and put his hat on the corner of Casey's desk. "I'm not sure. I've been making the rounds of Richards's known enemies. Fletch Monaghan dummied up, claimed to know nothing about any of it. Kurt Van Zandt said he didn't know anything, either. He was nervous enough to be lying, but maybe he's just scared I'd think he'd plot against Richards. He's got a yellow streak a mile wide."

Casey raised an eyebrow as he clasped his hands over his stomach. "Who else have you talked to?"

"So far, only King Arboneau. Richards rooked him out of thousands in property, and was behind the death of Arboneau's son. He claims to be afraid of Richards, but I felt hate coming off him like stink from a garbage pail."

Casey stared at Farrell, concentrating on every word. "Tell me more about the wife. Why did she come to you?"

"She had several reasons," Farrell replied. "The biggest was that with the police thrown off the case, there was no one looking for her daughter. Then there's her belief that one of Whit's former associates is behind it."

"And?" Casey held Farrell's gaze.

"She knew me when my scruples were a lot more flexible than they are now. She figures I can't be scared off—or pushed off the search."

"You could have told her no."

Farrell looked away. "I should have, but for some reason I couldn't." He paused. "Before she married Richards, she was my girlfriend. She left me for him." He paused again, smiling ruefully. "None of that makes it any of my business. I'll butt out now, if you say so."

Casey snorted. "Not this time. I've kept the case alive by investigating the murders, but I want to find that girl a lot more than I want to jail a bunch of hoods for killing each other." He opened a file folder on his desk and took out Jessica Richards' photograph. "She's a good-looking girl. Mature for her age." He glanced up at Farrell, frowning. "If she were mine, I'd have a hard time playing this so close to the vest."

Farrell grunted. "Richards is a pretty hard boy. Maybe he is worried, in his own way." He folded his arms. "I don't like this. I don't have a single decent lead."

"Don't be so impatient. You've already picked up information we didn't have. If you get any more hunches, play them. You're working for me, as of now."

Farrell let a grin steal over his face. "Do I get a tin badge, too?"

Casey blew a raspberry at him. "Not on your life. Who's left on your list of enemies?"

"I'm going to see Neil Gaudain. He's the nephew of old man Tarkington. Richards cheated him out of a sugar refinery years ago."

"And used the proceeds to help Sheriff Tim Marerro win his first election. I just got word that Marerro's detailed a squad of deputies to guard Mrs. Richards and his staff." Casey snorted. "With Marerro in his pocket, Richards has all the police protection he wants without worrying about them snooping into things he doesn't want looked at."

Farrell raised an eyebrow. "You know, even if Gaudain or any of these others I've talked to are involved in this scheme, there's still got to be somebody running the show. But who is he? Where did he come from?"

"That's a good question," Casey replied. "Whoever he is, he couldn't just show up with a new gang. Everybody in town would know about it in a matter of a few days."

"No. But he must be somebody strong enough that he could form an alliance with some locals."

Casey leaned his forearms on the surface of his desk. "Aside from the forensic evidence, we've only got one decent clue. The Negro custodian who was killed during the kidnapping dragged a very fancy tie clasp off the killer's shirt. We've learned that only a few Downtown stores sold it. I've been waiting for one of my men to call in with something."

"Maybe we'd better skip that lunch," Farrell suggested.

"My boy, one thing you need to know about police work is that it's essential to eat whenever and wherever you can." Casey keyed his intercom. "White. Are you there?"

"Yes, sir."

"Do me a favor, go across the street to the delicatessen and get us sandwiches and some coffee."

"Will do, Captain."

Casey leaned back and put his feet up on the desk. "Well, kiddo. How do you like police work so far?"

Thinking of the étouffé they were missing, Farrell said, "I'm glad I'm a civilian."

❧❧❧

The loose bracket on Jessica's bed proved to be a flat piece of metal about seven inches in length, tapering to a rounded point. It was a dubious proposition as a weapon, but as a tool it presented a number of possibilities.

Before going to sleep, she'd noticed a flat panel, about two feet square, near the floor of her closet. As the bed bracket came free in her hand, she found herself wondering if the panel might lead to an avenue of escape.

When she woke in the darkness, the panel was her first conscious thought. Seeing that light from the hall no longer seeped in from under the door, she got up, dressed, and turned on the closet light. She found that the panel was simply a piece of plywood, nailed to the wainscoting.

Retrieving the bracket, she inserted the rounded point into a crack between panel and wall, and gently exerted pressure. Little by little, the panel moved. The nails were rather short, and they came free noiselessly. She worked doggedly until she had pried all but one side free.

The sound of a key rattling in the lock gave her just enough warning to close the closet door, get back to the bed and pick up the movie magazine before the door swung open.

This time it was a dapper young man with narrow, fox-like features. His pale blue eyes slid along the contours of her body with undisguised lust. "Hello, babycakes."

Feeling that she could not ignore his presence, she spoke warily. "Good morning."

Like the big man the day before, this man carried a paper sack in his hand. A smear of grease discolored the brown paper on one side. He put it on the floor beside her feet, then stared down at her.

"Do—do you have any idea how long I'll be here?" she asked, forcing herself to remain still, maintaining a vocal tone that was flat and without emotion.

"Depends."

"Depends on what?"

"I might just decide to keep you here for a while. You are one juicy little broad, you know that?"

Her skin felt as though ants were crawling on it. She sensed that a wrong answer, a nervous laugh could spell disaster. "No. I—I didn't. Is that why I was…brought here?"

His right hand fell into his trouser pocket and reappeared with something in it. His thumb moved and six inches of chromed steel seemed to explode from within his fist. He grinned, his pale blue eyes lost in a deep squint that gave his face a rapacious, inhuman cast. As the grin slipped from his face, she noticed for the first time that his pupils were so small as to be non-existent. She had read that certain narcotics would produce that effect. She gripped the edge of the bed as she fought off panic.

"No, sweetheart. You're here because your old man is a cheap, four-flushing crook. You're here to make him pay. Sweet, ain't it?" He closed the knife, almost immediately snapping the blade back open. He repeated this, over and over as he leered at her.

A hot rush of anger drove the dizziness out of her. "Don't you dare talk about my father!"

Without warning he grabbed her by the front of her blouse and snatched her to her feet, bringing her face to within a few inches of his. "No? And what'll you do, you little bitch?" He threw his other arm around her waist, dragging her close to him. "You gonna tell somebody? You gonna scream or cry? I own you, and when I feel like it, I'm gonna show you how things are, get me?" He let go of her blouse and ran his hand slowly over her breasts and down her body, kneading her buttocks with his fingers. The heat radiating from his body sickened her.

Lying just beneath the revulsion and fear, however, she found rage festering. She wished she had the dull piece of steel in her hand. She wanted to hurt him.

When she didn't respond to his taunts, he shoved her abruptly away from him. As she fell, the look of cruel amusement came back into his eyes before he left the room. When she heard the key turn in the lock, she dropped her face into her hands and shuddered.

But her rage was still there, growing stronger beneath the terror. Recognizing it as a weapon, she surrendered to the anger, letting it overwhelm the fear. Stiffening her spine, she climbed to her feet and went to the food. She consumed the contents greedily, not caring what they were. She needed all her strength to escape and this was the fuel.

⚏

Skeeter caught the Esplanade bus within minutes of speaking to his uncle. Finding it nearly empty, he quickly moved to the colored section at the rear. As the bus passed Mystery Street, Skeeter stared, wondering what Mabel was doing. He remembered again her touch against his body, her lips on his, the sight of her tears.

Skeeter had seldom thought much beyond what he might do to entertain himself. Not having had a real home since his mother died, his life in the street had begun as an antidote to loss. After years of juke joints and unfamiliar bedrooms, he'd forgotten there was any other way to live. He'd sometimes sensed unspoken longings in Mabel, but had been too wrapped up in his own pleasure to ask about them.

Now he had the cops after him, a pair of men who wanted to kill him, and Mabel didn't want him around anymore. He recognized with a sense of wonder that those misfortunes carried an equal weight. Staying alive and out of jail didn't mean quite so much if Mabel was lost to him.

He got off the bus at City Park and transferred to a Carrollton bus. This one had more people on it, forcing him to stand back in the colored section with the domestics, gardeners, and other working stiffs. He imagined what it would be like to share their sense of purpose, to enjoy the knowledge that he had a home waiting at the end of the day.

At Howard and Carrollton, he left the bus and headed past the campus of Xavier University to Gerttown. He studied each street as he moved from block to block, paying particular attention to parked cars. Finally reaching Olive Street, he paused. There was plenty of activity within Howard's compound, but little happening on the street. Only a few cars were nearby, all of which appeared to be unoccupied. Holding his breath, he made a beeline for the office, walking steadily but without haste. Once through the door, he paused to peer back out at the street.

"You made good time," Howard said behind him. "See anybody as you come in?"

"Nary a soul. I cut through Xavier and come down Pine. Made a roundabout to throw anybody off. Soon as I saw the street was clear I come on over."

"Good," Howard said, putting a grease-stained hand on his shoulder. "I had Lonnie get a car ready and some of the other boys been watchin'. Cops ain't come back, and so far as I know, Frank Brown ain't, neither."

"This is the worst day of my life," he said shakily.

Howard reached inside his overalls and pulled out a long-barreled .38 Colt revolver. "You ain't lived very long yet, Skeeter." He laughed as he spun the revolver on his trigger finger. "Things can always be worse than they is."

Skeeter sank down in one of the office chairs. "I don't need nothin' worse, Unca Howard. I just want to get out from under this mess and get my life back."

"You'll be all right when you get to Houston," Howard said, sliding his gun back out of sight. "I got friends in the Fifth Ward who'll help you get on your feet. Change your name and nobody'll ever find you."

"I reckon."

"You don't sound too glad about it. Houston's a hell of a town, lots of opportunity for a smart kid like you. I know two, three bruthas over there with garages where you can make good money. Give you a month and you'll be livin' high, wide, and handsome with a new life."

"Guess I ain't got used to givin' up this life yet. Or some people…"

"Whoever she is, forget her," the old man said bluntly. "There's enough tail in Houston to keep a battleship fulla sailors happy." Howard put his hand on his nephew's shoulder again and spoke in a softer voice. "Boy, when white folk decide they want somethin' of ours, all we can do is fight, if we can, or run if we can't. This shit has 'gang' wrote all over it. You can't fight no white gang—none of us can. So you run, and stay alive."

Skeeter was too tired and dejected to argue with his uncle. "Reckon you're right. What time we leavin'?"

"After dark. Six o'clock, maybe." He went around to his desk and opened a drawer. "Here. You gonna need some money to get started, and you might feel better with this in your pocket." He handed Skeeter a roll of bills and a .41 Colt Army Special with the barrel cut to two inches and the butt wrapped in brown tape. "I burnt the serial number off with acid and the tape won't take your prints. If you have to use it, throw it in the first storm drain you come to."

Skeeter put the bills and revolver into his pockets. "Thanks, Unca Howard. I know you're goin' out on a limb."

Blessey waved a dismissive hand. "You're the only kin I got. C'mon up to the house. You can lay up there, have somethin' to eat before it's time to go."

"Yeah. I might could sleep a little." He followed his uncle through a breezeway toward the faded blue cottage.

⚜

Easter Coupé sat quietly inside the old Plymouth, stoically chewing a wad of gum as he watched the street. He continued to catch his mind wandering. He found that nothing about this job really made sense to him anymore. Sure, he killed people for money, but usually they were people who needed killin'. Skeeter Longbaugh was just a dumb kid. Killin' him was too much like going out of your way to step on a baby bird that had fallen from the nest.

It came to him that Skeeter and Patience had much in common. They were both young colored kids, neither had all the good sense they needed to get along, and circumstances had forced each of them into a seamy, dangerous existence. He shook his head violently to clear away those thoughts. How could he possibly confuse Patience with Skeeter?

He trained field glasses up the street and forced himself to watch patiently. Patience was a virtue. He had a lot of patience. Impatience was a liability.

Then it happened so fast he nearly missed it, the swift passage of a slender man across the deserted street. As Coupé focused the glasses on the man's face, he saw that his quarry had arrived.

The boy stepped quickly through the office door and out of sight into the gloomy interior. Coupé took a deep breath and put the binoculars down on the seat beside him. The moment of truth had arrived. What had seemed abundantly clear two days before was now a hopeless muddle in his mind. His instincts, honed by years on the street and in prison, told him to go in with his silenced .22 and take care of business. He'd done it before, many times, but this time was different. He felt a desperate urge to go sit in Kate's cool, dim bar and let her rub her thumb across his scarred knuckles again while he listened to the purr of her voice.

"Is that him?" Eddie Park asked, pointing at the figure walking quickly across the street ahead of them.

Merlin Gautier's lean jaw stretched as a grin spread across his face. "That's the pigeon."

"We can be over there in front of him before he makes the office," Park said, his voice tense with excitement.

"Hold your horses, sonny. We don't want to fumble the ball now." He pulled the microphone from the clip and keyed it. "Car Forty-six to Dispatch, come in, over."

"Dispatch, go ahead Forty-six."

"Alert Inspector Fifty-one that suspect just entered Blessey's. Will maintain position until he arrives."

"Roger, Forty-six. Wilco."

Gautier replaced the microphone and sat back, grinning at Eddie Park's nervous tension. "Relax, kiddo. We just about got this wrapped up in a pink ribbon."

Park cast a glance at his partner, shaking his head. "Sometimes I think you got no nerves, Merle."

"And you got too many. The boss has this figured. He'll surround this place and then we'll move in."

Park exhaled an impatient breath. "Yeah, I reckon."

Gautier chuckled, leaned back comfortably in his seat.

⌘

Farrell left police headquarters after sharing roast beef sandwiches with his father. The time with Casey had warmed him, and caused him to wonder if he would go back to Cuba after the first of the year. He didn't know how many years his father had left, and that thought was sobering.

He paused at the corner newsstand as the headlines from the latest edition of the *Times-Picayune* caught his eye. Under Art Frizell's byline, he read what little the reporter had learned about the murders of Jack Amsterdam and Butch Callahan. Art had dubbed the .22-wielding assassin "The Love-Tap Killer." Grinning, Farrell left a nickel for the newsie and took the paper along with him.

He had left his car two blocks from Police Headquarters out of necessity, but walking down a sunlit street in his hometown seemed the purest form of recreation to him at that moment. He strolled with his hands in his pockets, his mind wandering. He was within sight of his car when the gleam of a lost coin on the sidewalk caught his eye. He slowed his pace, leaned a bit forward to get a better look. As his head moved, something like an angry bee hummed past his ear and swept the gray Stetson off his head. In a split second, Farrell's subconscious recognized that bees didn't knock a man's hat off, knew a second bullet could be on its way, sent an order to Farrell's muscles that flattened his body on the sidewalk. As he fell, the second bullet came, whining off the sidewalk at his shoulder. He rolled instinctively into the cover of a parked automobile.

He waited for a moment, then crawled to the rear of the pale green Oldsmobile that sheltered him. From his vantage point at the rear fender, Farrell had a good view of the street. Traffic flowed past him, but no single pedestrian was in sight across the broad avenue. Sweet shooting for a pistol. Too sweet, maybe. He scanned the area for a vantage point from which a man might use a rifle, and saw there were many. Most of the buildings across the street were one- and two-story flat-roofed commercial buildings. Easy to gain access to and easy to escape from. He saw his hat nearby and pulled it to him. Two very small holes in the crown—a .22 for certain. He looked again across the street, checking the parked cars. It was impossible to tell the direction from which the shot had come. The shooter might be gone already, or just waiting for another shot.

He clapped the hat back on his head, got to one knee. The sunlight still glinted off the quarter that had saved his life. He picked it up, polished it on his lapel. "You and I will never be parted, sweetheart, no matter how hungry I get." He tucked it behind his show handkerchief.

Taking one last look over the trunk of the Oldsmobile, he got to his feet and sprinted down the street. Seconds later he was driving away, trying not to think about how close he'd just come to cashing in his chips.

Chapter 11

Jessica wasted no time prying the panel off the closet wall, but was disappointed to find it led only to another sparsely furnished bedroom. This one had a window, however, and she discovered that she was on the second floor of a rambling frame house in the midst of a meadow. The size of the property told her she must be somewhere at the edge of the city. Equally troubling was the sheer drop to a thick row of untamed and sharp-pointed shrubs.

Frustrated, the girl returned to the closet. She had crawled halfway through the opening when she happened to glance upward. She paused, turned her head sharply to get a better look. There was a trap in the closet ceiling.

She scrambled to her feet, pulling the wooden clothes rod loose from its brackets. Raising it to the perpendicular, she pushed the trap and saw that it moved. Trembling all over, she put the pole against the wall. She refused to confront the possibility that this might be anything other than a means of escape.

As she looked around for a way to reach the trap, her eye lit on the dry sink. Crossing to it quickly, she removed the pitcher, then lifted the cabinet experimentally. It was heavy, but it could be moved. Two minutes later, she found that it fit the closet with inches to spare.

With a sudden movement, she grabbed the sides of the closet door and climbed. The trap door rose under her fingers and fell back on a hinge, releasing a stale, dusty odor as she pulled herself through the opening. Her eyes darted quickly about the gloomy rafters until she found daylight leaking into the darkness.

All the years of gymnastics and dance she'd studied paid off as she lightly stepped from rafter to rafter, careful not to plant a foot wrongly between them. In no more than a minute she found herself in front of a metal ventilation louver that fit into the peak of the roof. Through it she could see a flat porch roof and a dilapidated rose trellis at the edge.

Planting her feet firmly, she hooked her fingers around the edges of the louver and put her back into lifting it. It made noise, but she was too far committed to stop now. She shifted right, left, up, and down, ultimately realizing that the metal was set into wood that had been milled to accept it. God damn it, she thought. To be this close...

As she moved her leg, the piece of metal in the pocket of her skirt thumped against it. She pulled it out, fitted it into the loose joint and pried experimentally. As she'd hoped, the wood was brittle and desiccated. She worked the bracket methodically, breaking wood off in small pieces. She lost track of time, focusing fiercely on the job.

She had broken away two sides of the triangle when she thought to look at her watch. Holding it up to the light, she saw that it was almost 11:45. If her jailer was feeding her on a schedule, any minute now he'd be there with lunch. She didn't give a damn about the food, but knew if he found her gone, he just might kill her before she could escape.

Turning regretfully from a job nearly complete, she worked her way to the ceiling trap and lowered herself into the closet. There was no time to get the cabinet back where it belonged, so she closed the closet door.

As Jessica turned from the closet, she got a glimpse of herself in the mirror. She was covered in dust and cobwebs.

Even if the dapper man were half out of his mind on cocaine, he'd surely notice a layer of filth all over her. She tore off her skirt, sweater, and blouse, and beat them against the bed frame until they were relatively clean. Time seemed to evaporate as she struggled to clean herself.

Pouring water into the bowl, she pressed her handkerchief into use as a washcloth. Her face and arms were nearly clean when the tumblers fell in the lock.

⚶⚶⚶

It was approaching 11:00 when Daggett and Andrews pulled up beside Merlin Gautier and Eddie Park. Daggett rolled down his window.

"He still in there?"

Gautier nodded. "Unless he's sprouted wings."

"Okay." Daggett took the microphone from the dashboard and spoke into it. "Inspector Fifty-one to Cars Eighty-nine and Sixty. Take your positions and watch closely. The subject may be armed." He put the mike back into the clip, then nodded to Gautier. "Let's go."

Andrews drove up the street, pulling to a stop just outside the gate to the garage complex. Park drove just past them, taking up a position adjacent to the cottage. All four detectives got out of their cars and took cover behind them. Through the gate, they could see mechanics stopping their work to stare nervously at them.

Daggett flipped a switch on his microphone and activated the loudspeaker. "Skeeter Longbaugh, this is the police. Come on out with your hands up. Mr. Blessey, you come out with him. Don't make us come in after you."

Inside the cottage, Skeeter jumped to his feet, his eyes flickering wildly. Blessey came past him with his teeth bared in a snarl. "Goddamn them fuckin' Uncle Toms."

"P-put the gun down, Unca Howard. They'll shoot us sure if they see it."

"Shut up, boy. I gotta think. That Daggett's a smart mothah-raper. He's prob'ly got cars stationed on the street behind my salvage yard, in case you try to climb the fence."

Skeeter put his hand on Blessey's shoulder. "It's no good, Unca Howard. Lemme go out before you get in trouble."

"Shit," Howard snarled. "I'm in trouble already if they find you here. C'mon." He grabbed the youth by the sleeve of his coat and pulled him into the center of the house. As Skeeter stared wide-eyed, he kicked aside a frayed rug and, with another quick movement of his foot, caused a section of floor to pop out of its moorings.

"Get down there and work your way to the side of the house. Listen close, 'cause I'm gonna draw them cops inside. When they do that, crawl out from under the house and slide into the next yard under the fence. The house is vacant, and so are the next two. Keep goin' until you reach Horrit Street, then walk out like you ain't got a care in the world. It's our only chance, so go on, now, git." He grabbed Skeeter and shoved him down in the hole. It was the work of a moment to close the section of floor and replace the rug. Daggett was yelling for them to come out again as the old man walked placidly to the front door.

❧

Skeeter's heart was hammering in his chest as he crawled under the house. Hearing the clatter of cops' feet above him, he quickly moved to the fence and under it.

Finding himself in a back yard overgrown with weeds, he continued to the next fence. He passed through two more yards until he reached the last one. He trotted down an alley, pulling up short at the edge of the house. None of the detectives were in sight. The compulsion to run was as urgent as a bladder full of beer, but he broke into a sedate stroll, rolling his shoulders like a man without a care in the world. When he turned the corner that would take him out of Gerttown, he began to breathe again. He was considering the theft of a car when a dirty brown Plymouth pulled up beside him. He tried to ignore it.

"Say there, fella, need a ride?" The voice was friendly, kind of country-sounding.

"Naw, man, I don't—"

The voice spoke again, low, soft, all business. "Get in the car, nigger, or I'll punch my initials in your back."

Skeeter froze, slowly turned his head until he saw the blocky, scar-faced black man staring at him over the barrel of a long, slender gun. Coupé pushed open the door. "I'll leave you layin' in the gutter if you don't move."

"Who are you, mister? I ain't done nothin' to you."

The black man's bared teeth were like those of a feral dog. "Get in the car." The words were hard, distinct.

Skeeter willingly gave up his soul to God at that moment. He'd wiggled and squirmed and connived with a criminal, all to end up where he'd started, trapped in a car with a strange, violent man. Ignoring the weight of the gun in his own coat pocket, he eased into the car and shut the door. He was trying to think when something hard struck him over the temple. Daylight brightened to fierce hues of yellow and red before it faded quickly to darkness.

⊗⊗⊗

Still shaky from his brush with death, Farrell headed Uptown on St. Charles Avenue. He turned toward the river at Jackson Avenue, then continued Uptown on Prytania. Two blocks up he eased the big maroon Packard to a stop under a pair of venerable oaks whose gnarled and knotted roots had turned the sidewalk into a roller-coaster track. A six-foot iron gate in an equally imposing fence was open, allowing him to reach the porch of the granite mansion unimpeded.

A push on the ivory button set into the door frame eventually brought an old man dressed in a morning coat, striped pants, and haughty expression. "Yes, sir?"

"I'd like to see Mr. Gaudain. The name's Farrell."

The old man looked him over with a thinly veiled air of suspicion. "May I ask the nature of your call?"

"Tell him Whitman Richards. He'll understand."

The old man's expression didn't change, but there was a sudden flash of light in his lusterless gray eyes. "One moment." He gently closed the door in Farrell's face.

Farrell set fire to a cigarette, smoking leisurely as he leaned his shoulder against one of the massive white columns. He'd smoked it about halfway down when the door opened again. "Mr. Gaudain will see you now."

Farrell sent the butt spinning out into the yard as he followed the old man down a long hallway to a library. A huge window let in light from a garden that boasted a fountain in which a bronze nymph gamboled under a shower spewed by bronze dolphins. In a leather club chair was a pale slip of a man who sat with his chin cupped thoughtfully in his hand as he examined the nymph. "She's lovely, don't you think?" he asked as Farrell approached.

"She'd be the star in any burlesque house in town."

Up close, Farrell could see the man's face. The skin had a fragile, rice paper look, his hair platinum. Farrell knew he was yet under forty, but he seemed older, and frail.

"Strange you should say that," Gaudain replied. "The model was a stripper on Bourbon Street who used the name Torchy LaFlamme. She was my fifth wife—for about ten months." He paused to allow Farrell to sit down in the chair opposite. "What about Whitman Richards, Mr. Farrell?"

"Someone's kidnapped his daughter. I have a suspicion that it's part of a plot to weaken him for a takeover."

Gaudain's dry, papery face twitched, almost smiled. "Dear me. Isn't that just dreadful." He paused to sip some port from a tiny crystal glass. "It's so nice of you to bring me the news."

Farrell got out his cigarette case, offered it to Gaudain, then selected one for himself. He lit it, watching Gaudain's face. "I guess this is all news to you."

"I've spent a lot of time and money trying to hurt Whitman Richards legally, Mr. Farrell. I've backed his opponents in three separate elections, backed Sheriff Marerro's opponents in two others. All told I've spent about a quarter-million trying to ruin that bastardly sonofabitch, and I suppose I'd do it again if I thought there was even the least chance. But kidnapping his child, dear me, no. I wouldn't even know how to go about such a thing." He sipped port. "Why are you telling me this?"

Farrell inhaled some smoke, then let it feather out his nostrils. "I'm no friend of Richards's, Mr. Gaudain. I might even dislike him as much as you do. But I used to be friendly with his wife, and she asked me to help find her daughter after Richards threw the cops off the case."

Gaudain laughed, shaking his head. "That sounds so like him. I'm sorry for his wife and child, but I don't know what more I can offer you, Mr. Farrell."

"Sure about that? I heard someone say that you were staying alive just so you could dance on Richards's grave."

"I am not, as you can plainly see, a man of action, Mr. Farrell. Nor have I ever consorted with thugs or gangsters. I might have once, but I didn't. I know nothing of the kidnapping or anything associated with it."

Farrell nodded slowly. "Well, knowing that is something, I guess. Richards has a lot of enemies. I think someone here is backing the play of a bigger man who's masterminding the takeover of Richards' territory."

Gaudain held up the decanter of port, offering Farrell some. When Farrell declined, he refilled his glass and took a healthy sip. "Well, I have heard that many people in this town have reason to hate Whitman. I am but one, not that my hatred is by any means inconsiderable. You see, I suspected from the outset that it was Richards who had my uncle killed, even though he masterfully cast the blame on another man, who subsequently left town to escape arrest."

"Sounds like a story I can believe."

Gaudain smiled. "It was the man who first approached my uncle about purchasing the refinery. My family opened the first one in this state, did you know that? And Uncle Charles was extraordinarily proud of that heritage. It was his life, you see. He couldn't possibly give it up."

"Who was this man?"

"Pete Carson was his name. A big brute of a fellow, but clever. It was he, the police later claimed, who lured my uncle to a meeting up in St. Charles Parish and killed him, left him for the buzzards."

Farrell sat a bit straighter, intrigued by the story. "Claimed? You don't think he did it?"

"Well, the entire thing was rather too neat for someone even as gullible as I to believe. It began with the note they found on my uncle's body which had set the meeting up. It was unsigned, but the handwriting was quite distinct. Then someone came forward who claimed to have seen an automobile leaving the area where my uncle's body was found. It was quite a distinctive automobile, a dove-gray LaSalle with dark green fenders. An informer later tipped the police that Pete Carson owned such a vehicle. When they investigated further, they found his handwriting on some papers filed with the Notorial Archives that matched the handwriting on the note."

Farrell rubbed the edge of his jaw. "Pretty damning."

Gaudain gave him a wintery smile. "Superficially, yes. A private handwriting expert I later had inspect the evidence pronounced it a forgery, albeit a stellar job."

"I see."

"When they went to question Carson, he had fled. The subsequent search to find him proved unsuccessful."

"You believe it's a frame-up, then."

Gaudain smiled again. "Well, consider this. The man who reported seeing the car in St. Charles Parish subsequently landed a plum of a job with the State Insurance Commission, a den of thieves run by a cohort of Richards'. The informer who tipped the police was later given a job with the sheriff, as the sheriff's personal chauffeur."

"This is beginning to stink."

"Indeed. Then Whitman proceeded to take advantage of my ignorance, driving away every other buyer who might have had any interest in my uncle's business. I blame myself for that. I've always been rather lazy and knew nothing of what the business was worth. Oh, he offered me a tidy sum, no error, but it was only a fifth of what I could have gotten from the others." He sighed. "I suppose my efforts to defeat Whitman are merely an outlet for my anger at myself."

"So nobody knows where this Pete Carson is now."

"Not precisely. It seems that a year or two later, a man was found cut in half on some railroad tracks in North Dakota. Body was terribly mauled and mutilated. But he had papers identifying him as Pete Carson."

Farrell raised an eyebrow. "So much for that idea."

"Perhaps. But you know, Mr. Farrell, I've never truly believed Pete Carson was dead. I made some inquiries about him. He was no fool. The police suspected him of any number of capital crimes, but they never found any evidence that would put him in jail. He was ruthless, intelligent, not at all someone who could be tripped up through any fault of his own. His luck was rather too bad to be credible."

"Meaning what?"

"I sent a private investigator to look into Carson's supposed death. He reported back that the body was buried without an autopsy. Furthermore, the undertaker who buried him said the man had somehow lost all his fingers—'perhaps eaten by scavengers' was his verdict."

"I get your drift. The body was probably an unlucky hobo that Carson used to cover his tracks." Farrell crossed his legs, rubbed a thumb along his jaw. "Tell me, Mr. Gaudain. If you went that far with your investigation, why didn't you turn what you'd found over to the police?"

Gaudain smiled. "Mr. Farrell, were you not acquainted with a police captain named Gus Moroni?"

Farrell blinked as his mind raced back to a night in 1936 when he'd gone into a dark house after a gangster named Ganns and his confederate, Captain Gus Moroni. He remembered vividly the bucking of the gun in his hand as he sent three bullets into the renegade police captain.

"Yes," Gaudain said softly. "I see you remember. You remember, as well, that Moroni was a blackguard, and that his boss, Emile Ganns, was one of Richards' supporters. Does that tell you anything?"

Farrell nodded slowly. "Moroni helped Richards cover everything up."

"Mere speculation, but you'll grant that there is some basis for it. Might I trouble you for a cigarette now?" He selected one from Farrell's proffered case, then leaned over to get the light. As he leaned back, exhaling the smoke luxuriously, he pointed a finger at Farrell. "If Carson still lives, I can think of no one who'd hate Richards more than he."

Farrell stared out the window at the gamboling nymph. "If you're right, the cops will never figure it out. Carson's bound to have changed some in ten years. With the police believing he's dead, there'd be no one looking for him to come back. Not even Richards."

"Oh, I'm certain Whitman knows who's stinging him."

Farrell's brow puckered. "Any idea why he framed this Carson?"

"Just thieves falling out, I suppose. We may never know, and of course, Whitman would not dare tell the police. He has too many secrets he has to keep hidden."

Farrell took in some more smoke, let it out gently. "I'm grateful to you for the help, Mr. Gaudain. If you're right, this is the first good lead in the case."

Gaudain put the cigarette between his lips, then smoothed an eyebrow with his finger. "Think nothing of it. It's quite stimulating to have such a famous brigand as yourself visit. I dare say you could tell *me* some good stories. Perhaps you'll come again and indulge me."

Farrell was silent for a moment, watching the other man. Finally he stirred. "It sounds like fair payment."

Gaudain made a dismissive gesture. "Not at all. I'm being quite selfish. If you should come again, I hope you'll tell me how all this turns out. Particularly if you have bad news about Whitman. I should very much like to hear some bad news about him."

Farrell stood and offered his hand to the languid millionaire. "There aren't very many ways for this to turn out, and most of them are bad."

Gaudain smiled dreamily. "Lovely. Simply lovely."

⧜

Farrell departed Gaudain's house warily, using the front porch pillars as cover until he could reach the shrubbery in the yard. When he reached the fence, he spent two full minutes examining the neighborhood until he was satisfied that no one was lurking within gunshot of him.

He drove back Downtown on Magazine, pausing at a telephone booth at the edge of the Lower Garden District. He caught Casey just as he was about to leave the office.

"I'm glad I caught you," Farrell said. "I've got a lead that only a cop can follow."

"And I've got one for you," Casey said. "That tie bar found at the Glasgo murder, one was sold to a man named Johnny Parmalee about three weeks ago. You know him?"

"Ex-prize fighter. Last I heard he was muscle, squeezing people who owed Diamond Phil Fanucci."

"Not anymore. He quit about two weeks ago. Told him he had a shot at something better and was going to take it."

"Really."

"There's more. Did you know Parmalee had a brother?"

"Uh-uh. He must be quite a bit younger than Johnny."

"About ten years according to his record. He was working for Fanucci, too, and he's got an arrest record that includes three arrests for assault with a deadly weapon. All three involved a knife."

"And Glasgo was knifed to death," Farrell mused. "That sounds like a very good lead, Dad."

"I think so, too. I sent men to their last known address—a hotel off Lee Circle—but they're both gone. Left no forwarding address. I've got their descriptions out on the air already, but I've got a hunch you'll turn something up on them before I do. So what've you got for me?"

Farrell laughed. "I learned one thing, and that's not to make an enemy of a rich, bored man. Neil Gaudain paid for his own investigators when his uncle, Charles Tarkington, was killed. It seems that Richards got our old pal, Captain Gus Moroni, to help him pin Tarkington's murder on a man named Pete Carson. Carson escaped arrest, and seems to have faked his death somewhere up north."

"That sweetens the pot a little," Casey said. "If Richards framed Carson, he'd have plenty of reasons to want to destroy him, and he might not be too particular about how he does it. I'll get a bulletin out to the radio cars."

"Don't go away yet," Farrell said. "I've got one other little tidbit for you."

"I'm listening."

"When I left you after lunch, somebody took a shot at me on Tulane Avenue as I was walking to my car. I didn't get a look at him, but the hole in my hat couldn't be anything but a .22."

"Mother of God." Casey's voice was a harsh whisper. "You all right?"

"So far, but I'll feel better when I know who this is."

"Be careful, son. I know I asked you to mix into this, but you can back out anytime. I'd rather have you alive than catch all the crooks in New Orleans."

"Don't fret, Dad. I'll see to it you get to the altar on time."

Farrell stepped quickly from the phone booth to the recessed entrance of a nearby jewelry store, melding his form to the shadows there. He saw nothing in any direction, but his sixth sense was as insistent as blood pumping from a severed artery. Whoever was stalking Farrell, he was still out there, looking for his chance.

Setting his jaw, the bronze-skinned man moved deliberately to his car, hit the ignition, then drove away.

∞

Georgia Miles Richards looked like almost any other pampered rich man's wife, but, unlike most, she'd been mistress to two criminals, each of whom had committed violence while she lived with them. For that reason, she was sufficiently familiar with crime to be less appalled by it than a more sheltered spouse. She was also fed up with waiting for some man to get her daughter back. She'd been to Farrell, Rob Landgon, and Whit, and so far none of them had delivered. She decided it was time to do something on her own.

Swearing her cook, Bessie Mae, to secrecy, she left the house through the kitchen. The garage opened onto a service alley, which allowed her to leave while avoiding the scrutiny of the two deputies who'd been detailed to watch the house. It appeared that neither of them realized that guarding the house included keeping a watch on the rear.

Lacking anything like a clear-cut plan of action, she headed Downtown. As much as she wanted to find her daughter, she also wanted someone to tell her what this was all about. Of course, some enemy of Whit's had stolen the girl, but who was it?

She had one friend left from the days when she'd come to New Orleans looking for adventure. Annie Riley had been merely an enterprising whore in 1921, but now she used the name Joyce Delessups and ran a high class bordello.

She drove through Downtown until she reached Canal, following that westward until she neared City Park Avenue. Across from St. Anthony of Padua church, she found the house she was looking for, a magnificent antebellum mansion with three floors and a gallery supported by smooth white columns. The woman who answered the door took her to Mrs. Delessups's drawing room.

"Georgia, darlin'," Annie Riley said, throwing her arms wide. "What's the respectable wife of a city councilman doin' comin' in this place in broad daylight?" She let loose a delighted bray as she hugged Georgia.

"I've got worse trouble than being seen at a bawdy house, honey," Georgia replied, kissing Annie's cheek.

"Sit down and tell mama all about it," Annie said, leading Georgia to the couch.

"Somebody's kidnapped Jess. I don't know who it is, but Whit does. He threw the police out of the house, and since then all he's done is fuck his secretary and leave sheriff's deputies on the front lawn."

Annie shook her head. "Men. They sure as hell are predictable, ain't they, honey? When did all this start?"

"They grabbed Jess on the grounds of her school yesterday morning. I don't know who or why. Whit's the only one who's even talked to the kidnappers."

Annie unstoppered a decanter of scotch and poured two healthy measures. She gave one to her friend, then took a bite out of her own. "Well, it's no secret that your hubby's stepped on a lotta faces over the years. Pickin' out the who from that list would take a crystal ball."

Georgia leaned back in the chair and placed the cool glass against her forehead. "Christ, this waiting is killing me. I just wish something would happen."

Annie raised an eyebrow. "Honey, I think you forgot how we used to do things when we were young."

Georgia looked at her sharply. "What do you mean?"

Annie shrugged. "Think about it. We wanted something to happen, we made it happen. I think you forgot how."

"I didn't forget everything," she replied soberly. "I went to the one man I thought could or would help. He said he would, but I've heard nothing from him."

"Who might we be speaking of, darlin'?"

"Wes Farrell. I figured if anybody could find Jess it would be him."

She laughed. "Yeah. If a third of the stories about him are true, he's half ghost and half Apache Indian." Her face grew a sly look. "Funny you'd think of goin' to him. What made you think he'd help you?"

Georgia felt heat growing in her face. "For old time's sake, I guess."

Annie's expression grew thoughtful. "That all? You didn't give him any better reasons?"

Georgia shot Annie an irritable look. "You mean like offer to sleep with him? You're damned nosy sometimes."

Annie regarded her soberly. "Don't be too tricky for your own good, Georgia. You ought to find some reason to get him to take you into his confidence. If he didn't still feel something for you, he'd of thrown you down the stairs. Remember, it's Wes Farrell we're talkin' about. He's either your best friend or Satan's stepson."

Georgia sighed as she put the glass on the table. "All right. Thanks for the advice, Annie. I guess I needed it."

Annie grinned at her coyly. "Advice? Was that what I gave you? We were just talkin', sugar. Talkin' like old girlfriends from the neighborhood. Come back and tell me when everything's over. I never got to ride the coattails of Wesley Farrell. Bet it'll be a hell of a ride."

Georgia shook her head as she stood up. "That's what I'm afraid of."

※※※

Skeeter returned to consciousness hearing water lap softly against the shore. He tried to move, but found his hands and feet tightly bound. The piercing aroma of rotting marine vegetation made him gag, setting off a sharp pain in the base of his skull. Somehow he managed to neither vomit nor pass out. After a while he was able to roll to his side.

His kidnapper sat stoically on the running board of the Plymouth. His hard features were twisted with some emotion that Skeeter had no desire to learn.

"Well, you finally come back to life."

"Why didn't you just kill me while I was 'sleep?" Skeeter groaned. "You get some kinda thrill outa seein' a man die?" Skeeter wasn't sure where all those bold words came from, but it was too late to take them back.

The Negro accepted the gibe with equanimity. "No, no thrill. A man named Johnny Parmalee sent me to shut you up, boy. I do those kinda things for money. I done it for a long time, and I found out that if you gonna kill a man, you best be able to look him in the eye while you doin' it."

"Yeah," Skeeter replied tartly. "I seen that yesterday when your boy, Joey, stuck his chiv into a brutha. He was looking ole Butterbean in the eye, all right. Now you out here cleanin' this ofay's shit up for him."

The big Negro's body stiffened. "Killed a brutha, you say? Was it a fair fight?"

"Hell, no. If that skinny li'l cracker hadn't of pulled the knife, Butterbean would of tore his cracker head off for him. Six kids and a wife he had, too."

The Negro said nothing as he lifted his long, slender gun from his lap. Skeeter braced himself, certain that his last moment had arrived.

"You know who I am, boy?"

Skeeter blinked. "Naw, man. I never seen you before."

The Negro's shoulders seemed to lift as a sigh left him. "The name Easter Coupé mean anything to you?"

"A righteous badman, they say. A killer born on Easter Sunday. That you?"

The Negro nodded solemnly. "All of that and more. Reckon I done killed fifty men in my time. Some in fights, some just 'cause they deserved it. Some I was paid to do."

Skeeter was intrigued in spite of his fear. Coupé was a famous man in the world the boy inhabited. "How much they payin' you to kill me, man?"

Coupé laughed mirthlessly. "A thousand semolians, boy, and a promise of easy livin' later on." He laughed again, causing the hair to stand up on Skeeter's neck. "You got any kin, boy? A woman?"

"Just an uncle. My mama died a few years back. My gal made me leave her 'fore somebody caught up to me. If I'd of married her when I should of, I wouldn't be in this fix."

Coupé shrugged. "I got no family, no wife, no kids. I got a house, two cars, and five guns."

In spite of himself, Skeeter was impressed. "Reckon you're a rich man, Mr. Coupé." He paused, cut his eyes away. "Why don't you go ahead and get it over with?"

Coupé looked at the pistol, bouncing it lightly on his broad palm. "I brung you out here to kill you and put your body in the lake. I done it many a time before this. Done it without thinkin' about it. This…this time is different."

Skeeter looked into Coupé's face. "Different how?"

Coupé rubbed a thick hand across his mouth. "I—I don't know." He stood, walked to within a few paces of Skeeter. Looking down with eyes that were wild and white, he brought the pistol level with the boy's head. Muscles bunched along the lines of his jaw as tightly clenched teeth began to show between his heavy lips.

Skeeter stared into the muzzle of the pistol, unable to tremble, weep, or pray. They remained in that tableau for what seemed an eternity before Coupé lowered the gun to his side. It took Skeeter a moment to register the trembling in the man's muscular body.

Without any warning, Coupé let out a hideous cry and threw the pistol out into the lake. Skeeter heard the faint plop of the gun landing in the water, but before he could react, Coupé was at his side, stuffing a handkerchief deep into his mouth. As the boy mumbled an inarticulate cry, Coupé lifted him bodily, placed him in the trunk of the Plymouth, then closed the lid. Inside the dark space, the baffled youngster heard the motor crank, then the sound of marl spurting from beneath the spinning tires.

∞∞∞

The telephone rang once again in the man's shabby room, and as usual, he let it ring a few times before answering it. "Yeah?"

"It's me," a soft voice said. It was clear the caller was speaking from a booth, because the sound of street noise came through the line.

"Did you get him?" the man asked.

"No. He moved just as I squeezed the trigger. There was no time to get a second shot."

The man's hard, rough hand bunched into a fist, quivering for a second. "Where is he now? You were able to follow him, weren't you?"

"Yeah, he didn't see me. He's inside a mansion on Prytania Street, a big place with white columns."

"Neil Gaudain's house. Can you get a shot from there?"

"No. I don't see how. There's no place to hide for a long shot, and he'll be on his guard against somebody walkin' up on him."

"No," the man replied, his voice full of regret. "He'd kill you sure. Stay with him. He's the only man in town who can upset our plans. Track him if you have to track him all night, but put a bullet in Farrell's brain before you come back here, understand?"

There was a long pause before the caller replied. "Yeah. I understand."

Chapter 12

Jessica pressed herself against the wall, trying ineffectually to hide herself behind her wrinkled blouse. As she held her breath, the dapper man entered. As before, he carried a brown paper bag. He stopped, gazed slowly about until he found her pressed up against the wall.

"Well, well, well," he said softly. "I was right. You ain't so little, are you, sugar?" He kicked the door closed with a negligent tap of his two-toned shoe, the sharp edges of his teeth just visible through his slitted lips.

"Please, go away and let me get dressed." Her voice sounded small and hollow. She somehow knew that even if she'd been dressed, it would have come to this eventually. He was a man who took his frustrations out on women and pretended it was sex. Something had happened to him today or last night and he didn't care anymore.

"Uh-uh, sweetheart," he said, pulling his tie away from his neck. "Now that I got you partly undressed, I might as well finish the job. Why don't you lie down there and get comfortable, hmmmm? We gonna have us a party." He unbuttoned the cuffs of his shirt as he moved in on her.

She didn't bother to answer. Her thoughts were of the closet, and the latch on the inside. She stepped nimbly to the cot and across to the other side, but he was watching for that, darting effortlessly in front of her. She knew she was going to have to fight and she braced for it.

He lunged at her, grabbing her around the waist as he attempted to nuzzle her neck. Jessica resisted him with all her strength, pounding his face with the heel of her hand while she fought to break his hold. His hands were like spiders, violating her in every way imaginable. Each of them was breathing heavily, their struggle wordless but for occasional grunts of pain.

Jessica found that he wasn't much heavier than she. They seemed about evenly matched as they struggled against one another. She jabbed a thumb at his eye, drawing a yell of pain. He retaliated, striking the side of her head.

The blow stunned her but the force of it knocked her out of his grasp. She stood in the center of the room now, gasping for breath, looking for an opening to hurt him. She realized that she would probably lose, but she wanted to hurt him as badly as she could. He made another sudden lunge, but she retaliated, stomping his instep. As he howled, she aimed a kick at his groin, barely missing. He roared, cursing her at the top of his lungs.

"Come on, you sissy," she taunted him. "A real tough guy, but you're letting a girl wear you out. Come on, you chicken bastard, come on and fight!"

He rushed at her, his rage making him careless. She sidestepped, swinging at his head. Her fist caught him in the ear, knocking him off balance. He fell hard, leaving a clear path to the door. She leaped past him, had the doorknob in her hand when she felt his hand on her ankle. Joey jerked hard, and she fell.

With the breath knocked out of her, she kicked and pulled to escape his clutches, but he was on top, crawling up her body hand over hand. She bore his full weight now. No matter how hard she bucked and writhed, she couldn't throw him off. Her breath was coming in ragged gasps and her vision was clouding over. She was losing.

Fully astride her, he captured her right hand in his left. The anguished sobs racketing from her abused lungs caught in her throat when she saw the knife snap open in his hand. He laughed like a maniac as he raised the knife and brought it down. I'm licked, she thought, her eyes locked on the gleaming blade rushing toward her face.

At the last possible second, a hard brown hand caught Joey Parmalee's wrist and bent it back. As her vision began to clear, she saw that a big, dark-blonde man was dragging Joey clear of her. With a careless swipe of his free hand, the big man sent the knife spinning across the room.

Joey screamed in pain, his feet kicking uselessly. The big man stared at him with savage delight as he smashed his fist into the younger man's face. Joey went limp, but the man hit him again, then struck him a terrific blow in the abdomen. Gradually the man's hideous grin relaxed. He shook Joey experimentally, then threw him out into the hall.

Jessica rose painfully up on her elbow, saw that her step-ins were ripped up one leg and her brassiere was torn half off her chest. She crawled to the side of the bed, trying to cover herself with her arms. She felt something soft against her body, and found the big man covering her with a blanket. As she clutched it to her throat, she stared up at him. "Who—Who are you?"

"I'm your Uncle Pete, Jessica."

"Uncle—Pete?"

He nodded. "I guess your daddy never mentioned me. Here, let's get you up on the bed."

<hr>

"Mr. Blessey, we know that Skeeter came in here. You're not doing yourself any good by staying clammed up."

The old car thief looked defiantly up into Daggett's angry face. "Way I sees it, I'm doin' myself plenty of good. You can't very well haul me in for harborin' a fugitive if there ain't no fugitive here, now can you?"

Gautier's narrow face had grown as sharp as an arrowhead. He took off his jacket and hung it on the back of a chair. "Iz, leave him in here with me and Sam for about ten minutes.

The old bastard'll shit words all over the floor when we get through with him."

"Knock it off," Daggett snapped. He started to walk out to the car, but on an impulse, he decided to give the old man one last try.

The old man sat with his arms folded, glaring obdurately at Gautier and Andrews. Daggett waved the other two back and confronted Blessey.

"Mr. Blessey, do you care what happens to Skeeter?"

It wasn't the kind of question the old man expected. He considered it, wondering if it were a trick. "I reckon so. He's all the kin I got."

"Then I want you to think about something. If he was an unwilling accomplice of the men who kidnapped that white girl, they're looking for him, and I think you know what'll happen when they find him."

The old man remained silent.

Daggett's face was like a thundercloud. "You don't give a damn as long as you keep your own ass out of the crack, do you?"

The old man's face twisted this way and that as he wrestled with himself. It was completely against his grain to trust a cop, but he recognized the continuing danger to Skeeter. He looked up at Daggett again, his eyes clear. "Was a man here earlier, callin' hisself Frank Brown. Claimed Skeeter sent him here to get his car worked on. I thought somethin' about him weren't quite right."

"Uh, huh. I'm listening. What did he look like?"

"Big fella, huge. His face looked like somebody carved it out of a block of coal with a dull chisel. Maybe six-four. Weighed two hundred and fifty pounds if he weighed an ounce. Had this bad scar runnin' along his jawbone here." He dragged his thumb along the right side of his jaw.

Andrews and Gautier looked at each other sharply. "Boss, I don't know but one man looks like that. His name's Easter Coupé," Andrews said.

Daggett's shoulders slumped. He figured Skeeter for a dead man already. "Gautier, get on the radio and get a descriptions of Longbaugh and Coupé out on the air. Sam, call the squad room and ask them to dig up anything on Coupé that they can find on file. Maybe we'll get lucky." As the two detectives moved to obey, Daggett turned his unfriendly gaze back on the old car thief.

"Mr. Blessey, for two cents I'd handcuff your ankles, hang you upside down from that door and beat your ribs in. There's not a person at headquarters who'd shed a goddamned tear if I did. I'm not gonna take you in because I can't pin anything on you, but I'll tell you this. If Skeeter winds up dead, you'll have to take the blame. There's nothing the law can do to you that'll be any worse than that."

He grabbed the old man's bib-front and dragged him to his feet. "But if I so much as catch you spittin' on the sidewalk after this, I'm gonna throw your miserable old ass in jail and fix it so you rot in there, you understand?"

The old man didn't like it, but he took it. "I hear you plenty good."

Daggett glared at him for a moment, then pushed him away with a growl of disgust. He turned and left the old man standing in the office alone.

⸎

"He's plenty slick, Whit," the short bald man said. "We done checked every fleabag hotel, every roomin' house, hell, we even been to see real estate leasing agents. We found he checked into the General Wilkerson night before last, but he checked out again next mornin'." He scratched the fringe of unkempt brown hair that grew beneath the pink dome of his head. "It's like tryin' to track a ghost."

Richards paced up and down the length of his office, rubbing the back of his neck. He'd lost two more men and fifteen thousand in cash in a Carson raid on a gambling den he owned near the Jefferson Parish line. With Amsterdam dead, his gambling operation was spinning into a shambles. "Somebody's hiding him, I know it. I just don't know who."

Vic shrugged nonchalantly. "So mebbe we oughta go shake a few people up. We might get lucky."

"Are you out of your mind? Don't we have enough enemies already?" He shook his head vigorously.

Vic crossed his legs, folded his hands peacefully in his lap. "Look, Whit. I know you're a respectable city councilman and all, and you prob'ly don't wanna dent that nice glossy picture you sold the suckers, but you gotta get wise to yourself. Jack's dead. Butch is dead. So far eight of our men is dead, and by my count we lost thirty, forty thousand bucks in two days. Experience tells me that while they're bleedin' us white, they're lookin' for a chance to send us to the same party they sent Jack and Butch to. I'm your man, always was and always will be, but I ain't sittin' still to get shot so's you can pretend you didn't get where you are by stealin'. Am I gettin' through to you yet?"

Richards stopped pacing to stare at the little bald man. He looked like Elmer Fudd, until you noticed the bulge of the .45 under his jacket. "All right, all right. I'm so worried about Jess that I'm losin' my mind."

"Don't give me that crap, Whit. All you're worried about anymore is that li'l blonde quail out there. You gotta be nuts, a man your age. Christ." He shook his head. "Get your head outa your ass, Whit. I know three, maybe five people who might just have the balls to back Pete up. I go hit them, and your problem goes away like heartburn after a Bromo."

"What people?"

Vic stood up, shaking his head. "Cut it out. You know what people. Even you only got so many enemies that can really hurt you." He turned and walked to the office door. "I'll call you in a little while." He opened the door and left the office.

Richards watched the door close, blinking uncertainly. In all the years they'd been together, Vic D'Angelo had always taken his lead. Richards was torn between anger at Vic's temerity and relief that someone was going to do something that needed doing. Without Jack and Butch he felt crippled. He sat down heavily in an armchair.

There was a brief rap at the door just before it opened and Rob Langdon entered. The slender young man frowned as he looked at his boss. "Whit—Whit? Look at me, Whit."

Richards looked up slowly. "What is it?"

Langdon ran his fingers through his hair, his mouth brittle with impatience. "Tell me what you want to do. We've got people lined up to see you on city business and others who want you for other reasons. The hall's full of sheriff's deputies and they frisk everybody who comes in. This is chaos. If we can't do business, people will start to lose confidence. You and I both know that can't happen. What do you want to do, for the love of Christ?"

"Who's out there? The real business, not those flannel mouths working for the city."

"Bandini and Lupo need help with that paving contract. Braden down at Public Works is giving them the run-around. Then there's Art DeLuca. You promised him exclusive franchise on that excursion boat business. He says that was supposed to be cleared up a week ago, but the Secretary of State's people won't talk to him. Besides him there's—"

Richards waved dismissively at his assistant. "That's enough. Jesus H. Christ."

Langdon's dark eyes held a look bordering on contempt. "Whit, I know how you feel, but you're a power in this town. You got a lot of people depending on you, and hell to pay if you don't deliver. We've got people we need to pay off, and we can't pay them off until we get paid off."

"All right. Fuck! You're a bigger nag than a wife. Send in Bandini and Lupo."

Langdon half-turned, paused. "Georgia's going out of her mind. Can't you do anything to make her feel better?"

Richards heard something in Langdon's voice, looked up sharply, his eyes with a cruel glint in them. "Working on you a little bit is she, Rob? Georgia's a gal who gets what she wants, so beware of her. Especially since she's taken you into her bed. Oh, yeah, I knew. How do you think I got where I am in this town, you little shit? You want to tell her something, then tell her that the half-brother I framed and double-crossed eleven years ago has come back from the dead. Tell her to stop worrying about Jess because he came back to hurt me. *Me.* Tell her the next time you share a quiet moment together. Now get out and send in Bandini and Lupo."

Langdon suppressed a shudder as he walked very carefully and quietly to the door, pausing as he put his hand on the knob. "You knew, but you said nothing. Why?"

"Maybe I just wanted to see if you'd try to double-cross me for her. Either she isn't as good as she used to be or you've got more spine than I thought. But nobody pulls the wool over my eyes, boy. Nobody."

Langdon opened the door and stepped through it. As he closed the door, Whitman Richards stood up from his chair, his pale face flushed and his dark eyes full of hot lights. He was still standing there when Bandini and Lupo entered.

∞∞∞

Farrell continued Downtown knowing that time was getting short. The longer this went on, the greater was the danger that Jessica might become a casualty or simply an inconvenience to the men seeking to destroy her father. He admitted to himself that the clock was ticking for him, too, as long as the sniper remained unchecked on his tail.

Finding Pete Carson was going to require all the manpower Casey could throw at it, but the Parmalee brothers were bottom-feeders. Wherever that kind went, they left a trail of slime behind for someone to follow.

Johnny had been a fighter, and probably still had friends and acquaintances at the fringes of the fight game. Farrell had, himself, trained to be a fighter long ago, and decided to see where that road would lead him.

He swung back to the east and picked up Tchopitoulas Street. New Orleans was a fight town, with more than its share of trainers and promoters. He stopped at a gymnasium near Jackson Avenue that was run by an old fighter named Red Chisum. Red remembered Johnny well enough, but hadn't seen him in a couple of years. He suggested Farrell try at a gym on Third Street run by a Spaniard named Parma. Parma sent him to a Negro trainer named Sugar Boy Wilkes. Nobody had seen Johnny Parmalee in some time, but Wilkes confided that a mutual acquaintance had said Johnny mentioned somebody from out of town asking him to do a job. Since Johnny wasn't much of a talker, Wilkes said, that nugget of info amounted to about a week's worth of conversation.

As Farrell followed the trail, he became aware of a Chevrolet station wagon behind him. He saw it the first time on Louisiana Avenue. Later it showed up in his rear-view mirror again on Annunciation. The third time he was certain it was the same car. The front bumper had been bent at a crazy angle on the right side. Farrell decided to leave the driver alone for a while. He'd made the mistake of getting too close. That meant he was human. If he was human, Farrell could take him.

He stopped at a bar on Octavia that he knew was frequented by ex-pugs. Talking to the bartender, he discovered that the man knew Johnny Parmalee and carried a scar from their last meeting. He was only too willing to talk. He mentioned a gym on Magazine Street, a few blocks west of Napoleon. Farrell thanked him and drove over there.

As the afternoon deepened, northerly winds blew an overcast over the city. Staccato bursts of hard rain lashed his windshield, the chill of it fogging the glass. Shivering, he cut on the heater, a thing he'd barely used in the almost year-round tropical heat.

Fifteen minutes later he parked the Packard in front of a two-story brick structure that had once been a movie theater. Now it was owned by Bucky Targo, a former heavyweight champ and trainer extraordinaire. As he paused to light a cigarette, the street behind him showed no trace of the station wagon. He felt the driver there, all the same. They had a connection that only death could sever.

He entered the gym, stopping just inside to let his eyes adjust. It was like most other places where aspiring fighters learned the craft. A regulation canvas ring dominated the center of the room. Around it, young men worked out on the heavy and speed bags, skipped rope, or worked out on weights. The air was permeated with the aromas of sweat and liniment, and just under those the coppery smell of blood. The combined stinks sent Farrell's mind back to 1917, when he had traded manual labor for eating money and boxing lessons in a place much like this.

The relative gloom of the large room gave way to harsh yellow light that illuminated the ring. A young white man and a stocky Cuban, both in silk trunks and leather headgear, bounced energetically on the balls of their feet as they feinted and parried. A half dozen of their peers watched in stoic silence as an older man kept up a torrent of abuse.

"Christ Jesus on a fuckin' bicycle, Devereaux, hit him, whydontcha? You waitin' for a fuckin' engraved invitation? No, Castillo, lead with your right, cover with your left. If Dev ever does throw a punch, he's gonna knock your fuckin' block off. Jesus!" He shook his head in frustration.

He was big, with shoulders like hams and arms the thickness of a normal man's legs. His midsection had gone soft, but he remained a powerful man who moved gracefully. He called time and ordered the young men to various work-outs. He was rubbing the back of his neck when he noticed Farrell. "Do somethin' for ya, mister?" There was no wariness in the question, but Farrell saw the man sizing him up, measuring his trim-waisted physique with a professional eye.

His thin-lipped smile suggested he did not consider Farrell an appreciable threat.

"You Bucky Targo?"

"I am. And who might you be?"

"Wesley Farrell. Can I talk to you for a minute?"

"What about?"

"Johnny Parmalee."

Targo sense of self-assurance seemed to slip. His eyes narrowed, darted from side to side to check for eavesdroppers. "We can't talk here with all this racket. Let's go inside my office yonder." He indicated a partitioned cubicle built on what had been the stage back when the place still operated as a theater.

Farrell nodded agreeably, followed the trainer across the noisy gym and up a short flight of stairs. Targo pushed open the door and indicated with his chin for Farrell to precede him. He closed the door, then lowered a set of grimy Venetian blinds over the single window. He turned to Farrell, his expression obscured by the gloom. "So what about Parmalee?"

"You already know, or you wouldn't have brought me in here."

Targo stiffened, his eyes blazing for the briefest of seconds. "What're you talkin' about? I barely know 'im."

Farrell's mouth parted and a hollow, mocking laugh escaped. "You're a liar, Targo. When you were fighting, Johnny was your sparring partner. When he got good enough to make a try at the title, you helped him train and got him a backer. He's got money tied up in your gym and he's helped you back a couple of young comers." Farrell's laugh sounded again. It had an edge like a headsman's ax. "He's a mighty obliging fella for a guy you don't know so well."

Targo rubbed a hand stupidly across the lower half of his face. He moved out of the corner on the stiff, leaden legs of an old man until he reached the desk, where he collapsed into a chair. "What do you want?"

"You can save yourself some grief by talking, Targo. Parmalee and his brother kidnapped a teen-aged girl yesterday and killed a man doing it." Farrell moved a bit closer to the desk, his voice dropping to a sharp, hypnotic whisper. "I don't give a damn about the Parmalees, but I want that girl. If I can get her back without hurting Johnny or giving him up to the cops, I will. It's up to him, really."

Targo turned slightly in the chair to avoid looking at Farrell. His lips worked like a man trying not to vomit. "I— I dunno where he is. I ain't seen him lately."

"You know where he hangs out. And don't bother with that address off Lee Circle. He moved."

The ex-boxer turned his chair again, putting his legs under the kneehole of the desk. His right hand was just out of sight near his leg. He raised his head and looked directly at Farrell, as though craving his immediate attention. "Yeah, well, there's a place or two he goes."

"Like where?"

"Like—" Targo's hand shot into view, a .38 revolver dwarfed in his huge fist.

Farrell seemed to know in advance that the gun was coming. His right hand ripped the bullet-pocked Stetson from his head and swept it into the ex-fighter's face. Targo grunted in surprise, his gun hand waving off center. Farrell moved in like a tornado, knocking the gun from Targo's grasp as he threw a crushing right into the man's jaw. As large as he was, the blow lifted Targo from the chair and sent him crashing against the wall. He lay there, shaking his head, his eyes large with shock. It took him a moment to remember he was Bucky Targo, three-time heavyweight champion of the world. Grunting, he lurched to his feet, his fists up as he moved in on Farrell.

Farrell's face was an image from a nightmare. His pale eyes blazed like molten silver as he brushed Targo's guard aside as though it were of cobwebs. His right smashed into Targo's chin, his left sinking elbow deep into the man's paunch. Breath whooshed out of Targo, but Farrell's attack on his belly was relentless. Three more blows sent the big man crashing to the floor. As he fell, greenish vomit shot out of his mouth to the dusty floor.

Without warning, the office door flew open and the room was suddenly full of loud male voices. Farrell met it with his Luger in his fist. "Get out!" His voice cut through the younger men's bluster and backed them out. Two tried to stand fast, but Farrell's feral stare above the dark maw of the Luger changed their minds.

Kicking the door closed, Farrell turned back to Targo. "All right, Goddamn you. Talk, and no more stalling or I'll rip the skin off your bones."

Targo remained on his knees, panting like a winded dog. "No more, please, no more."

"You can't save Parmalee, Targo. If I don't get him, the cops or Whit Richards's men will. With me, he gets an even break. What about it?"

"D-don't know where he is, swear it."

"Don't con me—"

"No, wait. There's—there's a place he goes. I'll t-tell you…"

Joey Parmalee was floating in dark water at the bottom of a deep well, treading to stay afloat. Water kept splashing him in the face from somewhere, getting in his nose and mouth, he turned his head this way and that, trying to escape but it was no use. The more he tried to escape, the more insistent the slaps of water were.

"Come out of it, kid. Come on, that's it." Johnny Parmalee sat on the edge of the bed where his brother lay, gently slapping him in the face with a wet washcloth. He stared at Joey's battered face with mingled feelings of disgust and regret.

"Christ—stop—stop hittin' me with that fuckin' thing." Joey turned his head to the side and pushed at Johnny's arm. He reached up to touch his face, and the movement stretched the bruised ribs. "Christ," he gasped, grabbing at his side. "Christ, I think he broke somethin'."

"Yeah," Johnny said softly. "He was tryin' to, the way I heard it. You're lucky he didn't kill you at that."

Joey looked at his brother's face, saw the disappointment in his eyes. "Takin' his side. That's just what I'd expect from you, Johnny."

Johnny got up, shoved his hands into his pockets. "You been at the coke again. You told me you were off of it."

With difficulty, Joey sat up, eased his legs over the edge of the bed as he sucked painful breath between his teeth. "I—I got bored. I needed some to take the edge off. Christ, he broke somethin' inside me. I feel like something's stickin' me in the lungs."

"Maybe you oughta try some more coke. Take the edge off the pain," Johnny said in a flat voice.

"You sonofabitch," Joey said through clenched teeth. "What'd you ever do for me except nag, criticize, treat me like some feeble-minded jerk?"

Johnny looked at his brother through heavy-lidded eyes. "It ain't my fault that mom and pop's car stalled in front of that train, Joey. That was as bad for me as it was for you. I wasn't but a kid my own self. Maybe I didn't always do right, but I tried to teach you how to be."

"Bullshit," Joey replied, running his fingers over his bruised face.

Johnny's face hardened. "So I ain't Saint Francis. All God give me to get along on was a hard head and my fists. I tried to live clean, but I didn't have no luck. I went to work for loan sharks to keep a roof over our heads and you out of the orphanage. Yeah, I ain't no saint but you never learned killin' from me. You never learned beatin' women or rape from me."

Joey's face was turned from his brother. He lay quiet, his damaged face sullen.

Johnny looked at him for a moment, squelching the sigh he felt building in his chest. When he spoke, his voice was soft. "Anyways, you better get your stuff and clear out. Pete said he didn't want you around."

Joey managed to stand up, his arm wrapped tightly about his damaged ribs. "You comin'?"

Johnny shook his head sadly. "I told you, I was sick of bein' a nobody. With Carson I got a chance, so I'm takin' it. It's time for you to grow up. You can do it if you try. You do that, you clean yourself up, maybe we can get back together again." He turned his head away from Joey. "I'm through nurse-maidin' you as of today."

Joey found his coat and shrugged painfully into it, then put on his hat. He saw that his valise was on the floor, ready to go. "Where's my rod?"

"In the bag. I took the shells out of it, so don't get any ideas. Just get in your car and go back to town."

Joey stared at him, his mouth working to spit out a curse, but nothing came. He picked up the valise with his good arm and walked past his brother into the hall. Johnny listened until he heard the front door open and close, then he let out a long, shuddering breath.

Joey limped outside, lugging his valise painfully to the shed where his Studebaker rested. It took him less than a minute to get inside and drive out of the pasture to Filmore. He took the road west through the park, stopping under a tree to think. While he thought, he got out his bindle of cocaine, used some of it. He hurt in so many places that the burn of the cocaine was like a mother's caress. He rested his head on the seat back, letting the drug take him to a place beyond pain, beyond humiliation.

When his heartbeat settled, he sat there, his thought processes now tightly focused. He opened his valise and found his .32 Smith & Wesson under the hastily packed clothing. From a box of cartridges in the glove compartment he loaded all six chambers, then replaced the gun in the valise. He knew what he wanted to do now. Turning the car around, he headed back east to Wisner, a street that would take him south into the city.

Chapter 13

Casey put his trepidation about Farrell's safety to one side and focused all his attention on Pete Carson. He knew nothing about the murder of Charles Francis Tarkington nor the possible complicity of Pete Carson, so, after getting Carson's record from R and I, he summoned his head of gang intelligence, Lieutenant Ben Guthrie.

Guthrie was a lean, fit man in his late thirties, but his snow-white hair and eyebrows sometimes caused people to mistake his age. He had been in gang intelligence since winning his detective shield in the late Twenties. Nobody in Casey's command knew more secrets and street gossip.

"I had to do some thinking when you mentioned Pete Carson, captain. That's going back a ways."

"Does anything exist that shows or even suggests a connection between Carson and Whit Richards?" Casey asked.

Guthrie grinned. "Before I answer that, let me tell you what I know that I can't prove. First, Gang Intelligence has been eyeing Richards since he first appeared in town in the late Twenties. He had money and he spent it to make more."

"Meaning," Casey said as he dug his pipe into his tobacco pouch, "that he invested in various criminal enterprises."

"Yep, but he was careful from the beginning. He would occasionally be spotted in public drinking with people like Big Tony Romero, Joe Dante, and Emile Ganns in a casual way, but he made a point to never be seen at any of their operations. The conventional wisdom is that he bought into booze, narcotics, and vice operations through go betweens. When gang leaders or their men took a fall, Richards was never around and there was nothing concrete to connect him."

Casey grunted as he set fire to his pipe. "Nobody ever said he was stupid."

"No, indeed. As he amassed enough money to build an empire, he took on men he could trust, like Amsterdam and Callahan, to oversee his gambling and vice operations while he stood back and played the upright public servant."

Casey squinted against a tendril of smoke that drifted past his eye. "So how did he keep contact with these people if he was at such pains to show no public association?"

Guthrie got out a cigarette and lit it. "We came to the conclusion some time ago that Richards and his key people are using unlisted telephone numbers subscribed under assumed names. These new rotary dial phones that have become available make it possible to make a call without even involving an operator. Those numbers are the kind of information you need a court order to get, and no judge is going to give it to you without a darn good reason."

Casey's mouth stretched into a taut, impatient line. "There's quite a few judges who owe their seats on the bench to Richards." He paused to puff smoke. "So how does this help us make a connection between Richards and Carson?"

"Strictly speaking, it doesn't. What we know we learned fairly recently, and by accident. My file clerk reminded me of it after you called."

Casey relit his pipe, knowing Guthrie enjoyed the process of revealing secrets a layer at a time. "Go on."

"A contact in the City Finance Department forwarded something interesting to us a few years ago. It was the cancellation of an allotment that Richards drew on his salary. It was going to a Mrs. Felicia Carson of New Iberia. The reason for the cancellation was listed as 'payee deceased.' That got me interested."

Casey felt a strange tingling in his blood, but he remained patient. "I can see how it might."

"I thought at first that maybe this was some woman Richards was keeping on the side," Guthrie continued. "So I contacted the sheriff's office there and asked them to see what they could find out about this lady. Turned out to be a sixty-eight year old woman—"

"Who was Richards' mother," Casey exclaimed.

Guthrie laughed. "I wasn't that quick, boss, but you're right. It seems that Mrs. Carson, born Felicia D'Abadie, was first married to a Cajun oil field roughneck by the name of Claude Richar', by whom she had a son named Jean-Louis. When Jean-Louis was nine, Claude was killed in an oil well explosion. Two years later, Felicia received a proposal of marriage from a railroad brakeman named Peter Carson, by whom she had a second son, Peter, Junior."

Casey started. "Jean-Louis Richar' is Whitman Richards, and he's also Pete Carson's brother?"

Guthrie nodded. "Half brothers. I had the sheriff's people look up the birth certificates and wire-photo them to us. It's the straight goods."

Casey leaned back in his chair, rubbing the back of his neck. "So how did the son of a Cajun roughneck end up being City Councilman Whitman Richards?"

Guthrie took a long drag on the cigarette, blowing it right back out again. "That's another story. I did some digging on this, skipper. I wanted to be sure. See, there's underworld gossip that when Richards hit town, he was still combing hayseeds out of his hair. He spoke better French than English. As the story goes, he realized pretty quickly that if he was going to make his way in the city, he was going to have to put up a more sophisticated front."

"He found somebody to teach him social graces, huh?"

Guthrie grinned. "In a manner of speaking. He took up with a prostitute who hailed from Boston. The story goes that she was the black sheep of an old Boston family. Anyway, she taught him to dress, how to talk, which fork to use—enough to help him get by until he could learn more."

"And he changed his name to go with his new identity. But where did he get the name Whitman?"

"That's the best part of the story, skipper. Seems this Boston gal had a sweet tooth, and a particular fondness for the Whitman's Sampler."

In spite of himself, Casey roared with laughter.

"That's the story, sir. When I got the information, there didn't seem to be much I could do with it, since Carson was dead according to the Minnesota State Police."

"But you filed it and your clerk remembered it. Nice work, Ben." He put his pipe in the ashtray and his expression grew sober. "That might be just what I need to stir the pot a little."

Guthrie's casual pose vanished as he leaned closer to Casey's desk. "Can I help hold the spoon?"

"Maybe so. Let's take a short ride and see if we can catch the councilman in his chambers."

⚒

"Man, if you're gonna kill me, just get it over with. If you ain't gonna kill me, lemme go. I was on my way outa town. Anyhow, the white gal ain't none of my business."

"Shut up," Easter Coupé replied crossly. "Sit there and keep your trap shut. I got to think this out."

Skeeter had been through a lot in the past two days. He had been running like a rabbit until this morning, but he no longer felt like running. He was angry to the point of fool-hardiness. "Think! Man, you slay me. I seen them kidnap a white girl, I seen that crazy white boy stick a knife in my friend's insides. I seen enough to have you all put in the chair six ways to Sunday. And you know what? I don't give a damn. Because of that ofay maniac, I done lost everything that matters to me, you hear?" He was handcuffed to a kitchen chair, but in spite of that, his outrage had the chair legs creaking and scuttling on the kitchen floor.

Easter Coupé turned, his face hideous with the emotions roiling inside him. "Damn you, shut up. I don't *want* to kill you. You ain't done nothin' to be killed for. That's the fuckin' trouble. I promised a man I liked and trusted that I'd do a thing to keep his ass outa the fire and agreed on a price. I ain't never gone back on my word before, not about business. But this time…"

Skeeter frowned thoughtfully as he listened. No one had ever told him about the meaning of a moral dilemma, but in listening to Easter Coupé he began to understand the concept. He spoke in a quiet, almost awed voice. "Man, you don't sound very happy."

The hardened gunman looked at his quivering fist, then opened it and looked at the splayed fingers. "You can do somethin' a long time and think it's a dandy idea," he said in a subdued voice. "Then a thing can happen and it don't seem so dandy anymore." He walked about the room, rubbing the back of his neck as though it pained him, seeming to talk to himself, rather than to Skeeter. "Every time I ever made a hit on somebody before, it made sense to me. I truly figured the man had it comin'. But you—hell, you're just a kid. You ain't been alive long enough to deserve killin'."

Skeeter felt disoriented. "What—what you gonna do?"

Coupé went to the kitchen cupboard, removed a flat brown pint of Old Overholt. He pulled the cork and took a long drink. "That's the problem. I made a deal and the job ain't over. Worst thing is, I give my word to a white man. Normally I'd never have no truck with a white man, but I thought I knew this one. I thought he was somebody who made sense." He drank some more of the rye, but it seemed to have no effect on his mood.

Skeeter understood now. He felt a strange pity for the other man. "If you don't kill me, they'll kill both of us. Sure as God made little green apples."

"Yeah," Coupé said in a harsh rasp. "Yeah."

⸎

"Why are you d-doing this?" Jessica asked, shivering under the sheet. "You say you're my uncle, but you've had me kidnapped and a man's been k-killed. It's—it's insane." Her composure was as tattered as her undergarments. Her lips quivered and speaking was clumsy for her. She stared, strangely dry-eyed, at the big dark blonde man.

"I'm sorry, Jess." Carson looked down at his feet. He hadn't felt ashamed of anything in years, but looking at the girl's bruised face touched something that he'd thought long buried. "It wasn't supposed to happen this way. I gave orders that you weren't to be harmed."

She laughed at him, the sound of it jarring even to her. "He was going to k-kill me, you son of a bitch. Explain to me how that helps you any."

He looked at her bleakly. "Your father framed me for murder eleven years ago, and he did it just so he could cut me out of what I had coming. Sooner or later, I had to come back to make it right. Kidnapping you was, well, it was just supposed to throw him off balance long enough for me to step in and jerk the rug out from under him."

She looked at him with her mouth open. "What? What are you saying? My father framed you for *murder?* You're insane. My father's a city councilman, a real estate magnate. Framed you? No, you're crazy."

He bit his lip, nodding slowly. "Yeah, it's tough to take. My own old man, your step-grandfather, he was no good either. It's a tough thing to know about your old man, but it's true. Whit's a grafter, a swindler, and he's had men killed so he could get rich. There it is."

She looked away from him, drawing her legs under her in a vain effort to put more distance between them. She shook her head over and over. "And what are you, Uncle Pete?"

He opened his mouth, but her question stopped him. He looked away, unable to look her in the eye. "I had that coming, I guess. But everything I said is true. I came back to get back what he took from me. Before it's all over, I mean to have it. One way or another. I'll let you go then. I don't want you to get hurt."

"You're too late," she screamed in a raw voice. "Get out. Get out and leave me alone."

He regarded her silently for a long moment, then nodded, backed out of the room. She heard the tumblers in the lock fall and then she was alone. She wept silently into the sheet, trying to make sense of the fact that her privileged life had been a sham, that all she'd believed had been a horrible lie. She wept for a long time, a silent, steady weeping that made up in intensity what it lacked in volume. Her courage had been tested to the limit and her confidence in her world had eroded almost to nothing.

The room was a blur in the midst of the weeping, but as her tears began to ebb and dry, a gleam across the room drew her attention. It was just under the bureau. She leaned forward, brushing at her eyes with the backs of her hands. As she got up and tiptoed across the room in the shreds of her underwear, she saw that it was Joey Parmalee's knife.

❄❄❄

King Arboneau finished putting rubber bands about the last stack of bills brought in by one of his couriers. It had been a good day so far in Treme. He'd collected $7,000.00. That was more than two working stiffs could make in a year, but the realization gave him little pleasure. At the age of sixty-three he should be retired, playing with grandchildren. Instead he worked long hours and felt the world closing in on him.

His son's death had been a monumental blow to him. When Tel had come into the world, it had been at the cost of his mother's fertility. There had been no other children, and his wife had died young, of disappointment, rather than cherish what she already had. That would have made some men bitter, but Arboneau had borne it with grace, and had lavished all his affection on Tel.

He wondered sometimes whether or not it would have made a difference if he'd made his living as an honest man. Tel wouldn't have been exposed to the kinds of men and women that Arboneau had needed to run an empire in the underworld. Tel had grown up to be a man who believed that being a man meant giving vent to a violent streak whenever he was tested or challenged. You taught him that, he thought. That was the kind of man you were.

His hand moved to the framed photograph of the young man and his girl on his desk. He took it in his rough hands and rubbed his thumbs softly over the images. The girl's name had been Linda Sue Mahoney. He had loved her almost as much as Tel had, but she was gone now, too, wiped away by the same stroke that took Tel. He had dreamed of the grandchildren they'd have, but that dream, too, was ashes.

It had taken him a long time, but he'd found some peace. He'd found Gabrielle in one of his brothels, and had brought her home to warm his own bed. When he'd seen how young she truly was, he'd been unable to go through with it. She'd become a surrogate child, and through her he'd found Cal Russell. Cal wasn't like Tel, but he was a pretty good kid, if not particularly intelligent. In the absence of a real son or grandson, Cal served. What a strange little family they were, but there was some happiness in their being together. It was something to be grateful for.

But lingering under the contentment, the hatred for Whitman Richards smoldered like a hot coal, always threatening to burst into full, destructive flame. Perhaps, with time, the ember would have cooled enough for him to ignore it, but that was before he had allowed himself to be pulled into this dangerous scheme to ruin his old enemy.

He had resisted at first. He was too old, too sick, too tired, to go to war with such a powerful man. What could possibly be gained by it, he had pleaded with his tormentor? How could he possibly prevail against Richards, who had defeated him so easily years before?

But the tormentor had spoken so reasonably, had argued so eloquently. He recognized now that he had opened the gate for the serpent to slither into his garden, and by so doing he had put himself on a path from which there was no return. Men had died and other men would probably die, because Richards would not give in so easily. He was too proud, too powerful.

Arboneau took a bottle of Four Roses from the desk drawer. He pulled the cork and drank directly from the neck. The part that bothered him the most was that now he had two enemies to contend with. The visit of Wesley Farrell had been like the knell of some distant bell, tolling his finish. He didn't know why Farrell cared about Whitman Richards or his trouble, but the old man was certain that there was more than Farrell had told him. Wesley Farrell wasn't the kind of man to sneak around looking for a chance to kick a man in the ribs. Farrell confronted his enemies, then proceeded to destroy them.

Farrell pretended to be a conscienceless criminal, but it was well known that he had friends everywhere. When people attacked or hurt his friends, Farrell always found out, and always came after the attacker. It chilled Arboneau to think that by setting himself against Richards, he had unwittingly challenged Wesley Farrell.

Now there was nothing to do but kill Farrell, or try to. Arboneau had already put in motion the machinery necessary to accomplish that. He prayed that he had acted soon enough, and that his instrument was up to the task. He nearly had Whitman Richards on the ropes, divested of his power. He had to stay alive long enough for Richards to understand who was taking everything away from him, and why. For that, he had to keep Richards alive, too.

∞∞∞

Daggett and his men spent hours searching Gerttown with a fine-toothed comb as they looked for some sign of Skeeter Longbaugh. However, their questions drew little but hostility or indifference from the denizens of that neighborhood. Splitting his team up, he sent them out to the very edges of the neighborhood to question the hustlers, vagrants, street people and tavern keepers.

Daggett and Andrews rolled out to Washington Avenue and pounded the pavement on foot, questioning even the Public Service bus drivers who traveled that route. Every question brought a negative response. They were in sight of the big white art deco building that housed the Louziana Lou mayonnaise factory when Andrews spotted a Negro huckster standing behind a mule-drawn cart filled with late harvest fruits and vegetables. "Let's ask the old man."

"We got nothing to lose."

The huckster seemed fantastically old to them, his red-brown skin as lined and seamed as a plowed field. His denim overalls were bleached almost white and sported a myriad of different colored patches. He wore a broad-brimmed straw hat that resembled a Mexican sombrero.

"He'p y'all?" he asked. "Got some nice watermelon here, sweet as a young gal's toes."

"No thank you, uncle," Daggett said. "We're looking for a young fella that we think passed this way."

The old man looked at them shrewdly. "Reckon you fellas be cops, huh?"

Daggett smiled. "That's right. But the kid we're looking for is in trouble that could get him killed unless we can find him in time."

"Dunno, but maybe. I been movin' around the neighborhood fo' a while now. What'd he look like?"

"Young, dark brown. About five-nine and skinny."

The old man nodded. "Seen a boy like 'at, two, three hours ago."

"See which way he went?"

"Well, hard to say on that. He were walkin' along when another fella drove up in a car, picked 'im up."

"Get a look at the car or the man drivin' it?"

"Well, sure. It were an old car, brown. Had Ply-mouth wrote on the hood. Driver looked like a big, husky fella."

Daggett felt the bottom go out of his hopes.

"Fust time I seed him in this part o' town," the huckster continued.

Daggett's head snapped around. "Say what?"

"The feller in the brown Ply-mouth. Fust time I seed him over thisaway."

"So...where do you usually see him?"

"Ever' Wednesday, I drive my wagon Uptown. See him at the end of Spruce Street, where it back up to the sewer woiks. He got him a green shotgun house and a go-rage in a block all by itse'f. Reckon ain't nobody else wanted to build no houses up ag'in the sewer department."

"No," Andrews said slowly. "I reckon not."

The old man was quiet for a moment as he scratched his grizzled head. "Likes strawberries and blackberries."

Daggett shot his partner a look, saw Andrews looking back at him, teeth showing beneath his dark mustache. "Old timer, next time I see you, we'll do some business. I got a yen for blackberries myself."

The old man nodded amiably. "That be right fine, mister. Yessir, right fine." He turned back to his mule and began to lead the animal up toward Washington Avenue.

Daggett and Andrews hoofed it back to where they'd left their squad car and put it in motion. Daggett keyed his microphone and put out the call to his other men. "We've got a possible location for Easter Coupé. We're heading down to the west end of Spruce Street near the Sewerage and Water Board plant. Subject is believed to be living in a green shotgun at the end of the block. Run silent and wait for further instructions." He put the microphone back into the dash clip and sat back, mopping his face with a handkerchief.

"Iz, I just thought of somethin'."

"Yeah?"

"He picked the kid up to kill him, right?"

"Probably."

"Think he's gonna take the kid home to do that? Don't seem to make much sense."

"No," Daggett replied flatly. "Let's find Coupé first. We'll cross that other bridge when we get to it."

Chapter 14

"There he is," the dark-haired man in the front seat said. "Looks like he ain't got a care in the world."

"In a minute, he won't," said the driver. They were sitting across from a commercial building on Howard Avenue where a crap game normally went on all day. Twenty minutes earlier, a tipster had called Vic D'Angelo to say that Fletch Monaghan was there making a killing.

"There he is," Vic said. He mopped his bald head with a linen handkerchief, then took his .45 from under his arm and worked a cartridge into the breech. "Ready, Riccio?"

"Ready when you are, Vic," the dark-haired man said quietly. He cocked both hammers of the double-barrel twelve-gauge in his lap.

"Hit the gas, Mike," the little bald man said.

The car squealed away from the curb, roared up the block. It came to a screaming halt opposite Fletch Monaghan. Monaghan knew instantly that something was wrong, clawed at the revolver on his hip. He had it clear, firing when the .45 and the shotgun belched flame from the side of the car. Buckshot and jacketed slugs caught the gambler broadside and hurled him to the pavement. Mike had the car racing away before the gambler's body hit the ground.

"Where to?" Mike asked as he turned a corner.

"Van Zandt," the little bald man said quietly. He mopped his head again. "We get him, then we go see Gaudain. I never killed a rich man before. Maybe we'll drink some high-grade scotch before we drop the hammer on him, huh?"

"You're the boss, Vic," Riccio said as he broke the shotgun and reloaded it.

Behind them, sirens howled like coyotes under a full moon.

⊗⊗⊗

It took Daggett and Andrews about twenty minutes to get through evening traffic to Spruce Street. At the end of the quiet avenue, butted up against the fence to the Sewerage and Water Board works, was the green shotgun house and garage the huckster had described. A yellow De Soto coupe was parked in front of the house. From their vantage point, they could also see the tail end of a brown Plymouth through the open garage door. The shades on all the windows were drawn, making it impossible to say if anyone was at home.

"What do you think?" Andrews asked.

"If I were Easter Coupé, I couldn't find a better place to live. Too bad for him we ran into the huckster."

Andrews scratched the back of his neck. "We got enough men to go in after him. There's nowhere for him to run."

Daggett took the microphone from the clip and keyed it. "All units, this is Inspector 51. We have the suspect's house in view. Two automobiles are present but no people in sight. Close on this position and wait for my signal."

Andrews quietly unlatched his door and got out of the car. He moved to the rear, where he opened the trunk and removed a Model 12 Winchester. Daggett got out on his side and waited as the other cars rolled quietly up the street and took positions adjacent to him. Several of the uniformed men moved around to the garage and took cover where they could see the back door to the house. Daggett looked across at Gautier and saw the man's narrow face split in a satisfied grin. He glanced back at Daggett and nodded.

Daggett removed the microphone and switched it to the loudspeaker. "Easter Coupé, this is the police. We know you're in there so come out, and bring Longbaugh ahead of you. Show us some empty hands and you won't be hurt."

Inside the shotgun cottage, Coupé and Skeeter both stared into the front of the house. Coupé remained seated, the bottle of rye still at his feet. Skeeter stared, sweat streaming down his face. "Man, what you gonna do now?"

Coupé laughed grimly. "What you think I'm gonna do?"

"You can't fight 'em. They'll kill you."

Coupé studied him, expecting to see fear. It shocked him to see the boy's expression was one of concern for Coupé, himself. "If they don't kill me, I go to jail until I die of old age. It ain't like I lived no upright Christian life. I got plenty black marks against me."

"But you didn't kill nobody," Skeeter said. "I can tell 'em you didn't. They'll believe me, man, I know they will. C'mon, untie me and let's go out there to 'em."

Coupé got up wearily from his seat, reached into his pocket and took out a key ring. "I'm hooked up with the wrong people this time, boy." He unlocked Skeeter's handcuffs and dropped them. "Time for you to go home."

Skeeter rose from the chair, rubbing his wrists. "Come out with me, man. You coulda killed me six times and you didn't. You ain't no killer, I'll swear to it."

Coupé opened the drawer of the end table and took out an envelope. He took Skeeter's right hand and pressed the envelope into it. "Listen to me, we ain't got time for a lot of talk. This here is a claim check for a suitcase at the Southern Railway terminal. You know where it is?"

Skeeter looked at him strangely. "Yeah, but—"

"Shut up and listen. Out to Toni Mereaux's cat house, there's a gal named Patience. I want you to give her half the money in the suitcase and tell her to use it to go back home and buy herself a dress shop or somethin'. Tell her there ain't no future working in a cat house, you hear?"

Too much was happening for Skeeter to even try to understand. He shook his head as though in a daze. "What're you doin', man? What're you talkin' about?"

Coupé caught him by the arm and pulled him into the living room. "Take the other half of the money and go marry that gal you was talkin' about. Have some babies. Take 'em to the country on picnics. Build a house for 'em to live in. Do all the things I never done." He reached the front door, unlatched it and pushed it open. "I'm sendin' the boy out," he called in a rough voice. "He ain't done nothin', you hear? I was hired to kill him to shut him up. He's straight, hear me? You got that, copper?"

Daggett stared across the yard. "I hear you. Your word's more than enough to clear him. Come on out with him and we'll go down to the station house."

"He's comin'," Coupé shouted, giving Skeeter a shove.

Skeeter emerged onto the porch. He paused, looking at all the armed men facing Coupé's house. He turned, stared back at Coupé. "Please, man, come on out. I'll tell 'em I ain't gonna swear out a complaint against you."

Coupé looked at him sternly. "Everybody's gotta pay the piper, sooner or later, kid. I done plenty of bad shit I didn't get caught for. It was just my turn, and that's okay. I lived every day knowin' this would come, sooner or later. Now go on." He leveled his .38 at Skeeter and cocked the hammer.

Skeeter backed away slowly, with his hands away from his sides. As he reached the yard, he walked toward Daggett, feeling numb all over. "Man, please don't kill him. He didn't do nothin', I swear."

Daggett grabbed Skeeter by the shoulder and shoved him down behind the fender. He had his gun in his hand now because he sensed the end was coming. "Coupé, come on out with your hands up. We won't shoot."

Coupé left the porch at a dead run. He was still running when shots rang out from several directions, cutting his legs out from under him. He fell hard, didn't move.

Daggett watched it unfold like a bad dream. He was screaming for the others to hold their fire, but it seemed to take forever for the shots to stop exploding around him. He was the first to the body, turning the big man over. He found a faint pulse and shouted for an ambulance.

"Why'd he do it?" Skeeter asked in an anguished voice. "Why'd he do it?"

Daggett felt sick to his stomach. He shook his head, not knowing what to say. He saw Coupé's revolver lying near his hand and picked it up by reflex. Thumbing the latch, the cylinder fell open to reveal daylight showing through all six chambers. Slowly, he stood, put the empty revolver into his coat pocket. "Come on, kid." He caught Skeeter under the arm, led him silently toward the squad car.

❧

Richards spent his day dealing with one petitioner after another. He somehow managed to resume his tough, manipulative persona. He got his tribute for every favor he granted, and with those from whom he wanted some concession, he bargained them to a sweaty standstill. Whitman Richards seemed very much in control of his fiefdom.

Rob Langdon efficiently ushered businessmen, city officials, and people of less respectable demeanor into Richards' imposing paneled office. He was part of each meeting, as steely-eyed and ruthless as ever when called upon. The rift between Langdon and Richards over Georgia seemed temporarily forgotten as the two men meshed seamlessly in the pursuit of money and power. Toward the end of the morning Langdon was less in evidence, but that had little impact on the rhythm of Richards' day.

The first rent in the fabric of a productive afternoon came at two when Sheriff Tim Marrero called.

"What is it, Tim? I've got somebody coming in pretty soon now so I can't talk very long."

The sheriff hesitated. "Whit, this may be nothing at all, but I thought I'd better call. Seems like your wife, she, uh, she slipped out the back of your house. Neither of my men knew she was gone until just a little while ago. Naturally, they called me pronto, but—"

"What the hell you mean, 'she slipped out the back'? You mean to tell me you assigned such a pair of fucking meatheads that neither of them thought to check the back of the house once in a while? You're kidding me, right?"

The sheriff sighed audibly. "I—I'm sorry, Whit. We questioned the cook, and all she knows is Georgia left about mid-morning and swore her to secrecy. Bessie Mae said she hasn't called in. Should I put her license out on the air?"

Richards' face was stiff with rage as he ran his fingers recklessly through his hair. "Sure, Tim, put it out on the air so the city police will know how bad you fucked up. God damn it to hell." He fell silent for a moment as he tried to gather his wits. As his anger cooled, he began to think straight again. "Look, Georgia probably went somewhere she didn't want me to know about. Chances are, since she sneaked out on your men, nobody else noticed her either. She'll come home when she's through with whatever it is she went out for. Are your men still at the house?"

"Yeah, and I sent two more over there."

"Then tell some of them to park their asses in the back yard. I want to know the minute she returns, you hear me?"

"Yeah, sure, Whit. I—I'm sorry as hell—"

"You're goddamned right you are. If anything happens to her, I'll roast you over a slow fire." He slammed the telephone down into the cradle, sat there drumming his fingers on the desk as he waited for his temper to cool. Finally he got up and strode to the reception area. He found it empty but for Catherine Landau.

"Where's Meredith?" he asked.

The older secretary looked up from a brief she was typing and peered at him over the rims of her spectacles. "She asked to go home. She wasn't feeling well."

Richards frowned. "Not feeling well?"

Catherine slowly turned her head back to the brief she was typing. "No. She, ah, she said she'd been experiencing spells of, uh, nausea for the past week or ten days. She thinks she, ah, might be coming down with…with something." She paused to push her glasses up on the bridge of her nose. "She, uh, asked me not to mention it to you, but—but it seems to be getting, uh, worse."

As Catherine's conversation dribbled to an abrupt conclusion, she quickly resumed her work, her fingers flying over the keys as she concentrated rather pointedly on the document she was typing. Richards stood there watching her when it finally hit him: Merry was pregnant. He felt himself go cold all over. Christ almighty, he'd thought she was taking precautions against that.

He turned and walked quietly back to his office, where he closed the door and sank into a chair. This was just the evidence of infidelity Georgia needed to take him to court and ream him out. He groaned aloud. He grabbed the receiver to his internal phone and jerkily dialed the two digits of Rob Langdon's office. It rang twice but it was Catherine who answered. "Are you trying to reach Mr. Langdon? He got a call earlier and left."

Richards blinked uncertainly. "A call? Who from?"

"He didn't say, just that it was urgent he take care of something."

"Oh. Certainly. No matter." He quietly put the receiver back into the cradle and leaned back in his chair feeling tired and off balance. He had only a moment to indulge the feeling before a knock sounded at the door. It opened before he could tell whoever it was to go away.

Frank Casey and Guthrie stood there. Casey led the way into the office without giving the councilman time to say anything. Guthrie shut the door behind them.

"What the hell do you want?" Richards demanded. "I told you to keep your nose out of my business."

"I'm sorry to tell you, councilman, but the evidence suggests that your business is now my business."

"I'm warning you, Casey—"

"Put a sock in it," Casey interrupted. "You're pretty slick, Richards, but even the slickest crook finally steps in the wrong patch."

"I'll have your badge, you sonofabitch."

"Not so fast, councilman," the red-haired detective replied in a calm, even tone. "What you want or don't want is immaterial at this stage. We're here in conjunction with what I'm sure will be a far-reaching investigation into civic corruption and murder."

Richards' face flushed bright red. His hands bunched into fists as he shot to his feet. "God damn you, I'll have the sheriff send deputies to throw you out on your asses."

"No," Casey said mildly. "You won't. There's a half-dozen uniformed officers stationed outside with orders to stop anyone who tries to come in here." He paused, took off his hat. "Those officers are men Sheriff Marrero fired after you bought the election for him. They have a certain distaste for sheriff's uniforms, if you get my drift."

Richards stood there with his mouth open, his fury making him speechless.

Casey took a seat in one of the expensive leather armchairs in front of Richards' desk and leisurely crossed his legs. "Have a seat, councilman. We've got a lot to talk about. For starts there's Pete Carson."

The blood drained from Richards' face. "What are you talking about?"

"Pete Carson. Your half-brother. The man you most likely framed for the murder of Charles Francis Tarkington."

Richards sank slowly into his chair, his eyes suddenly lusterless, like a man stunned by a sock full of wet sand.

"You've had a very bad week, councilman," Casey continued. "Two people you depended on are both dead, your daughter kidnapped, several of your operations knocked over, probably with significant loss of money…it's focused a lot of attention on your office that I'm sure you'd rather do without. You've made it worse by trying to cover it up."

Richards licked his lips. "I got nothing to say."

Casey shrugged. "Fine. I like to talk to a man who doesn't want to talk. You see, the police aren't masterminds. We plod, we trip over our own shoes, but we notice things, we make reports, and we keep files on everything. And we've always got people around with long memories, like this character. Say hello to Lieutenant Ben Guthrie from the Gang Intelligence Squad."

Guthrie gave Richards a two-finger salute off his hat brim, but Richards' eyes were still fixed on Casey.

"Lieutenant Guthrie, working on a tip, discovered your relationship to Carson. Another tip sent us back to the Tarkington case file, which reminded us that Carson was the prime suspect. He did a neat job of faking his death, neat enough to fool the rural police up in Minnesota, but not quite neat enough to convince us."

"You can't prove anything." Richards' voice was hollow.

Casey grinned humorlessly. "Are you sure? Once we lay your relationship with Carson beside the death of Tarkington and your subsequent purchase of the Tarkington sugar refinery at a below-market cost in front of the district attorney, I'll bet my pension that he'll order a full investigation. Once he does, I'll bet Guthrie's pension that we find other interesting associations, with more dirty money changing hands before it ends up in your pocket.

"The newspapers will have a field day," Casey continued. "And my guess is that once you're on the ropes, people you've swindled and extorted money from will come out of the woodwork like cockroaches in a house fire. Even if we can't convict you, you'll be ruined politically, and I happen to think that'd be a good thing all by itself." Casey got up and put on his hat, tugging the brim low over his eyes. "I wouldn't blame you if you tried to skip town, but if you do, I'll arrest you on a material witness warrant. My men at the railroad depots and the airport will be notified to be on the lookout for you from now on." He turned to leave, but paused at the door. "You might as well give Carson what he wants because he won't keep it long. His mugshot is in every radio car by now, and we'll get him too before it's all over. Have a good evening, councilman."

Casey opened the door, giving Guthrie time to favor Richards with an amiable grin and a gunman's salute. As the door closed, Richards snatched up his telephone receiver, then slowly put it back. With Langdon out of the office, there was no one to call.

⚜

The sight of the knife under the dresser was enough to reenergize Jessica. She fiddled with it until she understood the mechanism, then closed it and shoved it under the mattress. Within minutes she had repaired her underwear as best she could and lay down on the bed. Her watch told her it was late, but not late enough to attempt an escape.

She found that she wasn't tired. She'd been through a lot that day, but she recognized a resiliency in herself she hadn't known was there. She realized she had a good three hours before anyone would visit her again with food. She pulled her tool from under the mattress and walked to the closet. It was the work of a moment to push open the trap and pull herself through the opening. Her adrenaline was flowing again, and she felt stronger than ever.

Working her way across the rafters to the louver was like revisiting familiar ground. She felt the muscles in her legs respond as she stretched them from beam to beam.

When she reached the louver, she could see through the slits that the sun was low in the sky. She heard the cries of egrets and gulls somewhere nearby, and it suggested to her that she might be near water, perhaps Lake Pontchartrain. She slipped the strip of steel from inside one of her brassiere straps and set to work on the last obstacle to removing the louver altogether.

She'd worked her way through half of the ridge of wood holding the louver in place when she felt it begin to slip. She caught it in time to keep it from crashing out onto the roof. Finding that she had the strength to lift it, she carefully brought it inside the attic and propped it against the wall. A cool breeze swept through the opening, drying the sweat on her body, as she looked out on freedom. Twenty-five yards across the field lay a patch of woods.

The sound of geese came to her through the opening as she stared out at the field. As she watched, she saw the V-shaped formations flying toward her. Geese flew south, which meant she was looking more or less due north. If she'd guessed right, Lake Pontchartrain was somewhere beyond those trees. If she could get to the lake, there would be people to the east and the west, including the Coast Guard at West End and a police district substation at Milneburg.

Turning reluctantly away from the opening, she stepped cautiously back over the rafters to the trap. Five minutes later she was dressed in her school uniform. There was nothing to do now but wait, and hope for enough luck to see her to the grove of trees after she escaped the house. She'd never thought very much about luck before. How much was enough when you were betting your life?

⊗⊗⊗

Joey Parmalee's Studebaker rolled into Treme late that afternoon and stopped across the street from King Arboneau's grocery store. Pushing open the driver's door, Joey painfully pulled himself out to the sidewalk. Smoke from his cigarette curled lazily past a face that was a rainbow of red, purple, and yellow. He held his right arm stiffly against his body, barely able to tolerate moving. He limped across to the grocery entrance.

The girl named Gabrielle saw him when he was halfway down the aisle to the butcher shop. Her hands flew to her mouth. "Joey? What happened? Was you in an accident? Oh, you poor thing." She ran around the refrigerated meat display counter and put an arm around his waist to help him.

"Knock it off," he said gruffly. "I ain't dyin' or nothin'. I gotta see the King."

She put a soft, cool hand on his wounded face, made him sit down on a stool. "Just a minute, okay? Just stay here." She turned and ran up the stairs.

Joey sat there, dragging on the cigarette but finding small pleasure in it. Every bone in his body ached. He lost track of time, and perhaps consciousness, as well. The next thing he knew, he was looking up into a pair of fierce, impenetrable eyes.

"What are you doin' here? What happened to you?"

Joey was shaken by the violence of the old man's questions. It took him a minute to find his voice. "He—he's double-crossin' you, Mr. Arboneau."

"What are you talkin' about?"

"I—I heard him. Carson. He was on the phone, talkin' to Richards. Makin' some kinda deal with 'im. He's gonna cut you out. Johnny's in it with 'im."

Joey's revelation seemed to have no effect on Arboneau. "They do this to you?"

"Yeah. Caught me listenin'. They left me for dead out back of the house."

"Why would your own brother try to kill you?" Arboneau affected no attitude of surprise or disbelief. It was clear he was simply trying to get the story clear in his mind.

Joey painfully shifted his body. "My brother." He made a rude noise. "He ain't got no love for me. He kicked me around the whole time I was growin' up." He sneered as he looked back at the old man. "Johnny's sick of bein' nobody. He wants to be a big shot bad, bad enough to do anything, Mr. Arboneau. Carson's promised him his own territory once him and Richards has squared things."

The news shook Arboneau, but he maintained a sternly stoic visage. He had gotten into this to humble Richards and take back what Richards had stolen from him. He had known that Carson and Richards were half-brothers, but Carson's hatred had seemed too great to be undone by any appeal to kinship or financial gain. Perhaps blood was thicker than water after all.

As he silently stroked his chin, another voice came into his mind, the voice of his silent partner in this deal. The partner who, from the beginning, had been pushing for a redress beyond mere money and territorial power. He turned back to Joey. "Boy, I'm gonna let you stay here on the quiet. Stay in your room until I say different, hear me? I got some thinkin' to do."

Joey smiled painfully, but there was a glint in his eye that was both hopeful and sardonic. "Yes, sir. Glad to be workin' with you, Mr. Arboneau."

Arboneau said nothing, watching as Gabrielle helped Joey from the room. He had experience enough to know a jackal when he saw one, but he reluctantly admitted that a toothless old lion might find a use for a jackal. When he was alone, he pulled his telephone to him and asked the operator for an Uptown number. It rang several times before the owner picked up.

"Yes?" the soft voice said.

"You're going to get what you wanted after all," he said.

"What do you mean?"

Arboneau told Joey Parmalee's story in a flat, bitter voice, leaving out nothing.

"I could say I told you so," the soft, husky voice said. "But there's no time. We need to get someone out of the way first."

"I'll see to it," the old man said.

⊗⊗⊗

Farrell left Targo with the sense that he at least had a direction in which to go. But he wanted more. The Parmalees weren't leaders, they were followers. Somebody had brought them into this caper, but who? Surely not Carson. Johnny had been an aspiring boxer eleven years ago, and Joey would have been a mere child. That meant there had to be a middleman, but who? He was certain of Neil Gaudain's innocence, but that left the three others he'd talked to, and perhaps some he had not discovered.

He was startled by the sound of sirens overtaking him. He pulled to the curb to let the ambulance pass, then continued on his way. Before he'd gone another block, he had to make way for two police cars. He heard other sirens ahead of him, too. Led by his curiosity, he drove in the direction of the excitement. He came to an intersection where he saw the ambulance at the curb and several police cars around it. A man lay on the sidewalk. Near his out-flung hand Farrell saw a revolver lying. He pulled to the curb, cut the engine, then made his way to the crowd of curious bystanders.

"Cripes," a man said loudly. "I ain't heard so many guns go off since I was in the Argonne back in Seventeen."

"Who is it?" someone demanded urgently. "You see it?"

A large man in a bow-tie and shirtsleeves left a nearby tavern, pushing his way to the center of the crowd. He stopped suddenly with his hands on the shoulders of the men in front of him. His mouth opened in shock. "Aw, God, it's Monaghan. Doctor, is he okay? Is he gonna make it?"

Farrell couldn't hear the reply, but he saw the bartender's shoulders slump. He watched as the man turned slowly and stumbled back out of the crowd. Farrell worked his way through the tangle until he reached the bartender's elbow. "Excuse me, you a friend of Monaghan's?"

The man turned, his face stiff with shock. "What?"

"Monaghan. Are you a friend of his?"

He nodded. "We were partners in this joint here."

"Had he said anything about being in trouble with anybody lately? Or maybe had he run into an old enemy? Look, it's important."

The bartender heard the urgency in Farrell's voice and stared at him for a moment. "No. Fletch kept his nose clean. He'd of told me if there was any trouble."

"Sure of that?"

The man nodded. "Sure enough. What's it to you?"

"I think somebody just made a big mistake because he's scared." He paused, frowning. "I'm sorry about Monaghan. He was all right." He turned to leave before the bartender could engage him in further conversation.

As he walked to his car he considered the possibility that someone with an old grudge against Monaghan could have chosen today to pay off the score, but Farrell doubted it. What made more sense was that Richards had decided to hit anyone who could possibly be connected to the kidnapping of his daughter and the murder of his cohorts. It was a desperate move, and a stupid one. If Carson got wind of this, he might go underground, taking the girl with him.

He reached his car and paused. Once again he felt that strange presence nearby. He looked around, spotting the old Chevrolet wagon a block down. At the sight of it, the urge to confront a real enemy became too much to resist. The skin over his cheekbones grew taut and his eyes took on a hungry look. He walked toward the old car, unbuttoning his jacket. When he reached back on his hip for the Luger, the driver cut the wheels hard and sent the station wagon in the opposite direction. As Farrell watched him go, it took all of his willpower not to empty his gun at the retreating car.

He felt heat simmering in his blood as he returned to his car, gunned the engine into life, then tore away with a shriek of tortured rubber.

Chapter 15

It was dark when Farrell pulled into the parking area behind his club. He took the metal stairs two at a time in his haste to get to a telephone. He'd already entered and walked halfway across the kitchen floor when he recognized instinctively that he wasn't alone. Acting on some wordless mental cue, his right hand drew and leveled the Luger as he stepped suddenly into the living room.

"You won't need that for me," Georgia said. She sat on the sofa with her shoes off and legs tucked up under her. She put a cigarette into her mouth and drew on it until the tip glowed bright red.

"I haven't got time to visit, Georgia, and anyway, what the hell are you doing here? I told you to wait at home."

She glared at him. "You know, I'm getting good and goddamned sick of all you big strong men telling me where to go and what to do. My daughter's been out there for almost two full days and not one of you has done or said anything to make me feel any better about it. Instead of ordering me around, why don't you tell me what you know?"

Farrell stared at her for a long moment before the fierce look on her face reminded him of other times. He relaxed, put the pistol away. "I'm having a drink. You?"

"Yes, but no more of that fucking Pernod. Scotch in a tall glass with plenty of ice."

Farrell laughed as he went to the taboret, remembering once again what he had liked about her. It was only the work of a moment to put ice and scotch into two glasses and take one to her. "Season's greetings, baby."

"Bullshit." She grabbed the glass and took a healthy taste. "What about Jessica?"

"Jessica's a pawn in a gang takeover. Quite a few years ago, your husband set up a man named Pete Carson, to take the fall for a murder. Carson apparently faked his death to throw the cops, and probably Whit, too, off his trail. I think he's made a deal with some local hood to back him in a takeover attempt."

"Who's the local hood?"

Farrell shook his head. "So far all I know is that a couple of loogans named Parmalee are involved. I've got a line on them that I'm following up tonight."

Georgia shook her head irritably. "Great, but why kidnap Jessica? Why not just kill Whit?"

Farrell snorted humorously. "Baby, don't ever get mad at *me*, okay?" He shook his head, grinning. "I've got a theory about that. Whit's a big man in this town, but not just because he's a smart crook. He's built up a network of city and state officials, cops, and political grafters that makes it possible for him to manipulate state laws and local regulations. He uses that power to extort money and gain influence, allowing him to maintain a more or less legitimate front. If he dies, the network dies with him."

Georgia blinked, shaking her head. "All this time I thought he was just another crooked politician. You make him sound like a cross between Capone and Woodrow Wilson."

He smiled grimly at Georgia. "You gotta admire what he's done. He plays his cards right and he could be governor one day. And that's just the reason that Carson wants him alive."

Georgia looked at him blankly. "I don't get it."

Farrell pointed a finger at Georgia. "Think, beautiful. Carson hasn't been sitting around for the past ten years just so he could kill your husband. He wants what Whit made, and he can't have it without Whit."

Now Georgia laughed. "Men," she said in a tone that was half admiration, half pity. "So this Carson is using Jessica to pin Whit to the wall. That's really funny."

"Why funny?"

"Because Whit's been fucking his secretary for the past ten months. He's goofy in love with her. If Carson had kidnapped her, Whit would've folded up like wet cardboard." Her mouth opened wide for a rich peal of laughter. "So what are you planning to do, mastermind?"

"I'm already doing it." He stepped across the room and picked up the telephone receiver. Giving the operator the number for police headquarters, he waited patiently until he got a voice. "This is Wesley Farrell. I need to speak to Captain Casey. Yes, it's urgent."

A moment or so passed before his father came on the line. "Where are you calling from, Wes?"

"I'm at home right now. Did you get word of the hit on Fletch Monaghan a while ago?"

"Yeah. It looks like Richards decided to fight back. He may have hit a snag, though."

"How's that?" Farrell asked.

"Vic D'Angelo and some of his boys tried to hit Kurt Van Zandt, too, but his luck ran out. D'Angelo killed Van Zandt's partner, Lenny Raskowitz, and wounded both of his bodyguards, but the rest still managed to kill D'Angelo's men and wound him. D'Angelo's under guard in the hospital. Van Zandt's in protective custody by his own request."

"Does he know anything about Carson?"

"No," Casey replied. "But he'd spill his guts if it would keep him safe. He's not part of this."

"What about D'Angelo? Is he talking?"

"He's making like a clam. He won't even admit to knowing Richards or Carson." Casey paused for a moment to get his breath. "What have you learned so far?"

"Not much, only the name of a place Johnny Parmalee visits almost every night. I'm going over there in a little while to see if I can pick him up."

"What about the sniper?"

"I don't know. I think I saw him at the scene of the Monaghan kill in an old station wagon. When I went for him, he beat it. Maybe now that I'm on to him, he'll steer clear of me. I wonder if he really knows what he's doing."

"If he's the one who killed Amsterdam and Callahan, he knows. You shouldn't be going after Parmalee alone. How are you going to watch your back?"

"I'll manage," Farrell said.

"You're nuts. Let me put some men with you."

"Where I'm going a city dick would stick out like a boil on Miss America's nose. Let me play this my way."

"Sometimes I think you want to get killed," Casey said bitterly.

"You know better than that," Farrell said in a chastened voice. There was a moment of silence before Casey spoke again.

"I shouldn't have said that, son. I'm sorry."

"Forget it. You learn anything new since I left you?"

"And how," Casey replied, the rift already forgotten. "Ben Guthrie found out that Richards and Carson are half-brothers. That piece of information links Richards to the Tarkington murder. I was over there with Guthrie just a while ago to let him know the jig was up. You should have seen his face."

Farrell smiled at his father's enthusiasm. "Maybe I will later, after we get the girl back."

Casey sighed. "Good luck, son, and good hunting."

"See you later." Farrell hung up the receiver, turned to see Georgia looking at him speculatively.

"Since when did you get so chummy with the law?"

Farrell rubbed the back of his neck. "That's not important. What the cop told me is."

"What is?"

"Carson is Whit's half-brother. That connection gives the cops the leverage they needed to pin Whit to the wall on the Tarkington angle. They went to his office and lowered the boom on him."

Georgia shook her head, a strange little smile on her lips. "He framed his own brother. Even I didn't think he was that big a louse." She turned her gaze back to Farrell, saw the pale light in his eyes that had once frightened her so and almost trembled. "So what will you do next?"

"I've got a tip as to where a man named Johnny Parmalee might be tonight. We're pretty certain he's one of the men who grabbed Jessica. If I can get my hands on him..." He left the thought unspoken while he finished his scotch. "At any rate, I can't hang around talking to you all night."

"I'm going with you," she said abruptly.

"Not on your life. Forget it."

She got up and walked to the window. "I can't forget it. It's my fault she's in this fix."

Farrell made a face. "C'mon, Georgia. It's got nothing to do with you."

She continued to stare out the window. "It's got everything to do with me. It was marrying Whit that caused this. Sure, he loves Jessica, all right, but that doesn't change the way he's lived his life. People respect Whit, they fear him, but I've never heard anyone say that they liked or admired him." She half-turned, her face pale against the darkness outside. "I've kept up with you, Wes. Sometimes I get gossip from people I used to know. I read the papers. You turned into a pretty decent kind of guy."

Farrell felt foolish. "Knock it off, Georgia. I was a two-bit hood when you knew me. I ran whiskey past the Coast Guard, I made a living playing cards, I even owned some cat houses. Besides, what's this got to do with me?"

"Have you still got that picture of Jess I gave you?"

"Look I haven't got time—"

"I said have you got the picture?" Her voice rose suddenly, her features contorted with strong emotion.

"Yeah. Yeah, I've still got it."

"Give it to me." When he gave it to her, she caught him by the hand and dragged him into the bathroom. She shoved him in front of the mirror, then held up the picture. "Look at it."

"I did look at it," he said peevishly.

"No, goddamn you. Look at her eyes, then look at your own, and the shape of your chins and your noses. Look!"

Farrell looked at the picture, studied it. He looked at his reflection, then cut his eyes back to the photo, really looking at the girl's eyes for the first time. A wrenching shudder went through him. "No. No." He turned and caught Georgia by the arms, pulling her to him. "No. Goddamn you, no."

She stared back at him without batting an eyelash, her mouth tight and hard. "Yes. I found out I was pregnant with your kid and I ran. I didn't know what the hell you'd say if I told you. Whit came along at just the right time. He wasn't as hard as you, at least not then. He didn't frighten me the way you did. With him, I thought—" The tension drained out of her body and she dropped her eyes from his. "I don't know what the hell I thought. I was twenty years old. I'd run away from home and I was knocked up. So I ran away again."

Farrell looked down at her, his eyes going out of focus. His fingers relaxed and Georgia slid out of his grasp. She sat down on the toilet seat, looking up at him with moist eyes. "You want to know the crazy part? She's like you in a lot of ways. Stubborn, intense. She plays to win and almost always does. Lately I've wondered what it would've been like, having you around to see her grow up."

Farrell felt limp and rubbery. Without knowing it he sank to the edge of the tub and sat on the bath mat. "I have a kid. I have a kid." His mind jumped back to the night he'd discovered he had a father, and had listened to that father talk about losing him and always wondering where he was.

A tear escaped the corner of his eye and dribbled over the sharp line of his cheek.

Georgia nodded slowly, her eyes cast downward. "Silly, isn't it. You looked like such a bad risk and Whit like such a good one. Now he's got men who want what he's got badly enough to—to—" She buried her face inside her cupped palms, her shoulders shaking.

From the time he'd understood what it was to live with the knowledge of his mixed racial heritage, Farrell had always meant to remain childless. He and Savanna had talked about the burden of bringing a child with two bloods into the world. Along with the desolation he felt at not knowing Jessica he felt the sting of the burden he'd unknowingly placed on her. He reached out a tentative hand, placed it lightly on Georgia's bowed head, smoothing the hair. She looked up at him.

"You hate me now."

"No."

"I'm sorry for what I did. I stole something from you. You should hate me. I hate myself sometimes."

He sighed, shrugged. "I'd have made a lousy father."

A small, breathy laugh escaped her. "You can't know that. Children make you better. They force you to stop being selfish. Now that Whit and I are finished, I'd like her to know you, as much as you can stand to be known. What I can't do anymore is just sit at home wringing my hands. You've got to let me help you find our child."

Farrell felt like someone waking up in another man's body. He looked at her for a long time, nodding slowly. "You've got guts, Georgia. I always said so. Put your shoes back on and go powder your nose. We may be out late."

❊❊❊

King Arboneau got a cigar from the box on his table, bit off the end and spat it into the corner. He lit it carefully, using the match to toast the wrapper. He smoked it in silence as he looked at the photo of Tel and the pretty girl he might have married. He'd have enjoyed living in the same house with their love. The knowledge that Gabrielle was upstairs copulating with that weasel, Joey Parmalee, was like a distorted image of his lost dream.

So much lost, so much time gone by, never to be recovered. He recognized now that this had been a stupid play, needlessly complex. He had a strange premonition that he had been maneuvered into something that had now taken on a life of its own.

It had taken him months to figure this all out. It had been an accident, really, that got it started. A tin-horn gambler, Dink Iacono, had come to New Orleans with an unbelievable story. He had seen Pete Carson, alive, in Seattle. Because Iacono was a blowhard and braggart, Arboneau had been reluctant to believe him at first, but the gambler's insistence eventually won him over.

The King had sent the one person he trusted above all others to Seattle with Carson's photograph. Three weeks later, a long distance call in the middle of the night from that confidant had confirmed Dink Iacono's story. Carson, now calling himself Big Mike Hayden, had put together an organization out there and was doing nicely for himself. Arboneau had barely dared hope that Carson would be willing to throw away everything he'd built just for the chance to return and get even with Richards. It was a lot to ask, so much so that after the initial contact was made, Arboneau himself made a secret trip by plane to Seattle in order to discuss a plan. It was a risky gamble, but it paid off. Carson seemed to hate Richards even more than Arboneau did, and suggested the possibility of not just overthrowing Richards, but keeping him alive in order to use him as a pawn. That part of the plan had required considerable negotiation, but eventually was grudgingly agreed to by Arboneau's silent partner.

The old man puffed the cigar contentedly. They had planned everything, from the manner of kidnapping Jessica Richards to the time and way Carson would enter the city.

Arboneau had known, however, that at some point the plan would become unstable. In the end, violent people trust only violence, and chaos always follows. He had just learned from contacts on the street about the hits on Monaghan and Van Zandt. Only Vic D'Angelo's capture had protected Arboneau himself from the eventuality of Richards' wrath.

Now, reluctantly, he accepted that the plan to keep his enemy alive, to use him as a pawn, was finished. If Carson had double-crossed him, then the half-brothers would become partners again—in death. It was not as satisfying to Arboneau, but at least blood would be answered, finally, with blood. Perhaps he and his surrogate family could survive, if he moved quickly and his luck held.

He left the room and walked through the building to Gabrielle's bedroom. He knocked on the door lightly. After a brief span of seconds, the door opened a crack.

Gabrielle smiled shyly. "Yes, Daddy King?"

"Tell Joey I need him."

⊗⊗⊗

Coupé had been hit in the chest, shoulder, and both legs by the police fusillade. Daggett realized that if he didn't go into shock before the ambulance arrived, there was some possibility he might survive. He shouted for a blanket and elevated Coupé's legs with a satchel he kept in the trunk of the squad car. Skeeter knelt beside the wounded man, talking to him in a low voice.

"How you doin'?" he asked.

Coupé's eyelids opened slowly. "Damn. I ain't dead."

"No, sir. Sergeant Daggett thinks you might live. I told him I'd testify for you, tell the judge you didn't do all them bad things. I'll say it was a mistake."

Coupé almost smiled but a surge of pain turned it to a grimace. "Fool kid. Lyin' to the judge ain't gonna help."

"Easter, what was all that 'bout the gal at the cat house? Patience?"

Coupé breathed painfully for a moment. "Don't know her las' name. Just a baby whore I saw las' night. Somebody I wisht I'd met a long time ago. She thinks my name's Frank Brown." He laughed briefly.

"And you wanna just give her all that money you got stashed? You could use it for lawyers and such."

"Abe Lincoln hisself couldn't get me off, boy. If I help you and her get a fresh start, maybe things'll go easy for me when I go before Saint Peter."

Skeeter shook his head. "Man, you are some crazy."

As Daggett watched Coupé and Skeeter, he heard the sound of a siren approaching. He walked to the curb and stared down the street. Eventually he was rewarded with the sight of an ambulance's blinking red lights. He removed his hat and waved it like a flag until it came to a stop.

"Where is he?" the intern yelled over the dying siren.

"Over there," Daggett replied. "He's got four slugs in him, so you'd better hurry."

As the intern rushed past, the driver and an orderly came directly behind with a stretcher. Daggett watched them work over Coupé as he tried to swallow the brassy taste in his mouth. He walked over to his squad car and sat on the running board beside Skeeter Longbaugh.

"You all right, kid?"

Skeeter shook his head. "I never seen nobody get shot. Knowin' him—I dunno, it makes it worse somehow." He turned his head to look at Daggett. "It was like he was just sick and tired of it all."

Daggett nodded. "It happens like that sometimes. I'm sorry we had to shoot him. When he rushed us with the gun, there was nothing else to do."

"Yeah, I know. I could see in his eyes he was gonna do it. I wish—" He put his head in his hands and shivered.

The sound of the ambulance doors slamming made Daggett look up. He watched as the ambulance driver drove up into Coupé's yard so he could turn around. The rear wheels tore long strips in the grass as he hit the accelerator and roared back in the direction of Carrollton Avenue.

"I'm sorry I got to bother you right now, Skeeter, but we're still looking for the Richards girl. Do you know where they've taken her?"

Skeeter shook his head. "Uh-uh. The big Parmalee, Johnny, was drivin' us to the hideout yesterday mornin' when there was an accident and I run off in the confusion. I wasn't thinkin' about nobody but myself. I was afraid Joey Parmalee was gonna kill me first chance he got."

He had Daggett's attention now. "You're sure about that? Joey Parmalee was the other man?"

"I ain't gonna make no mistake about that, Sergeant. I was standing as close to him as I am to you when he stabbed Butterbean. He was grinnin' like a crazy man."

"But they never told you where they were taking you, or who they were working for?"

Skeeter shook his head mournfully. "I'm sorry, Sergeant. It's my fault, them gettin' the girl, but I don't know any more than I just told you."

Daggett clapped him lightly on his bent knee as he stood up. "Okay. Just relax until we get ready to go Downtown. They'll have to get an official statement, so they'll ask you to tell the story all over again."

"You think I could use a telephone when we get there?"

"You want to call the girl who works for Ma Rankin?"

"Yes, sir."

Daggett smiled. "I'll fix it." He walked up to the house and met Andrews coming out on the porch. "Find much?"

Andrews shrugged. "If they find anything in there to connect him with any other crime than this one, I'll be surprised. Man ain't hardly got nothin' in there. A few sticks of furniture, a few plates and cups. No radio, no magazines or books. Three pistols and a shotgun and his shaving gear is about it."

Daggett shook his head. "Let's take the kid Downtown. I've had as much of bein' a cop as I can stand for one day."

⚬⚬⚬

The Red Dog Club wasn't a burlesque theater like many of those along Bourbon Street. It had pretensions to being a nightclub with exotic entertainments. Farrell held Georgia's elbow and gently steered her through the lobby into the main floor. A bored-looking man with a pencil-thin mustache gestured with a menu at a table along the far wall.

As they made their way across the floor, the club band played a song full of brass and cymbals while a bottle blonde moved around the stage rhythmically shedding her clothing. Her face had all the expression of an ironing board, but she moved her body with practiced ease, showing off each part in perfect time to the music.

"Christ," Georgia said. "I didn't know there were still dives this crummy in New Orleans. I'm behind the times."

"You sure are," Farrell said as he held her chair. "They keep Canal Street clean for the tourists, but down here it's still just a place to separate the sailors and other suckers from their dough." He pulled out another chair and sat down.

Farrell watched the stage as the band reached a crescendo. The dancer was down to a g-string and a sequined brassiere, which she ripped free. The crowd whistled and hooted as she flaunted her breasts and made the tassels glued to her nipples twitch and roll.

"A guy could get an idea in this place," Farrell said.

Georgia snorted. "You were born with that idea, boy."

Their banter was interrupted by the appearance of the master of ceremonies, a broad-shouldered man in a tuxedo. "All right, ladies and gentlemen, let's hear it for Kitty East, the Sadie Thompson of New Orleans. Yeah!" He clapped ecstatically, encouraging the crowd to make more noise. As the applause died, the MC made a few stale jokes as he led up to his introduction for a dancer called Pearle La Rocca.

As the music started, a redhead with long, tapering legs slid onto the stage. Unlike Kitty East, this girl was an acrobat, throwing her narrow-waisted, high-bosomed body across the stage in a variety of hand-stands, rolls, and cartwheels. Her costume, scanty to begin with, began to fall away. Taut muscles rippled and writhed beneath her tan skin. It was enough to make a regiment of soldiers burn their camp to the ground and ride the officers to Montana.

But Farrell was watching the door. As the tempo of the music quickened, he saw a man enter. Johnny Parmalee had gotten older, but he was still built like a steam shovel. His square, rugged face had a strangely poignant look, as though he had said goodbye to something he once cherished.

"Georgia." Farrell spoke just loudly enough for her to hear. He turned his head very deliberately in Parmalee's direction. "That's our man in the gray hat."

"He's a sad-looking man," she said.

"Maybe he's got reason to be," Farrell said, thinking of the man's lost hopes for a shot at a title fight, ten years shaking down losers, and a drug addict for a brother.

"What are we going to do?" Georgia asked.

"We have to get him out of here," Farrell replied. "And we've got to do it without starting a brawl."

Georgia nodded, her eyes narrowed thoughtfully. "He wouldn't be inclined to fight if somebody else was in the picture. Like a woman." She cut her eyes at Farrell. "You remember how I helped you get the drop on that Greek in Algiers Point back in 1923?"

In spite of the tension, Farrell smiled. "We really took that Greek to the cleaners, didn't we, baby?"

The endearment brought a flush of pleasure to Georgia's face. Farrell recalled anew what he had felt for her so long ago, this woman who was the mother of his child. He recognized that even after a separation of eighteen years, they had a bond that was unshakable.

"Okay," he said. "We've got to play this carefully. Parmalee's not like the Greek. He's spent a third of his life hurting people for money. If we're clumsy, we could end up with a handful of nothing, understand? This guy is the only person I know who can take us to Jessica."

She sobered immediately. "I'll be careful. I'm smarter than I was with the Greek." She got up, smoothing her dress. Without a backward glance, she made her way along the edge of the room. Farrell saw the determination in her face, and silently wished her luck. He turned his gaze to where Parmalee stood, and when he looked again for Georgia, she was nowhere in sight.

Chapter 16

"Yes, sweetheart, I'm stuck here for a while longer," Casey said into his telephone.

"A fine how-do-you-do," Brigid said. "We're getting married tomorrow and you're stuck at work."

"Not all night," Casey said with a comical purr in his voice.

"Honestly," Brigid said. "I wanted to have a quiet dinner together, our last date, so to speak."

"Well, if you can wait another hour or so, we can still make it. Don't forget, Antoine's is open late."

"Antoine's?" Brigid now had a purr in her own voice. "Well, maybe I'll let you off the hook after all. How much longer do you think you'll be?"

Casey consulted his watch. "Well, I might be able to make it there by eight. Why don't you have a piece of cheese and a glass of wine to tide you over."

"All right. 'Duffy's Tavern' is on the radio in a few minutes. I'll let that keep me company until you get tired of playing policeman. I love you, Frank."

"I love you too. Don't drink too much of that sherry or I'll have to arrest you for drunk and disorderly." They shared a brief laugh before hanging up. Casey began hurriedly going through the reports piled on his desk. He had read half of them when Inspector Matt Grebb knocked.

"It's open," Casey called. "Hi, Matt. What's up?"

"Sorry to bother you, chief, but we got some new information on the Amsterdam killing."

Casey sat up quickly. "Give it to me."

"One of the patrol car guys in the neighborhood of the Amsterdam murder got a piece of gossip a little while ago from a girl who does some trade at the Bella Creole Hotel."

"Did she see or hear anything useful?"

"She was outside the dump between the time Amsterdam was shot and the time the first patrol car arrived. She claims she saw a girl, a redhead, late teens or early 20s. She was with a young guy, slight of build, come out of the alley beside the hotel."

"She get much of a look at him?"

"Yeah," Grebb replied. "She said he looked wrong for the place. Young, slender, in a suit and tie. Wore a dark hat down over his face, but he was wearin' glasses. She saw the light hit them as they reached the mouth of the alley."

Casey rubbed his chin. "She see which way they went?"

"She claims they walked two blocks up, got into a sedan and drove away. She didn't get the license, but she said there was something funny about them."

"Funny how?"

Grebb scratched his ear. "They didn't touch or hold hands or nothin'. The girl kept her distance. The man walked stiff, with his hands in his pockets."

Casey tugged at the corner of his mustache. "Delgado found red hairs on the bed with Amsterdam. That's the hooker, and the man with the glasses must be the shooter."

"Doesn't sound like anybody local. Maybe somebody Carson brought from out of town." Grebb paused as he scratched his ear. "Y'know, I been thinking about Richards and this Carson being brothers. I had me a brother. We beat the hell out of each other on a regular basis. Always competing with each other, I guess, tryin' to see who was top man." He shook his head.

Casey nodded. "If that's what this is all about, the top man will be the one still standing when this is all over."

⊗⊗

Jessica knew from her watch that it had to be dark outside by now, but it was difficult to tell just what her chances would be of making it out unseen. There were a lot of footsteps in the house, men talking in loud voices. There was a radio playing somewhere, and a gruff male voice singing along to some tune she didn't recognize.

She lay on the bed with her arms folded behind her neck, willing herself to relax. It would do no good to make a break and get caught. Be patient, she counseled herself. After all, the home you left never really existed.

Thoughts of home led her to thoughts of her parents. She loved both of them, but as she'd gotten older, she'd sensed the tension between the couple, seen the looks that had let her know that there was no love, and sometimes little liking, between them. She'd heard girlfriends sometimes talk about their parents and their fights, about the fathers with "a little something on the side" that kept them from home some evenings. Her own father was a big, virile man, and Jessica had no doubt he had his own "something on the side," since he and her mother hadn't shared a room in years. She wondered if she could get her mother to talk honestly to her, when things got back to normal.

Normal, she thought with a wry smile. What would be normal after this? You've been kidnapped, witnessed a murder, nearly been raped and killed. And now you're lying here with a switchblade knife in your pocket. You were just a babe in the woods two days ago, Jessie Girl.

A knock sounded at the door and she sat up quickly, her heart hammering against her ribs. "Who's there?"

The tumblers fell in the lock and the door opened. To her relief it was Pete Carson with a bag of food in his hands. "Dinner's a little late tonight, but at least the waiter has better manners. Can I come in?"

She shrugged. "It's your house, Uncle Pete."

He entered the room and pushed the door to, but not completely closed. He put the bag of food on the floor at her feet, then stepped back, leaned a hip against the dresser. "Go ahead, before it gets cold."

She opened the bag and found a hamburger wrapped in grease-stained butcher's paper and a bottle of Coca-Cola. He stepped over long enough to snap the cap off with an opener on a pocketknife, then resumed his place.

"Thanks." She unwrapped the burger and took a bite. She was pleased to see that whoever had cooked it at least knew what he was doing. "Good," she said through the bite.

He nodded, almost smiling. "I'm letting you go soon."

She tried not to show her surprise. "You are?"

He nodded. "Your old man hasn't got any choice except to give in. I've got you, my men have hit his operations and stolen his money, and he's lost several of his key men. All that's left is for me to show him my ace in the hole. Once I do, he'll know he's licked and give me what I want."

She swallowed the bite and looked at him strangely. "Which is what?"

Carson grinned. "Money, power. The usual things. He knows now I can take everything that matters to him, that I could grab your whole family if need be."

She took a sip of the Coke and blotted her lips with a paper napkin. "You say my father's a criminal, like you."

He nodded. "A lot of what he's got today I helped him steal. We worked pretty well together—for a while."

"So you're no better than he is."

Carson's face hardened. "Maybe a little. I've done plenty of bad things, but I never killed anybody and shifted the blame on somebody else. That's what he did to me—killed a man named Tarkington and then put me in the frame."

She swallowed another bite of burger. "And what did you do to him? You must've done something."

His easy grin returned. "You're no dummy, are you, sweetheart?" He shrugged. "Maybe I was a little dishonest about some of our money dealings. But he could've called me on that. He didn't have to set me up for the electric chair. I didn't short him that much."

"You came to hurt him. Did it ever occur to you that anybody else would be affected by your grudge? Every time I look at him from now on, I'll know he's a thief." Anger rose in her like a sudden fever and her voice coarsened. "I feel like my blood's tainted. My mother—what about her? What was she? A dance-hall girl? A stripper? Or maybe the female half of a badger game?"

Carson saw something so savage in her pale green eyes that he had to look away. "Georgia's life is her own business, kid. You'd have found out about your old man sooner or later. New Orleans is a small town and people like to gossip." He stepped away from the bureau, a big strong man, still very sure of himself. "Get a good night's sleep." He turned to go, but paused at the door. "I'm sorry, Jessica. I was only out to hurt Whit."

"I'll put that under my pillow tonight," she said bitterly. "Maybe if I'm lucky a fairy will come along and leave me a nice, shiny quarter in its place."

Carson stood there for a moment, not looking at her. Finally he slipped out and closed the door behind him.

⊗⊗⊗

Farrell smoked to pass the time while kept his eyes on Johnny Parmalee. Perhaps ten minutes after she'd left Farrell's table, Georgia appeared at the entrance. She looked the club over with a predatory smile on her lips, her eyes lit with a devastating sparkle. After a short pause, she approached Parmalee with a subtle swagger in her walk. He tried to ignore her, but she was having none of it.

Georgia took the stool beside him and began to engage him in conversation. Farrell gave the big man credit for trying to ignore her. Georgia ordered herself a drink, then got

Parmalee to light her cigarette. It proved a useful strategy, because once the ex-boxer got a good look at her face, he was hooked. His neck and shoulders lost their hangdog posture as he let himself be drawn into Georgia's web. Ten minutes and another drink later, Parmalee did just what Farrell expected him to do. He spoke to the bartender, and a moment later the maitre d' arrived to conduct them to a secluded table away from the noise.

Farrell saw them seated, then gave Georgia time to distract Parmalee further. When he judged the leg-breaker sufficiently enthralled, Farrell drew his gun, camouflaging it with his hat as he got to his feet.

Judging by the hoots and whistles from the crowd, the stripper onstage was giving them their money's worth, thus ensuring that no one paid any attention to Farrell's progress. Georgia, wearing all of her clothing, by now had Parmalee's rapt attention. Farrell reflected that Parmalee had somehow gotten past the questions of why a classy dame like her was in such a crummy dive, and why she had chosen him as her paramour. Farrell almost felt sorry for him.

As he approached from Parmalee's rear, he noted that Georgia had captured his right hand in hers, and was seductively rubbing her thumb over his scarred knuckles. She held his gaze, her smile full of promises. The ex-boxer didn't notice Farrell's presence until the bronze-skinned man stood at his elbow. Parmalee turned his head, saw the muzzle of the Luger just visible under the brim of his hat.

"Don't do anything stupid, Johnny. Just go on acting like the luckiest man in the world."

Parmalee stared into the bore of the gun, then raised his eyes to Farrell's. "You're Wes Farrell, ain't you?"

"Uh, huh."

"What's your beef? I ain't done nothin' to you."

"No, but you kidnapped this woman's daughter, and we want her back, now."

"Hey, you're—"

"Save it, Johnny. I know you're hooked up with Pete Carson and somebody else. I also know you're doing all you can to overthrow Whit Richards and take over his action. I know your brother killed the custodian at Sacred Heart. I know just about all of it except where the girl is. Take us to her and I'll tell the cops you cooperated."

Johnny pulled his hand from Georgia's, his expression bitter at her betrayal. "Thanks, loads. Kidnapping's a Federal beef. I'll get twenty to life, if I'm lucky."

"Things are tough all over, Johnny. The snatch racket's as dirty as they come, and you know it. You're no schoolboy. Now get this. You're going to stand up very slowly, both hands on the table. You wearing a gun?"

Parmalee's mouth tightened. "My hip pocket."

"I'll take it as you stand up. You walk ahead of me, slowly, like a guy without a care in the world. Try to run and I'll shoot both legs out from under you."

"You're holding all the cards—for now," Johnny replied in a dull voice. He put his hands on the table, pushing himself erect, pausing as Farrell relieved him of his .38.

Farrell backed up a step, covering Parmalee. "Georgia, when we start walking, you fall in behind. We'll put him in my car and take him to police headquarters."

"Okay, Wes," she said. She was fine. Her voice was firm and steady as she stood up.

Farrell's pale stare captured Parmalee's eyes and held them. His face had edges that would cut paper, and his bronze skin glowed with dark blood. Even if he hadn't known Farrell's reputation, Parmalee recognized that his life was dangling over Hell by a thread. He put on his hat and started slowly across the room. Farrell followed, with Georgia on his heels. Their procession had all the gravity of a funeral march, but the audience was too mesmerized by the ecdysial antics of Betty Lou Bussey, "the Bourbon Street Tiger Lily," to pay the somber party the slightest heed.

They reached the sidewalk without incident, but Bourbon Street was a seething mass of giddy nightclubbers. Farrell dashed any hopes Parmalee had of an easy escape by hooking his left arm through Johnny's right, jamming the muzzle of his gun into the ex-boxer's ribs.

"That way," Farrell indicated with a sharp jerk of his chin. Parmalee could do nothing but comply.

It was slow going, but they reached the corner of Iberville without incident. Farrell nudged Parmalee around the corner, sending him in a northwest direction. Free of the crowds, Farrell let the big man loose as he slid his gun into his coat pocket.

"We're parked two blocks up, Johnny. Let's get this over with."

"Give me a break, Farrell. I'll tell you where the girl is. You don't need me to get her. Pete never meant to harm her. He's there alone. He'll have to give her to you."

"You rotten bastard," Georgia hissed. "Is she all right? If she isn't, I'll flay the skin off you."

"Keep it moving," Farrell interrupted. "You can talk and walk at the same time. This was all a stunt to make Carson rich, isn't it?"

"Yeah," Johnny replied bitterly. "Nothin' else. My brother and me, we was hired to snatch the girl and then knock over enough of Richards's operations to make him think he had a gang war on his hands."

"So it was you two who killed the men at the shoe repair shop?" Farrell gave Parmalee a gentle nudge.

"Joey did that, the stupid, kill-crazy punk. Sky high on nose candy, he don't give a fuck about anything or anybody."

"He kill Amsterdam and Callahan, too?"

Johnny looked blank. "Who? What you talkin' about?"

"Don't play dumb, Johnny. Richards's two top men were gunned down within hours of the kidnapping. If you didn't do it, who did?" As the words left his mouth, Farrell heard the hum of a motor grow suddenly stronger behind him. Before he could react, Georgia cried out in alarm.

Farrell shoved Parmalee against a shop window as he swung to meet the threat. He registered the wooden body of the station wagon first, cursed his stupidity at being caught flat-footed on a dark street. Light reflected from a pair of rimless glasses beneath the low brim of a hat as a lance of yellow flame burst through the open car window. Farrell felt the electric hum of a bullet sing past his ear. Already off balance, he fired twice, but the shots went wild. He struggled vainly to regain his footing, knowing the other man had all the time in the world to make a clean shot. He was faintly conscious of Parmalee breaking away, of Georgia screaming, but all his concentration was focused on bringing his gun to bear on the man in the station wagon. He squeezed the trigger, felt the gun buck in his hand a fraction of a second behind the muzzle blast that flared in his face from the other man's gun. Farrell ground his teeth, knowing the other man couldn't miss, knowing he was dead and would never look into his daughter's eyes. All his rage, frustration, and disappointment erupted from him in a furious roar as Georgia threw herself in front of him.

The bullet struck her, bouncing her body onto Farrell's. He caught her as they collapsed on the sidewalk. He fought his gun past her and emptied the magazine at the station wagon that now retreated at a furious clip. The silence that followed was deafening.

Anyone who had been within a block of them had melted into the night, leaving that part of Iberville as lonely as Marie Laveau's tomb. Farrell pulled Georgia to him, turned her carefully so he could see the wound. Blood welled from a hole above her left breast.

"Georgia? Georgia, can you hear me?"

Georgia's eyelids fluttered. "Wes—save her. Save-our-ch-child, for God's—"

Farrell went cold all over as she stopped talking. He pressed his fingers against her carotid artery, found a weak, thready pulse beating there. Flexing the muscles in his legs, he swept the woman's body up into his arms and ran to his car a half-block away. He prayed she'd last the six-block trip to the emergency room at Charity Hospital.

※※※

Carson sat in an armchair with his eyes closed. Johnny had gone out to get a few drinks and the men Arboneau had sent over had returned to the city after it was clear they weren't needed. It amused Carson to know that he'd tied a knot in his brother's tail, and he now sat alone in this quiet parlor like an honest working stiff. If he knew his brother, Whit had probably worn a hole in the carpet by now.

All told, this caper had gone pretty well. A couple of people had gotten killed, but that was the way it went sometimes. It was bothersome that Arboneau had brought the younger Parmalee into this game. It made Carson doubt the old man's judgment. However, it wasn't Arboneau who had brought Carson into this, but Arboneau's partner. Arboneau had an organization and the will to use it, but it was his partner who had the plan. He smiled, thinking about their meeting in Seattle. The plan had been laid out in front of him like a photograph, and the utter ruthlessness of it had sold him immediately.

The telephone rang, interrupting his reverie. He frowned, pulled the instrument to him. "Yeah?"

"Are you alone?" a soft, muffled voice asked.

Carson raised an eyebrow. "I was wondering when I'd hear from you. Where the hell have you been?"

"I told you from the beginning how this would be. There was no time for anybody to take a vacation in the middle of it. But it's almost over now. I'll be out to see you, soon. Maybe this evening."

Carson's lips bent into a smile. "I'm looking forward to it. We're almost at the finish."

"That we are, Pete. Sooner than you think."

Chapter 17

Whitman Richards paced the floor of his office like a caged animal. Rob Langdon was still missing and that knowledge only added to his sense of disquiet. Richards had called Rob's apartment several times, but to no avail. The athletic club Rob belonged to and a bar he frequented had all been called, but in spite of messages left and pleas to have his calls returned, the phone had remained silent throughout the afternoon and into the evening. He began to suspect that he might have been wrong about Rob. He had called home several times, too, but Georgia remained among the missing. Had she and Rob run away together? Even worse, were they mixed up in this scheme of Pete's? He wouldn't put that past Georgia, not the way she felt about him.

He continued to pace, running his fingers restlessly through his thick, dark hair. Failure was a stench in his nose. You sat around day-dreaming about love and roses while a man you should've killed sneaked into your town and ruined what you spent twenty-five years building. Christ.

He felt hollow inside. Days of terror for his missing daughter and impotent fury at his unseen enemies had drained him of his juice. A man can rationalize failure up to a point, but let him finally lose respect for himself and he is as surely defeated as though taken prisoner on a field of battle. As he stood feeling sorry for himself, the telephone startled him back into the here and now. With a shaking hand, he picked up the receiver. "Hello?"

"Mr. Richards, this is King Arboneau calling."

"A-Arboneau?"

"That's right. I'm responsible for bringing your brother back to town, but of course, you know that already."

"I-I don't understand."

"Pardon me if I laugh. You understood well enough when you ruined me. You understood perfectly well when you had my son assassinated."

"Y-your son? He made threats against me. What was I supposed to do, old man? What would you have done?"

The silence in the open phone line seethed for a moment, then Arboneau spoke again, in a chillingly calm, rational voice. "I did what I should've done years ago, Richards. I arranged to have your daughter taken away. I sent people to rob you and kill your employees. And here's one more thing I've done. Here, listen." He put his receiver down noisily. Sounds of a struggle followed, then the rattle of the receiver being picked up again. Then came a cry and a voice he knew.

"Whit? It's—it's Rob."

"Rob? Where are you? What's—"

Rob's voice jittered with terror. "Whit, listen, they got me. And—and—"

"And what? Tell me, man."

Langdon's words seemed to stick in his throat. "They've got—Meredith—too."

Richards almost cried out in despair but somehow he kept control of himself. "No. No, that's not possible. The sheriff's deputies—"

"They—they forced me to call Marerro, Whit. I told him to pull the deputies off. That—that you wanted it done."

"*Oh God, no,*" Richards cried. "Tell him—tell him—I'll give him whatever he wants. Anything—Rob? Rob?"

Rob spoke, but not to Richards. It was pitched at a level of hysteria that matched Richards' own. "*No—Don't! Don't sho*—" A pair of sharp cracks lacerated Richards' ears, then came the sound of a woman shrieking in terror.

"Merry—Merry—God damn you, Arboneau, put Merry on," Richards cried. "Put her on."

Arboneau laughed dryly. "Now that you know what I'm capable of, do you feel more like cooperating?"

"No," Richards moaned. "Please. Don't kill her. I'll do whatever you ask. Just don't kill her."

"Listen carefully, Richards. I'll give you some instructions."

⊗

Casey drummed his fingers on his desk blotter as he held the telephone receiver to his ear. "Yes, doctor. Yes, I understand. We'll be waiting for your call." He hung up the telephone and squeezed the bridge of his nose. He tried not to think of what Brigid would say about missing dinner. "He said they're still working on her, Wes. He wouldn't hazard a guess on the outcome."

"That's great," Farrell said in a dead voice. "And Parmalee is probably halfway to Kansas City by now."

Casey swiveled the chair and looked at Farrell as he stared out at the dark street. "But you're still alive, and that's pretty good news to me," he replied softly. "We aren't licked yet, son. Not yet."

"I wish I could believe that."

Casey heard something in Farrell's voice that he didn't quite recognize. "What's got you in such a stew?"

Farrell turned from the window. "Before Georgia and I went out for Parmalee tonight, she—she told me—something."

Casey leaned forward, straining to hear what Farrell wasn't saying. "You can talk plainer than that."

Farrell took the photograph out of his shirt pocket and handed it to his father. "Take a good look at that picture and see if it reminds you of anybody."

Casey's brow became furrowed as he took the photo from his son. He spent a couple of minutes shifting his eyes from the picture to Farrell's face and back again. "Wait a minute. You're not saying that this kid's—"

Farrell nodded. "I've done the math several times already. Jessica's going to be eighteen in April. Georgia left me in September 1924. She couldn't have been more than a month or so along, but she knew she was pregnant." He turned and looked at his father with a sad smile. "Now that you're a grandfather, have you got any words of wisdom?"

Casey stood up to put his hand on Farrell's shoulder. "Since I met you, son, life has sure been an adventure." He laughed softly. "I wish your mother was here now."

There came a knock at the door. The pair turned to find Israel Daggett standing in the door. "I've got Skeeter Longbaugh's statement, Captain. It fills in a lot of holes, but not the one we need. Apparently Coupé never talked to him about the gang's hideout or who's leading the gang."

Farrell lit a cigarette and blew out a cloud of smoke. "I don't see how you guys stand this waiting."

Daggett grinned. "We don't. We just learned how to make it look like we do."

Farrell drew on the cigarette again, then relaxed, letting the smoke slowly escape his nostrils. "Is the kid still here?"

Daggett shrugged. "Yeah. We only just finished with him a few minutes ago."

"Can I talk to him?"

Daggett looked at Casey, who squinted and rubbed the back of his neck. "It's okay with me."

Daggett jerked his thumb. "Let's go see him, then."

The lanky brown man led them downstairs to the Negro Squad, which occupied several rooms at the back of the second floor. There they found Andrews and Longbaugh at a desk sharing a roast beef po'boy sandwich.

"Skeeter, this is Mr. Farrell and Captain Casey. They've got a few more questions for you."

Skeeter put the remnants of his sandwich down in the wrapper and wiped his mouth on his shirt cuff. "Don't know what else I can tell you that I ain't already."

Farrell smiled with a reassurance he didn't feel. "I know you've been through it a hundred times, but humor me a little, okay, kid?"

"Yes, sir."

"Start at the beginning, and don't leave anything out."

"Yes, sir. I was comin' home after bein' out all night, and I found the Parmalees in my house."

"Just waiting for you."

"Yeah. Said they needed me to get 'em on the school grounds. I was scared stiff."

"They say anything on the way to the school?"

"No, sir. Only that they'd been told 'bout Miss Jessica's job in the office and how she got there through the cloister."

"They say how they knew?"

"Nosir, but everybody there knows her. They coulda watched from the gate and seen her do it every day, reg'lar as clockwork. Anyways, they wanted me to stop her in the cloister, distract her, like."

Farrell lit another cigarette from the butt of the first. "They grabbed her and carried her out. Then what?"

"Well, that's when Butterbean seen us and started into hollerin'. Joey Parmalee stabbed him and he dropped. His brother was some mad about that, but he was in a big hurry to leave, so we got in the car and drove off."

"Okay," Farrell said. "Now you're in the car with them for what, fifteen minutes or so? What went on between them?"

"Well, I could see they didn't like each other much. Johnny'd pick on him some, but Joey, he'd come back at him. It was strange, like he was scared of his big brother, but couldn't stop himself from comin' back at him. Scared me, I'll tell ya. Anyways, Johnny, he just kept drivin', stickin' to the limit."

"What did they argue about besides killing you?"

Skeeter shrugged. "I wisht I could say for sure. I was concentratin' on stayin' alive more than I was listenin' to 'em snap at each other. Joey was mighty disagreeable. Then come the accident and I made tracks."

Farrell frowned, trying to think of something else to prod the youngster's memory. "Nothing else, huh?"

"No, sir. I sure wish there was."

"Okay. Thanks, kid. I'm glad you made it." He turned and walked away with Casey at his side.

"Skeeter, I guess you'd like to make that call to your girlfriend, wouldn't you?" Andrews said.

Skeeter broke into a smile. "Reckon so. Reckon Mabel's been real worried." He got up to reach for the telephone, then stopped, blinked, shook his head as though trying to remember something.

"Hey, man? What's eatin' you?" Andrews asked.

The boy turned suddenly. "Mr. Farrell."

The excitement trilling along the edge of Skeeter's voice spun Farrell about on his heel. "Yeah?"

"I just remembered somethin'. Joey was in such a hurry 'cause he had him a date with some gal named Gabby."

"Gabby?" Farrell closed his eyes for a moment, his body tense with concentration. When he opened them, the picture was there in his mind: the pretty, pale-skinned young girl in King Arboneau's butcher shop. The girl named Gabrielle. And with her, a slight young man wearing glasses. "I think I've got this figured out."

⊗⊗⊗

It was past ten-thirty when Richards left his office. The stark emptiness of Carondelet Street was heightened by the rhythmic clack of his leather heels on Gallier Hall's marble steps. His skin was slick with a feverish, alcoholic sweat. Meredith's face flashed before his eyes, tormenting him.

He drove across Poydras Street, through the business district to Canal, on into the Quarter. The sounds of hot jazz from honkey-tonk doorways clashed jarringly against his ears, and the garish glow of the neon signs took on a nightmarish quality. The smells of beer, smoke, and cheap perfume came through the open car window like an evil miasma, clinging vilely to his skin. He mopped his clammy face with a handkerchief, but moments later the slimy alcoholic sweat returned. High pitched feminine laughter reached out at him from the sidewalks, taunting him as he fought to get his car through the weekend traffic.

He continued across Esplanade Avenue into the Faubourg Marigny, leaving the raucous Quarter behind him. Passing through one long shadow after another, his journey took on the qualities of a sickroom nightmare. He reached inside his coat and found there the reassuring weight of his Remington automatic, the sole remaining vestige of his early criminal life. Almost the only thing he had left from that time, save Georgia. How had that gone wrong? he wondered. Had there been some unheeded warning in the souring of that love that one day the rest would sour too?

Suddenly he was crossing Elysian Fields into Bywater. The narrow streets were flanked on each side by tiny shotgun cottages jammed up against each other. Infrequent streetlights served only to make the crowded neighborhood more forbidding. Something was familiar about this area, but what? Haven't been here in, what, eight, ten years?

As he drove past a cluster of warehouses, something flashing up ahead drew his attention. Drawing nearer, he saw it was a railroad crossing, and in the open field beside the tracks was the Chevrolet station wagon Arboneau had mentioned. Parked just beyond was a late model Studebaker. The silhouette of a man could be seen in the driver's seat. He crossed the tracks, pulling to the curb.

Hastily he scrubbed the sweat from his face with the limp handkerchief, throwing it on the floorboards as he opened his door. He slid out, swiftly transferring his gun to his overcoat pocket. He stepped out into mist that swirled about his knees. He knew where he was now. He remembered the loud-mouthed kid slumped with his neck broken in the

Pontiac sedan, the shrill whistle of an approaching train piercing the night.

As he walked toward the station wagon, he saw a man behind the wheel. The man turned his head slightly, light reflecting off his spectacles. Richards paused, frowning at the familiarity of the profile. No, it couldn't be. That wasn't possible. He walked more slowly, his hand wrapped about the butt of his gun. Merry had to be in the back of the station wagon. Then the creak of hinges reached him and the fat man stepped out of the passenger side of the car.

"That's far enough," the fat man said.

"Arboneau? Where's Meredith? Where's my daughter?"

The fat man stepped away from the station wagon, his movements slow and heavy, but there was authority in the way he held his head, moved his arms. "You know this place, don't you Richards? Can you remember my son's face."

Richards' eyes darted around wildly. "Your son. This is where your son was killed."

A phlegmy laugh reached him. "This is where the train hit his car, but he was already dead. Do you remember? He called you a blood-sucking worm and a coward who had other men do his killing for him."

The pale winter moon cast a gray luminescence on the old man's baggy face. His deep-set eyes were lost in shadow, giving his expression a hideous, skull-like aspect. Richards felt the sweat on his face again, gripped the automatic tighter inside his pocket as he shoved the safety off with his thumb. "I didn't come here to talk about ancient history. Where's Meredith and my daughter, Goddamnit?"

Arboneau shook his head wearily. "I have hated you for many years, Richards. You took away everything that mattered. I sat up nights trying to find ways to get even with you, to hurt you as badly as you hurt me. Now I see what a pitiful wretch you are, I wonder why I bothered."

Arboneau crooked his finger. "Come here, Richards. Come get what you came for." He walked around to the rear of the station wagon, lifted the tailgate and stood away.

Richards staggered to the rear of the station wagon, stopped dead as he stared inside. He stood there for a long moment, blinking, not believing. A look of ineffable sadness came over him for the briefest of seconds before he stretched out his hands in a gesture of supplication. "Oh, no," he said in a small voice. He took a step forward, but the sharp snap of a .22 staggered him. Already dying, he somehow took another step as a second shot cracked. Whitman Richards fell slowly backward into the mist, an arm still extended in that strange, final gesture. Miles away, a Louisville & Nashville engineer sounded his whistle as a slow freight approached Bywater crossing.

⧓

Carson was drinking coffee in the kitchen of the farmhouse when he heard the car skid to a stop in the back yard. Snapping a .38 from the spring clip under his arm, he rose and threw open the back door. He saw Johnny leap from the car in his haste to get inside.

"What the hell's wrong with you?" Carson demanded.

"We got trouble. I stopped in at the Red Dog Club on my way back here from town. Wes Farrell stuck me up with the help of that girl's mother."

Carson's mouth tightened. "Farrell? I thought he ran a nightclub."

"You're a li'l outa touch, Pete. He's got friends on the cops now, and he spends half of his time bird-doggin' for them. But that's not the worst of it. He knows about you, about Richards bein' your brother, and all about Joey and me pullin' the snatch. I gotta figure if he knows all that, the cops know it too, by now."

"Jesus," Carson whispered. He was silent for a moment, staring off into the dark barnyard, then he blinked, cut his eyes back to Johnny. "Is he on your tail?"

Johnny licked his lips nervously. "No. At least I don't think so."

"What the hell does that mean? Snap it up, Johnny. We're standing under the gallows."

Johnny's mouth worked for a moment, his expression registering confusion. "Something happened back there. We was a block or so off Bourbon on Iberville. Farrell was takin' me to his car, givin' me the third degree. This old station wagon—a Chevy, I think—rolled up on us. The driver cut loose at Farrell."

A peculiar expression crossed Carson's face. "A Chevy wagon? You get a look at the driver?"

Pete shrugged. "Not a good look. It was dark and there was lead flyin' back and forth pretty good. Mighta been a trick of the light, but it looked like the guy wore specs. Anyhow, Farrell was tradin' lead with the guy, so I got the hell outa there. Farrell might be dead. I saw him go down as I turned to run."

Pete was no longer listening. He was too busy trying to understand how Farrell knew all about him and his plans. Carson knew the station wagon well enough to recognize the old man's hand in this play, but if Arboneau knew all about Farrell's interference, why hadn't he tipped Carson off? A very prickly and unpleasant idea began to form in Carson's brain, a thought that maybe the old man was playing a different game than he and Carson had agreed upon.

Carson had sensed that all the cards weren't face-up on the table. Arboneau's emissary had spun a pretty tale of how they'd topple Richards and take over his empire, but there had been something seething beneath the clever talk that he hadn't quite gotten. He recognized that his own desire to out-wit his half-brother had blinded him to the pitfalls of partnering up with strangers. He looked up to see Johnny watching him anxiously.

"Pete, Farrell said something else I didn't get," Johnny said. "What?"

"He asked if Joey and me had killed Amsterdam and Callahan. I didn't know what he was talkin' about."

Pete's face froze. "Amsterdam and Callahan? Dead? We weren't supposed to be killing anybody, particularly Whit's top brass. You're tellin' me they're dead?"

Johnny looked confused. "It's what he said."

Pete understood now. Revenge. That's all it was ever about. Arboneau and his little pal didn't care about Whit's power or money at all. He lifted his eyes to the big man. "Better come inside and get ready to leave. This thing is about to blow up in our faces."

"What're we gonna do?"

"Leave town. You'd better come with me up to Seattle. I owe you that for getting you into this mess."

Johnny looked relieved. "That's white of you, Pete. What about the girl?"

"That was my mistake. We'll take her as far as the city limits, then let her go. We'll drive to Baton Rouge, get on a train and head north."

Johnny nodded. "I need a rod. Farrell took mine."

"There's a spare in the drawer of the living room table. Get moving, and bring the girl down with you."

As Johnny moved to obey, Carson fought off a wave of defeat. Whit was going to take this hand after all.

❈

After Skeeter spoke to Mabel and told her everything was all right, he passed up Andrews' offer of a ride to Ma Rankin's house. He caught a bus in front of police headquarters and rode it to Charity Hospital. It took him a little while, but eventually he found where they were keeping Easter Coupé. By introducing himself as Coupé's second cousin, he gained admittance to the Negro gunman's room. He looked for police guards, but soon discovered there were none.

The big man lay on his back, his torso swathed in bandages. His legs lay outside the sheets with casts from the knee to the ankle. Skeeter drew up a chair to the bed.

"Mr. Coupé," he whispered. "Mr. Coupé, it's Skeeter Longbaugh."

Coupé stirred, his eyelids flickered. He stared through narrow slits for a moment, then a smile slowly spread across his face. "Hey, man. How the hell you doin'?" He spoke with a slow, thick tongue.

"Fine. How you doin'?"

Coupé grunted. "They say I ain't gonna die—yet. My luck ain't worth a tinker's damn." He laughed softly.

Skeeter was moved by his courage, and put a hand on the big man's wrist. "I'm sure sorry how this worked out. Is there anything I can do for you?"

Coupé slowly shook his head. "Nothin', boy. Just do like I tell you. Get that money from the train depot and split it with Patience. Tell her it's from Frank Brown. She don't know my real name."

The germ of an idea began to form in the back of Skeeter's mind. "Mr. Coupé, how much money you think might be in that suitcase?"

Coupé grunted sleepily. "Dunno. Reckon it might be fifteen, eighteen thousand. Maybe more. Hard—to—s-." He drifted off to sleep before he could complete the thought.

Skeeter remained beside him for at least a quarter hour, thinking. After a while he left the unguarded room and went down to the hospital lobby to use a telephone.

Chapter 18

As Farrell had suspected, R & I had an arrest record for one Gabrielle LaPaglia, age seventeen. Her parole officer listed her address as Arboneau's store in Treme. Farrell and Casey reached the neighborhood a bit before midnight Saturday. Leaving Casey's police cruiser, they ascended the exterior staircase to the second story of the ramshackle building.

Casey looked at his watch as Farrell knocked. "I hope you called this right. Brigid is going to kill me for standing her up."

Farrell said nothing as he pounded the door insistently. He continued pounding until the noise elicited a response.

"Who's there?" The voice was small, childish, and apprehensive.

"Police, Miss LaPaglia. Open up, please."

The door opened a crack and a narrow slice of face eyed them. "Police? What do you want with me?"

Casey held up his shield. "We need to talk to you, miss. Open up, please."

The door opened slowly. Gabrielle stood half-hidden behind it, clutching a worn terry cloth robe to her throat. Her long, red hair hung loose to her shoulders.

Casey shot a glance at Farrell as he walked into the room. Farrell followed, his eyes taking in everything as he shut the door behind them. Gabrielle skirted them like a skittish animal.

"Miss LaPaglia, you work for King Arboneau."

"Y-yes. He give me a job and a place to live. He's been g-good to m-me."

Casey gestured for the girl to sit in the room's only chair, then pulled up a stool so he could talk to her at eye level. "Miss, we have good reason to suspect that Mr. Arboneau's behind a kidnapping and several murders."

Gabrielle's eyes flickered from Casey's up to Farrell's frigid stare. She flinched, cut her eyes back to Casey's. "Daddy King owns the grocery store where I work. I don't know nothin' 'bout any of that."

Casey cupped his chin in his hand and regarded her kindly. "That won't wash, Miss LaPaglia. We don't know the name of Arboneau's trigger man, but an eyewitness saw him leave the Bella Creole Hotel Wednesday night after the murder of Jack Amsterdam. The killer was described as a young male, slight of build, wearing glasses. He was in the company of a young woman, with long red hair worn loose to her shoulders."

Gabrielle's jaw was tight and her eyes blinked rapidly. She squirmed in the chair, trying to draw away from the detective's relentless voice.

"We've got another witness who works at the Bella Creole," Casey continued in his calm voice. "He brought the call girl up to Amsterdam's room in exchange for part of what Amsterdam was to pay her. Since she got out without giving him his cut, he's understandably upset with her. He's in a cell at parish prison and he's identified your mug shot."

Gabrielle's face began to crumple and tears slipped from the wells of her eyes, running quickly over her pale round cheeks.

Casey knew he had her. "We've compared the fingerprints from your prostitution arrests and they match some of the prints we found on the hotel bed, Gabrielle. Right now you're looking at accessory to murder."

"I didn't wanna do it, mister, I swear. Daddy King promised me when he took me in I'd never have to lay with nobody again. I didn't even know what they was gonna do until they done it, I swear." She pounded her knee with the flat of her hand as she sobbed out the confession.

Casey caught the hand and patted it soothingly. "Listen to me, Gabrielle. I believe you didn't kill Amsterdam. We'll work that out later. Right now, I want to know where they're holding a girl named Jessica Richards. She's the daughter of the man I told you about. She was kidnapped to hurt her father, but things are coming unglued now, and I'm afraid for her life, you understand? You help us find Jessica, we'll help you. Hush now, hush." He gave her his handkerchief and continued to pat her hand.

Casey's patience and calm voice gradually soothed the distraught girl. As the sobs subsided, she developed a case of hiccups that brought embarrassed giggles from her. She pushed her long hair back from her face and looked at Casey shyly. "Heard him talkin' to a man he called Pete day before yesterday," she said. "There's some men out at an old dairy farm Daddy King owns out on Filmore somewheres. Reckon that's where they'd keep her." She paused, her thoughts momentarily distracting her from her fear and distress.

"Are you sure?"

"Pretty sure, but if not, there's another place in Bucktown. He took me and Cal there fishin'."

"Cal's the kid with the glasses?" Farrell asked.

"Uh, huh. Cal's like me, he ain't got nobody. We been— we been kind of a family, the three of us."

Casey nodded patiently. "Can you take us to the farm?"

Her face froze as she recognized the implication of what she'd revealed. "You ain't gonna hurt Daddy King and Cal? They're all I got, mister. Please, don't hurt 'em."

"Get dressed, Gabrielle," Casey said. "We'll wait right here."

The girl stepped into a bedroom and partially closed the door. Farrell pushed his Stetson off his forehead, rubbing his face. He saw his father staring at the far wall. "What're you looking at?"

Casey motioned him over and pointed to a framed photograph. "I believe that's Tel Arboneau."

Gabrielle, now in her street clothes, came up behind them. "Daddy King has pictures of his son all over the house. He misses him somethin' awful. He wanted Tel and his girlfriend to get married and give him lots of grandchildren." She paused to pull a blue cable-knit cardigan over her blouse. "I hope I can get married one day and give Daddy King all the babies he wants. I so want to make him happy. He's done so much for me."

Casey turned from the photograph to stare at the girl. She returned his look with an earnest, almost wistful expression. "Nobody can make another person happy, Gabrielle. Happiness is something you have to make for yourself. I hope you will, when this is over. C'mon, we need to get going."

Farrell remained silent, noticing that a gleam of something that might have been understanding had just appeared in his father's eye. He had stood beside him, seen and heard what Casey had, yet that understanding had eluded him. Casey took Gabrielle by the arm and led her to the door, Farrell following silently behind.

⊗⊗⊗

As midnight drew near, Jessica heard fewer sounds. She decided the moment to escape had arrived.

In the act of opening the closet door, Jessica heard the harsh sound of the tumblers falling in the bedroom door latch. She leaped away from the closet, turned to find Johnny Parmalee standing in the hall looking at her.

"What do you want?" she asked.

"C'mon, Pete wants you downstairs."

"Why? Is he going to take me home?"

Johnny Parmalee searched her face, saw the marks of the fight she'd had with his brother. He winced involuntarily. "My brother do that to you?"

Her hand went to her face. "Joey?"

Johnny nodded, unable to hide the chagrin he felt. "I did my best to raise him right, but I guess I did a lousy job." He held out a hand. "C'mon. Pete's waitin'."

She felt hope drain away as she left the room. They found Pete slipping into his jacket.

"What are you going to do with me, Uncle Pete?"

Pete put his hat on as he faced her. "There's some kind of trouble brewing, so we're gonna have to leave here." He placed a small automatic in his hip pocket, obviously trying to keep the worry from his face. "I'll drop you off at the edge of town. It's finished, all of it."

She was unable to keep the irritation from her voice. "So that's it? You kidnap me, keep me a prisoner for three days, and just like that it's over? What bullshit this is."

Pete nodded. "I can see why you'd feel that way, Jess. This turned out to be a bad idea, all the way around. You got a right to be sore."

Jessica had her mouth open to speak when the sound of a powerful automobile engine cut through the night silence. All three people froze for an instant. Johnny spoke first.

"Who the hell is that?"

Carson's expression suddenly went calm and deliberate. "There aren't many people it can be. Bring Jess along."

Carson led the way into the front room. He pulled the edge of a drape away from a window and peered out. "It's King." He turned and cut his eyes at Johnny. "It looks like he's got that four-eyed shadow of his and your brother's with him."

Johnny's face flattened, the skin around his eyes and mouth suddenly pale. "I told him not to show his face around me again. Four-eyes is probably the one who almost got me killed tonight when he made the hit on Farrell."

Arboneau yelled Carson's name, called for him to come out. Carson looked at Johnny, made a motion with his head. He went to the door and stepped out on the porch. Johnny followed, taking up a position beside him.

"What're you trying to do, King? What happened to the plan we worked out? Nobody said anything about killing Amsterdam and Callahan. Is that what got Farrell snooping into this? If he knows all about us, probably the cops do, too. The whole operation's blown."

Arboneau's small black eyes were invisible in the shadowy folds of his face. "You ask me what happened to the plan? That's funny, Carson, after what you've pulled. But it won't work. You see, I got my vengeance. Not quite the way I planned, but I finally have it."

Carson stiffened. "What are you talking about?"

"I mean all debts have been paid. Show him, Cal."

Cal slid from under the wheel and walked to the rear of the station wagon. Johnny watched his brother. Joey's eyes were lost in shadow, but his insane grin was the tip-off that he was carrying a full load of coke. Johnny felt something inside him collapse as he wrapped his fingers around the butt of his .38.

As Cal opened the rear of the station wagon, something dark and bulky fell into the yard. Joey's jittery laugh sounded as he turned it over with his foot.

Jessica had been standing just behind Pete, staring, feeling the tension swirl around her. Clouds drifted past the moon, letting a dull silver light illuminate Whitman Richards' face. "Daddy!" She flung herself past Carson and Parmalee to where Richards' body lay. Her incoherent screams split the autumn darkness like the wild shriek of a wounded animal. She cradled Richards' head in her lap, her body convulsing with sobs.

As Carson looked down at the remains of his brother, a raging heat crept into his face. "It wasn't enough you had to kill Amsterdam and Callahan, you had to kill him, too? Who the fuck said you could order a hit on my brother?"

Arboneau ignored the raw words as though they were casual remarks about the weather. "You reap what you sow, Pete. I got into this because I believed both of us wanted to even the score with Richards. It was a good act, or maybe I was just too blinded by my own hate to see clearly. It never occurred to me that you'd make a separate peace."

Carson's mouth fell open. What Arboneau said to him made no sense. "What the hell are you talking about? There's no separate peace. You've been had." His head jerked in Joey's direction. "Did you get this pipe dream from that rape-fiend hophead? He wouldn't know the truth if it bit him." As Pete's hand flew to his gun, Cal Russell anticipated him. He fired three times over the back of the station wagon, blasting Carson against the house.

Joey's hand moved in a blur, but his brother was faster. Johnny's gun slammed twice, staggering the younger man. Joey, his eyes hot and savage, aimed deliberately at his brother and fired. Johnny dropped his gun, his left hand flying to his head. He teetered, then fell at Arboneau's feet. Joey's laugh echoed triumphantly until the shock finally reached his brain. He struggled to stand, looked at Arboneau with a puzzled expression as he slid to the ground.

The few seconds of violence had silenced Jessica. She stared wide-eyed from the shelter of Richards' body. Arboneau surveyed the destruction with calm satisfaction as he grabbed Jessica's wrist and snatched her to her feet. It was then that he heard the sirens in the distance. He understood that in spite of his efforts to shield himself from complicity in this mess, everything was coming apart. He turned to the girl, intent on killing her when an idea struck him.

"Cal, we'll use the boat in Bucktown. Hurry."

Cal's face was pale but he moved decisively. He was under the wheel by the time Arboneau dragged Jessica into the back seat. With a squeal of tires, the station wagon shot away into the night.

When everything was quiet, Pete Carson stirred. As he stared dazedly about at the litter of corpses, he recalled the castle in the sky he'd been building for the past several months. It occurred to him that he'd been suckered in the worst way a man can be. Painfully, he regained his feet, staggered to Richards. "Your kid was right, Whit. I had this all wrong from the start."

He lifted his head as the sirens grew louder. Russell's slug had broken his collarbone, but had gone all the way through. It hurt, but he could still navigate. He was pressing a handkerchief against his wound when he heard a low moan. He staggered to where Johnny lay and knelt beside him, sliding his hand under the ex-fighter's head. "Johnny, you all right?"

Johnny groaned again, put a hand to the bloody smear on the side of his head. He opened his eyes, blinking until Carson's face came into focus. "J-Joey?"

Carson shook his head.

"Christ. Jesus Christ." The words were like something ripped from Johnny's soul. "It's all gone now. It's all gone."

Carson looked over at his own brother's body, saying nothing for a moment, then he put his arm under Johnny's shoulders and lifted the big man to his feet. "C'mon, kid. There's a north-bound freight leaving the Illinois Central yards in an hour, and we're gonna hitch a ride in one of the boxcars."

In less than a moment, they were inside Johnny's Chrysler heading down a dirt road away from the approaching sirens. Carson cast one last look in the rearview mirror, then turned his eyes forward again. He'd come in with nothing, and he'd leave the same way. Save for the regrets.

⁂

Casey, Farrell, and Gabrielle were passing City Park when they heard from the Milneburg district radio cars. "We just missed them, Captain. Richards and Joey Parmalee are dead, but still warm enough to breathe. No sign of Carson, Johnny Parmalee, Arboneau, or the girl."

"Roger, stand by," Casey said. He cut his eyes at the frightened girl seated between them. "All right, Gabrielle, it's got to be Bucktown. Where?"

"Just past the docks where all them fishin' boats tie up," she said in a dull voice. "There's a road leadin' to a cottage with screen porches. Daddy keeps a motorboat there." She looked up at Farrell, feeling a chill come from the shadow obscuring his face. "Please don't kill 'em," she whimpered. "I know they done bad, but please don't."

Farrell's voice issued from some dark hollow place where light and hope had no place. "King's dealt the cards. He's got to play them now."

Casey keyed his microphone as he turned into Robert E. Lee, gunning the engine toward West End. "This is Casey to all units. We believe Arboneau is headed to a house just west of the Bucktown docks. I'll get there ahead of you, so be on the lookout for us. Run silent, repeat, run silent." As the other units rogered his message he floored the accelerator.

"They'll be hard to take in the open, particularly if they're already getting the boat underway," Casey said. "They've got nothing to lose by fighting it out."

"I'll distract them so you can flank them from the shore," Farrell replied. "When they see me coming, in the open, chances are they'll make a lot of noise about killing Jessica. I'll do my best to keep them talking."

"Or they'll use her as a shield so they can kill you," Casey said. The words came from him in a tone of dispassion he didn't feel.

"I thought about that," Farrell said. "If Jessica was just another girl, maybe I could hold back, play it safe."

"Yes," Casey said, finishing the thought. "But she's not just any girl." He knew his son too well to think he'd hesitate when so much was at stake. He remembered too well the night Farrell had fought his way through a raging storm and into a dark house full of armed men when Casey's life had been in the balance. Pride and fear grew a lump in his throat, silencing him as he sent the police car hurtling through the rural darkness. Holy Mary, Mother of God, he thought. Pray for us sinners, now, and at the hour of our deaths.

✖✖✖

The glow of a false dawn brightened the eastern sky as Cal Russell left Robert E. Lee Drive for the Old Hammond Highway. The smell of open water and decayed marine vegetation came to Jessica through the open car window. She was frightened, profoundly sad, but simmering beneath that was a rage festering. She didn't know what this evil old man planned for her, but the sight of her father's corpse had driven away any hope she had of surviving this.

Cal slowed the car as the Bucktown docks came into view. The sound of marl beneath the tires was eerily like the crunching of bones in a wolf's jaws. Arboneau grabbed Jessica by the arm and showed her his gun.

"Listen to me, girl. I've got a boat down here. We're going down there together and get into it. I'd be happy to keep you alive in case I need a hostage, but if you give me any trouble, I'll kill you."

She stared back at him, glad he couldn't see the hatred she felt. "You're going to kill me anyway."

"Maybe, but not yet."

Cal brought the car to a stop alongside a weathered cottage with a broad screened porch. Arboneau shoved open his door and worked his ungainly body outside. He motioned with his gun for Jessica to follow him.

"That way." He gestured toward the back.

With Cal in the lead, the trio continued around the side of the house into the back yard. A long pier jutted out into the inlet, beyond which lay the expanse of Lake Pontchartrain. The moon was low in the sky, creating the illusion of a long, glimmering path leading across the water to the horizon, a silvery road to nowhere.

As Cal ran to the end of the dock to start up the boat's engines, Jessica remembered other times at the lake, trips to the amusement park or the beach. Her dad had brought her here to cruise the lake in his Chris-Craft or to catch crabs. All gone now, down that empty silver road.

Jessica looked back the way they'd come, ignoring the hard circle of Arboneau's gun muzzle in her back. She was tired of this. She wasn't afraid to die anymore. Maybe it was time to push it to the finish here and now, where her mother could find what was left of her. Her hand brushed the pocket of her skirt, unexpectedly finding the lump of Joey Parmalee's knife. Her hand was in the pocket when something distracted her. A night bird maybe? No, there it is again.

A tall, unfamiliar man appeared at the foot of the dock. He walked with a casual, unhurried step that was somehow implacable. His hands hung loose at his sides, but the threat of violent action seemed implicit in his carriage. She stared at the place where his face should be, but only a hard gleam was visible.

"Arboneau. King Arboneau."

Arboneau, distracted by Cal's preparations to make way, jerked about at the sound that crackled through the air at him. He looked about frantically, moving the muzzle of his gun like a diviner. "Who's there? Who's out there?"

"You remember me, King," the shadowy figure said. "I'm the guy you told the long, sad story to, remember? About how you didn't know a thing about a kidnapping or any of the other trouble Whit Richards was having. I'm the one you told that you were nothing but a beaten old man who'd lost his nerve."

"Farrell? Is that you, Farrell? You got it wrong. I didn't want to kill him. I was betrayed by people I trusted. I wanted to bleed him white, until he was nothing but a dried out husk like…like me." Those last words were spoken wistfully, surprised that his life, which had once held such promise, as if could have come to so mean an end. "It was Carson. He lied to me. He lied."

"None of that matters now, does it, King? You're the last man standing. Let the girl go and take your chances."

"No. Never," the old man cried. "Stay back or I'll kill her. I will, damn you, I will."

Farrell's bitter laugh reached down the dock to where the old man stood, his knees shaking with terror. "No you won't, King. You push a button so people like Joey Parmalee and the four-eyed kid with the .22 can do your dirty work. You can't do it by yourself. You're a weak old man, remember?" Farrell's coarse jeer hurtled through the dark like a missile, rocking Arboneau's nerve. "Is that your killer in the boat, old man? If it is, he's in a fix. He can't get a clear shot at me from where he is, and he can't get to the dock without stopping my bullet."

"Stay back," Arboneau screamed. "I mean it."

"Daddy King! Daddy King!" Handcuffed in the car, Gabrielle's wail of despair lanced through the night into the old man's heart. He looked down at Cal, who waited to do his bidding. Tel was dead, and King understood that he'd now led his substitute family to disaster just as certain.

Farrell saw the indecision in Arboneau and decided to press his luck to the breaking point. Unbuttoning his jacket he stepped onto the dock, advancing on Arboneau with a slow, steady tread. "You can't get past me, King, and you can't get anywhere in that boat. The Coast Guard's already on the way and they'll have the inlet blocked before you get there."

Jessica had borne all of this stoically, but her face was no longer that of a teenage girl. Farrell looked at the set of her mouth, the pale hatred simmering in her eyes and he recognized an undefeated spirit. A shiver of fierce pride went through him. He blinked back tears he couldn't explain as he smiled at her.

"Jessica, my name's Wesley Farrell. I'm a friend of your mother's, and I'm going to take you home."

"Then do it," she yelled. "I'm goddamned sick of being pushed around." As she spoke, a length of steel seemed to explode from her fist. She stabbed it down at Arboneau's leg with all her strength.

As the blade penetrated the fat of his thigh, the old man screamed, throwing his arms wide. Freed of his grasp, Jessica threw herself prone against the weathered planks.

As the girl pitched forward, the Luger appeared in Farrell's hand, jumping in his fist as though alive, illuminating the dock with flares of hot red light. Arboneau's body arched as the slugs ripped his chest. Casey, firing from the yard, hit Cal Russell in the neck as Farrell's last shot tore through the young man's skull. As the noise of the explosions died, Farrell was suddenly aware of the calm slapping of water against the dock pilings.

He walked down the dock to where Jessica lay, his heart thudding in his throat. She stirred as he reached her. He knelt down, placing a soft, tentative hand on her head. "Are you all right, Jess?"

She let him help her to her feet, looking past his shoulder to where the bodies lay. "No. I'll never be all right again. They killed my father."

Farrell trembled as the word reached his ear. Its meaning was different to him now. He left his face blank, spoke to the girl in a cool, dispassionate voice. "I'm sorry, Jess. Really sorry."

She looked up at him, staring as she reached up to touch his face with her fingers. The gesture was strangely familiar to him. "I don't know you. Why—how—?"

Gabrielle, freed from her shackles by Casey, rushed past them, sobbing. She knelt first beside Arboneau, who groaned loudly, shaking his head back and forth in pain. She looked past him to the edge of the dock, where she saw Cal for the first time. A strangled cry erupted from her as she went to the dead boy, cradling his ruined head in her lap. Her mouth hung open, but all the sounds of grief had been driven from her.

Sirens drove silence out of the fishing village, but Farrell didn't hear them as he looked down for the first time at the daughter he'd found. "C'mon, Jess. Your mother's in the hospital. She'll want to see you when she wakes up." He cradled her arm in his and led her from the dock toward the house.

Sergeant Ray Snedegar and Inspector Grebb trailed Casey to the end of the dock where Gabrielle mourned the loss of her family. She'd taken Cal's glasses from his face and was running her fingers through his lank brown hair. She talked to him about something they'd done and asked if he remembered. Casey holstered his gun and held up his hand so the men behind him wouldn't intrude on the girl's grief.

"More work for the coroner," Snedegar said.

"And we're less one crooked city councilman," Grebb replied. "This kid with Arboneau?" he asked.

Casey silently reached down to pick up Cal's glasses and the .38 Harrington & Richardson revolver he'd carried. He put them into his pockets as he stared thoughtfully at the grisly tableau. "Looks like it. Better get the doctor to give this girl something to calm her down. We've got a lot of talking to do before the night's over."

Epilogue

Farrell pushed the doorbell button inside the expensive apartment building on Philip Street in the Garden District as Casey stifled a yawn.

"God, I'm getting too old for this job. You're liable to have to say the wedding vows for me this afternoon."

Farrell squeezed his father's shoulder, grinning at him. "You're not getting off as easily as that. Brigid expects a wide-awake bridegroom, not a stand-in." He pushed the button a second time.

The door opened a crack, revealing a sleepy blue eye. "Who's there?" a woman asked.

Casey showed his badge. "Police, Miss. May we come in?"

The eye opened wider. Hastily, Meredith Baker removed the burglar chain, and threw open the door. "What's the matter?" Her face wore a look of mild alarm.

As she stood in the door, Farrell took her in for the first time. Her short blonde hair, tousled with sleep, cupped the contours of her face like downy feathers. Her flawless skin glowed with health, setting off the cornflower blue eyes and soft pink lips. One kiss from that mouth, a man's brains would melt and dribble out of his ears.

Casey took off his hat as he walked through the door. He turned, his face sad, apologetic. "Miss Baker, I've got some news about Councilman Richards. It's—well, it's kind of tough. Maybe you should…sit down."

Farrell closed the door very softly. Taking off his hat he walked past Meredith Baker to the little breakfast bar that separated the kitchenette from the living room.

Meredith lifted a hand to her mouth, the knuckles just brushing her soft lips. A mild tremor went through her body, just visible through the pale, pink negligee she wore. "W–Whit? Something's…happened to Whit?"

Casey's mouth stretched and pursed with the effort of what he must say. "I'm afraid he was killed last night."

Her eyes blared as a long choking sob tore itself from her throat. Farrell quickly caught her as she sagged and helped her to a chair. She moaned like someone in the throes of death as Casey stood rigidly by, his eyes downcast. They remained like that for a while as the young woman sobbed uncontrollably.

"I'm sorry, Miss Baker. I'm truly sorry."

Finally she raised her tear-streaked face to Casey. "How. How did he d-die?"

"He was murdered."

Her mouth contorted, broke, contorted again. "Why?" The word was pitched high with her pain. "Why would anyone kill Whit?"

Casey sat down across from her, placing his hat on the coffee table. He took an envelope from his pocket and placed it on the table beside the hat. "It's a long story, but I'll give you the high spots. You'll pardon me for mentioning this, but it's well known you and Richards were having an affair."

She held up her head, her eyes flashing. "We loved each other very much. We were going to be married."

Casey nodded gravely. "That being the case, I suppose Mr. Richards let you in on the fact that he was a gangster, a corrupt politician who'd made millions through graft."

Her pink lips quivered, stretched into a bitter line. "He was honest with me, about everything. He was a strong, powerful man who took what he wanted. He was no better or worse than other powerful men."

Casey's mouth turned up at one corner. "You'll pardon me if I don't admire him to the extent you do. It was his own corruption that started this. Years ago he had a man named Tarkington killed. The reasons don't matter, but he arranged the murder and then framed his half-brother, a man named Pete Carson, for the crime. Carson escaped, faked his death, and disappeared."

"I don't see why you're bothering me with all this," she glared. "I just lost the man I love and all the dreams we shared. Can't you leave me alone?"

Casey waved a placating hand. "Just bear with me, miss. Sometime after the Tarkington murder, Councilman Richards had a run-in with a small-time gangster named King Arboneau. He used his political connections to ruin Arboneau, and later he had his son, Tel, murdered because Tel had threatened him. This would be about eight years ago."

"You make it sound as though this town is crawling with gangsters and fiends," she said harshly.

"We're no worse than most cities," Casey said mildly. "But we're getting off the track. You see, Arboneau discovered Carson's whereabouts. Arboneau was too weak to tackle Richards on his own, so he tracked Carson to Seattle and convinced Carson to join him in making a power grab.

"This tickled Carson to death," Casey continued. "He'd done all right for himself, but nothing like what Richards had done here. Carson's idea of true revenge was to get Richards under his thumb, use his contacts and organization, and rake the profits into his own pockets. It appears that Arboneau was in favor of that, too. After all, he'd been reduced to running a lot of penny-ante action in Treme."

She got up from her chair, running her fingers through her hair as she walked to the kitchen. "I need some coffee. Would you like some? It's fresh."

"Good idea," Farrell said. "We've been up all night. Can I help you?"

She waved him back to his seat as she got cups, saucers, sugar and cream on a bamboo tray. "You seem to have it all figured out, then. This Carson and Arboneau are responsible for what happened."

"In a sense," Casey said. "They put things in motion, but they aren't really responsible for the way things turned out."

"How so?" she asked, pouring coffee into the cups.

Casey rubbed his chin. "Carson and Arboneau had their eye on a goal, but somebody with a High Standard .22 automatic kept cropping up, getting in the way of that goal."

She frowned, her eyes registering confusion. "I don't get you. I thought you said Arboneau was responsible for Whit's murder."

Casey shook his head primly. "Neither Arboneau nor Carson were aware of it. Carson probably wasn't even in town when Jack Amsterdam was lured to a room by a prostitute and murdered, or when Butch Callahan was caught in front of the one place he felt safe and gunned down. Even if Carson heard about it, he didn't know what it meant to him."

"It's funny the way the killer worked," Farrell said, speaking for the first time. "Amsterdam and Callahan had been with Richards from the beginning. They had a hand in everything he did. The way they were killed, it's almost as though with each killing, the gunman was sending a message to Richards, warning him that his turn was coming."

Meredith shivered, caught the edge of the counter. "This is so horrible—I don't see why I have to hear all this."

"Bear with me, Miss Baker," the detective said. "A police investigation is a complicated thing, particularly when it's about murder. And in spite of all the window dressing to the contrary, murder was what this was all about, from the beginning."

She looked at him sharply. "Isn't that obvious? Whit's dead and so are all these other men."

Casey shook his head slowly. "It wasn't obvious to Carson and Arboneau. Like the killer, they wanted revenge, but only the kind you can get from a man who's your prisoner. They wanted everything Richards had, but they needed for his organization to survive, and for that he and his top men had to remain alive, at least for a while."

Farrell got up from his chair, took the tray of coffee things, and carried them to the coffee table. He gave his father a cup and took one for himself. Meredith seemed not to notice.

"The kidnapping of Jessica Richards was the tip-off that two games were going at once," Casey said as he sipped his coffee. "She was leverage to get Richards to play ball. Richards played for time while he sent his men all over town looking for Carson, who by then had revealed himself. Richards was being torn in two pieces by then, his daughter kidnapped and Arboneau's men robbing his illegal gambling, prostitution, and narcotics operations. Within forty-eight hours, his whole empire had been disrupted."

"Some of his men tried to hit back," Farrell added, "but because they didn't know Arboneau was Carson's ally in the city, they wasted their strength striking out at the wrong men. They ended up getting killed or captured by the cops, leaving Whit completely isolated."

Meredith took a napkin from a pile on the breakfast bar and blew her nose. "I can't believe it," she whimpered. "He was so strong, so—alive."

"He was pretty tough," Farrell agreed. "But like every man, he had his weaknesses. His daughter was one of them. It's funny, though, that Carson made the choice he did."

"What choice?" she asked from behind the napkin.

"Yesterday Whit's wife said something. It was something like 'Whit's goofy in love with his secretary. If Carson had kidnapped her, Whit would give up everything he had.'" Farrell tugged thoughtfully at his earlobe. "Carson was a careful planner. His men knew just where and when to grab

Jessica. But they could've grabbed you a lot easier, Miss Baker, with a lot less trouble."

The hand holding her napkin fell to her side as she stared wide-eyed at him. "What a horrible thing to say."

Casey sighed. "Horrible is the word, because the killings got nastier as the killer went along. Late yesterday Rob Langdon was lured away from the office and kidnapped."

"Rob? Rob lured away? Do you mean to say—?"

"That's right, Miss Baker. It's safe to say that Langon was forced to tell Richards that the gang had you, too. I suspect he was killed to send a clear message to Richards."

"Oh, Rob. Oh, God, no."

"Yes. We found his body with Councilman Richards' in Bywater early this morning. Both shot with the same gun." Casey got out his pipe and began to pack it. "Wes, why don't you give Miss Baker a cigarette. Some smoke would do us all good." He put the stem in his mouth and applied a match to the bowl, puffing clouds of sweet smoke into the room as Farrell offered his cigarette case to the young woman. She took one, put it shakily to her mouth and held it for his light.

"It took us quite a while to get a line on this killer," Casey continued. "Several witnesses described him as a slightly built young man who wore glasses. He was seen leaving the Bella Creole Hotel in the company of the prostitute who lured Jack Amsterdam to his death, and he was seen again outside Vesey's bar before Butch Callahan died."

"He tried his hand with me, too," Farrell said. "I was a little luckier, but he shot Georgia Richards trying to get me last night." He inhaled a lungful of smoke, then blew it out in a big gust. "We tracked him to Bucktown last night where he and King Arboneau were making a getaway with Jessica Richards."

Meredith took a shaky drag from the cigarette, let the smoke out jerkily. "Did—did you get him?"

Farrell nodded. "We got both of them. He won't be shooting anybody else."

Her shoulders slumped as a sob escaped her chest. "Thank—thank God. At least Whit can rest in peace."

"I doubt it," Casey said. "I've been trying to imagine how he must've felt in the dark last night, down by the railroad crossing. He'd come there to get you back from Arboneau, Miss Baker. He was ready to give it all up to get you back. He must've loved you very much." Casey took the pipe from the corner of his mouth and put it in an ashtray to cool. "I doubt a man can know peace when he stares into the back of a station wagon and sees the dearest thing in the world to him rise up from behind a corpse, point a gun, and shoot him twice. Hell can't be much worse than a disappointment like that."

The cigarette fell from Meredith's fingers as her mouth dropped open. "Wha—what are you talking about? I was here—all night. Waiting for Whit."

Casey picked up the envelope that lay beside his hat. Very slowly he opened it and shook out a photograph. He held it up so Meredith could see it. "This came from King Arboneau's house. It's a picture of his son, Tel, who was killed by Whit Richards eight years ago. The pretty girl beside him is his fiance, Linda Sue Mahoney. That's your name, isn't it?"

She stared at him, her face as still and impenetrable as a frozen lake. She said nothing.

"You're quite a girl, Miss Mahoney," Casey said. "Men fall for you like pole-axed steers and do whatever you want. The trouble is they all end up dead." He stood up. "You'd better get dressed. We've got to take you Downtown."

Casey had only a second to dodge the coffee cup Linda Sue Mahoney threw at him. As her right hand moved in a blur to an open drawer, Farrell snatched a bolster from the chair beside him and snapped it backhanded at the woman. It hit her with surprising force, staggering her back against the stove. She tried to bring the .22 automatic back to bear, froze at the sight of the Luger trained on her. "I'll give you five seconds to decide whether you want to go on living," Farrell said.

She stared into his eyes for the full five seconds before she let the pistol clatter to the floor. As Farrell kicked the pistol toward his father, she drew her knees up to her chest, wrapped her arms about them, and slumped against the wall. "I should have made you kill me," she said in a flat, toneless voice. "Everything that mattered for me died a long time ago."

Casey picked up the murder weapon, then moved to Farrell's elbow. "Revenge for Tel was all you wanted, wasn't it?" Farrell said.

She nodded dumbly.

As Farrell stared down at her, he thought about Jessica and Georgia, and about second chances. The murderous fury that had driven him for the past twenty-four hours ebbed away, and he felt the stirrings of something he finally recognized as pity. "Let her go, Frank."

Casey's head snapped around. "What? What the hell are you talking about?"

Farrell lowered his Luger as he turned to face his father. "What the hell has she done, when you add it all up? She wasn't in this for the money. She rubbed out some thieves, murderers, and political grafters, or gave us the excuse to do it. There's not a single body in the morgue that anybody will miss."

"Are you insane? Did you get a rap on the skull that knocked your brains out?"

"No," Farrell said, sliding the Luger back into his waistband. "But maybe something knocked some in. You got the murder weapon there, and you've got witnesses that think Cal Russell killed Amsterdam and Callahan. Everybody who could contradict that is dead except for Gabrielle, and she's not going to talk, particularly if you tell her that her freedom depends on keeping her mouth shut. Besides," he said, with a sardonic edge growing in his voice, "if you let Miss Mahoney go, think of the paperwork you'll save. As of now the case is wrapped up, and you'll get to your wedding on time."

Linda Sue Mahoney had stopped crying. She looked up at Farrell, her mouth hanging open.

Casey looked at Farrell, at Linda Sue, then at Farrell again, his mouth wrinkling with impatience. "Damn you," he growled at his son. "Miss Baker, I don't know why I'm doing this, but I'm going to walk out of here. I want you out of this city within twenty-four hours, you understand?"

Linda Sue Mahoney nodded dumbly as she allowed Farrell to pull her to her feet.

"Let's go get some breakfast, Frank." He touched two fingers to the brim of his hat and smiled at the young woman. "Merry Christmas, baby, and a Happy New Year." He took his father by the arm and pulled him out of the apartment. By the time they were back in Casey's police cruiser, Linda Sue Mahoney was packing her bags.

⊗⊗⊗

At five-thirty that evening, the newly married couple sat in the bride's apartment with Farrell listening to a network radio broadcast from New York City. Marcel was late, but Savanna had already called to say she was on the way. She had given Farrell a dubious look when he'd delivered the invitation, but as Farrell expected, Savanna's adventurous nature elicited an acceptance.

"I still don't get how you figured out that Cal Russell wasn't the one who murdered all those men," Brigid said as she handed Casey a fresh drink.

"Well, I'd seen the photo in Arboneau's living room," Casey replied, "and that had my mind working, but it was seeing Gabrielle with Russell's corpse that told me we didn't have the right man."

"All right, Sherlock, tell us the secret," she said.

"The witness who'd seen Gabrielle and the killer leaving the Bella Creole said that they were walking apart, stiffly, not touching. Gabrielle had just been through a pretty terrible thing, and Cal was like a brother to her. She'd likely have clung to him for comfort of some kind. When she saw him dead at the dock, she went to him, put his bloody head in her lap. When we got her back to the station and settled her down, she was ready to talk."

"So Gabrielle was the mysterious call girl at the Bella Creole Hotel."

Casey smiled. "Very good, my dear. But she didn't go willingly. Meredith forced her to borrow some of Russell's clothing and then took her down to the hotel where Jack Amsterdam liked to meet his ladies of the evening. Meredith kept the disguise to use on Callahan the next afternoon."

"I'm still not clear why she started off with those two men. Why not just kill Richards?" Brigid asked.

Casey shook his head. "People's minds get twisted up after so many years of hating. She'd spent a long time trolling for back-alley gossip, and had learned it was Callahan who had lured Tel Arboneau to Vesey's bar with an offer to betray Richards. He got Tel drunk, then he and Amsterdam killed him before leaving his car where the train could broadside it." Casey paused to take a sip of scotch. "I think, too, she wanted to take everything that Richards had before she killed him. She got Langdon to leave the office, ostensibly to get a prescription for nausea from the drug store. She had already told him she was pregnant with Richards' child, and had asked him for his help. It was a simple matter to take him prisoner and force him to lure Richards to his death."

"Did I understand that Arboneau helped her kill Richards?" she asked.

Farrell yawned and stretched. "That part of the story is a little confusing to us, even now. It sounds like Joey Parmalee had a falling out with Carson, then went to Arboneau and told him Carson was pulling a double cross with Richards. It was just enough to make him do what Meredith had been after him to do all along."

Brigid laughed. "This Meredith must be quite a girl."

"She's a knockout," Farrell agreed. "And she spread it around. It wasn't just money or revenge that lured Carson back from Seattle. She had remained with Arboneau for years, keeping Tel alive in his mind, never letting him forget what Richards had done to them. The old man talked quite a bit before he died. I think he was a little in love with her, too."

"A real black widow," Brigid said. "Everybody who loved her got it in the neck."

"All except Carson and Johnny Parmalee," Casey agreed. "We've got the FBI and the United States Marshal's men looking for them, but Carson's good. We might never get either of them."

"Have you had a chance to see Georgia?" Casey asked as Brigid excused herself for a moment.

"She was so weak that they wouldn't let me stay very long," he replied. "But she was alert enough to know everything was all right." He paused to take a sip of his drink. "She took Whit's death harder than I thought. Maybe he meant something to her after all."

"Women are funny creatures, Wes," Brigid said as she returned from the kitchen. "We have an infinite capacity to love a man and hate his guts at the same time."

Casey patted her hand. "Contrary is what you are, but you're still adorable."

The doorbell rang and Farrell went to open it. Savanna, dressed in an elegant purple suit and wide-brimmed lavender hat, stood in the doorway, her expression a little stiff, but with a strangely eager look in her eye. He smiled, took her by the arm, and brought her inside to where Casey and Brigid stood waiting.

"Savanna Beaulieu, this is the new Mrs. Casey," he said.

"Call me Bridy," Brigid said. She held out a hand, and Savanna, after a brief hesitation, grasped it warmly.

"Out in the parishes they call me Rosalie. Savanna's just a nickname I picked up somewhere."

"How about some scotch?" Casey asked, holding out a highball glass.

Savanna looked at him gratefully as she took the glass. "Perfect timing, Captain."

Somehow the happy mood and blending of personalities overcame the strangeness of the circumstances. Marcel arrived with a bouquet of flowers, and within a half-hour the five were talking easily over plates of cold cuts and cold salads. Casey was telling the newcomers about King Arboneau's conspiracy when the bell rang yet again. Brigid answered and found Jessica Richards standing in the hall.

"Is Mr. Farrell here?" the girl asked.

"You're Jessica, aren't you?"

"Yes, ma'am."

"Come in, honey. We're having a little party."

Jessica blushed. "I didn't mean to intrude. I can talk to him tomorrow."

Brigid waved a dismissive hand. "Nonsense. Come in and have a sandwich with us. We're celebrating my wedding day, so all comers are welcome."

"Oh. Congratulations." She held out a hand to the older woman.

From his vantage point across the room, Farrell had seen the girl and stood up. Savanna, seated beside him, saw Jessica's face and uttered a low whistle. "Holy Mother of God, she's the spit image of you."

Brigid led Jessica into the living room and introduced everyone. Jessica recognized immediately that in this group of brown and white people there had to be a story. She wondered if she could stay long enough to get to hear it.

Farrell took her by the hand and led her into a corner of the room. "You look pretty good for having been locked up for almost three days." He sat her in a vacant chair and gave her some ginger ale. "Your mother's doing all right?"

Jessica nodded. "I think so. She's pretty tough."

Farrell laughed softly. "Yeah, she is that."

"She—she said some things to me a while ago. She said I should—get to know you. Do you know why?"

Farrell sat on an ottoman and took her hand in his. "Maybe she's woozy from the anesthesia. Talk to her again later. See what she says. People say a lot of funny things when they're doped up."

She looked at their intertwined hands. "You risked your life for me last night. I still don't understand why. My mother said—" She looked into his eyes, searching for an answer to her questions.

He rubbed his thumb lightly over her hand, not hearing the noise of the radio and the others laughing and talking behind him, as though he and Jessica were in another place entirely. "Your mother and I were pretty close a long time ago. It's kind of a long story to explain just how we knew each other." He shot her a quick look. "Life's kind of complicated sometimes. Maybe—" He was trying to think of how to proceed when he heard a sudden tense undertone in the voices behind him and the sound of the radio being turned up. He turned his head and heard the anxious voice of the network announcer come through the speaker.

"Ladies and gentlemen, this is Robert Trout speaking to you from CBS Radio headquarters in New York with a special bulletin. Sources in the Hawaiian Islands have begun to report to us that the American naval, army and air corps bases there have been attacked by aircraft of the Imperial Japanese Navy. Many of the reports are unconfirmed at this point, but what we do know is that there has been considerable destruction and loss of life. That is all we know at this point, but we will continue to interrupt regular programming this evening as new information comes in. We now return you to our regularly scheduled program."

"Dear God," Brigid said, her voice hushed. "What does it all mean?"

Casey looked up from where he stood at the radio, his face gone slack. "I think it means things are going to be different from now on."

Jessica looked at Farrell, her eyes trusting him. "I see what you mean."

12:30 A.M., Monday, December 8th, 1941 on U.S. Highway 90

Easter Coupé opened his eyes and felt the sensation of motion. He blinked, wondering if he were dead and on his way through the dark to Hell.

"He's awake," a man's voice said beside him.

"Hey, man, how you feelin'?" It was another man's voice.

A soft light switched on, momentarily blinding him. After a moment of blinking, things became more distinct. The first thing he saw was an unfamiliar colored man looking down at him. He grinned at Coupé. "'Bout time you woke up. I was gettin' lonesome here in the dark."

Coupé was certain now that he must be dead. "Where am I? Who are you?"

"They call me Lonnie," the man said. "Mr. Blessey's up front drivin' the hearse."

"Hearse? If I ain't dead, what the hell am I doin' in a hearse?"

The scrawny old man laughed from the driver's seat.

"Man, you are one lucky motha-fuckah. All the people in New Orleans you go to kill, you pick the one boy who's gonna feel sorry for you after."

Coupé shook his head, trying to clear it. "Man, what the fuck's goin' on? How'd I get out of the hospital?"

"You can thank Skeeter. After he got your suitcase fulla money from the railroad depot, he got in touch with a gal name of Patience Delachaise. Seems the gal didn't want no part of your money 'less some of it was used to help you out. When Skeeter found you was too bad hurt for the cops to bother guardin' you, he called me and we got some people together. We come in dressed like undertakers, covered you up with sheets, and wheeled you right outa there." He cackled delightedly. "Right now, you done passed Sulphur, Louisiana. By sunup, you'll be in Houston, in the Fifth Ward some-wheres. Got some friends there who'll take care of you 'til you back on your feet again."

"And you doin' all this outa the goodness of your heart, that right?" Coupé asked.

"No, fool. Skeeter give me five grand to get you out. I'd of left you for the hangman, but for five thou I'll bust Capone outa Alcatraz. Oh—he give me a thousand to give back to you, so's you'll have a stake."

Coupé rubbed his face, his mind whirling. "Damn."

"Got one more thing for you, too," the old man said.

"What's that?"

"Got the address of that Patience Delachaise, in Lake Charles. Said when you was all right again, to write her. Said she'd like to see you again for some damn reason. Women. I swear, you can't understand nothin' about 'em."

Coupé felt a smile grow on his face. "No. Reckon you can't."

To receive a free catalog of other Poisoned Pen Press titles,
please contact us in one of the following ways:

Phone: 1-800-421-3976
Facsimile: 1-480-949-1707
Email: info@poisonedpenpress.com
Website: www.poisonedpenpress.com

Poisoned Pen Press
6962 E. First Ave. Ste 103
Scottsdale, AZ 85251

—